THE UNIQUE MAGAZINE   ISSN 0898-5073

Winter 1989/90   Art by Vincent Di Fate

Published quarterly by the Terminus Publishing Company, Inc., P.O. Box 13418, Philadelphia PA 19101-3418. (4426 Larchwood Ave., Philadelphia PA 19104-3916.) Application to mail at second class postage rates pending at Philadelphia PA and additional mailing offices. Single copies, $4.00 (plus $1.00 postage if ordered by mail). Subscription rates: Eighteen months (six issues) for $18.00 in the United States and its posessions, for $24.00 in Canada, and for $27.00 elsewhere. The publishers are not responsible for the loss of manuscripts, although reasonable care will be taken of such material while in their possession. Copyright© 1989 by the Terminus Publishing Company, Inc.; all rights reserved; reproduction prohibited without prior permission. *Weird Tales*® is a registered trade mark owned by Weird Tales, Limited. Typeset, printed, and bound in the United States of America.

THE EYRIE

VDF

Welcome to the sixth issue of "our" *Weird Tales®*, the 295th issue overall. The Terminus *Weird Tales®* (as fans are calling it) has now survived longer than any previous revival of The Unique Magazine, and we're working hard to better even the Main Sequence, 1923–54, in quality, if not in longevity.

The last few months have been a busy time for us. We finished work on a promotional piece (done jointly with *Aboriginal Science Fiction* and *The Magazine of Fantasy and Science Fiction*) which will go out to nearly a quarter of a million science-fiction, fantasy, and horror readers. And too we're hard at work on the next couple of issues, which offer David J. Schow and Nancy Springer as Featured Authors. *And* we are giving serious thought to the 300th issue . . . which is coming up amazingly fast. You can bet your eyeteeth *Weird Tales®* #300 will be something special!

Subscriptions pour in at a great pace. We have over 3600 subscribers as we write this (July, 1989). That may not seem like a lot (most magazines have tens of thousands of subscribers, after all) — but for a small magazine of modest capital which started less than 2 years ago, it's downright astonishing.

Those of you who have been with us since the beginning will remember our promise: when we have 4000 subscribers, we will increase frequency of publication to bi-monthly, 6 issues per year. It's great news, then, that we're so close.

But — we might not make it to 4000 sub-

scribers. At least, not for a few issues yet.

Why? Because for many of you, your subscription ends with this issue. If the card enclosed with your copy says "Please renew" — **PLEASE** take a moment to do so *now*, while you're thinking about it. That will help us immeasurably; believe us, it's a lot of work to send out letters asking for subscription renewals!

Most magazines in the field expect a 60%–70% renewal rate among subscribers. We think a 80%–90% renewal rate is realistic for *Weird Tales®*. After all, this *is* The Unique Magazine, and it prints stories you just won't find anywhere else. With the demise of *Rod Serling's The Twilight Zone Magazine* and impending shut-down of *The Horror Show*, *Weird Tales®* becomes the only professional magazine of horror and the fantastic in the United States. If you like fantasy and horror short stories, this is the place to turn. And as you know, we have the best artwork to be found in any magazine, bar none.

So for those of you who've been with us since the beginning — thank you. We've tried to make *Weird Tales®* something special again: great fiction and artwork, quality book paper, design, and binding — all at an affordable price. (Other publishers have told us we should be charging on the order of eight dollars a copy — but that's simply too much money for a magazine. Even though the cover price has increased, we have held subscription rates to 6 issues for $18.00, or 12 issues for $34.00.)

If your subscription expires this issue,

4

please join us — again.

We were a bit disappointed recently when the editor of one of the "Year's Best" annuals not only failed to include anything from *Weird Tales*® in her fat "bug-crusher" of a book (to use Gardner Dozois's incredibly precise technical term) but remarked amid a survey of the horror field for 1988 that nothing in *Weird Tales*® seemed particularly scary.

Alas. Well, *we* thought that Brian Lumley's "Fruiting Bodies," Alan Rodgers's "Emma's Daughter," and Tad Williams's "Child of an Ancient City" were pretty damn scary, thank you. So apparently did you, Readers, from your responses.

This is not to argue with the distinguished anthologist. But her remark did get us thinking about what precisely a horror story *is* and what *Weird Tales*® is supposed to be publishing.

First, not all our stories are horror stories. We publish — and want to continue publishing — all sorts of odd and off-trail fiction, most (but not all) of it fantasy. Is Felix Gottschalk's "The Wonderful Wall-stretcher" in our Spring 1988 issue fantastic? We're not sure, but it seems to be about the mental process of fantasy, and certainly it is not the sort of story you will see in, say, *The New Yorker*.

The original *Weird Tales* (1923–54) published all sorts of fiction, including galaxy-spanning space operas by Edmond Hamilton, slapstick humor (e.g. Robert Bloch's "Nursemaid to Nightmares"), and Lost Race adventures. The sort of pulp fiction emulated by the Indiana Jones films appeared in our pages, the best-remembered specimen being *Golden Blood* by Jack Williamson (1933).

While it is unlikely that the present incarnation of the magazine will publish pure space-opera (unless it is somehow "weird," as Gene Wolfe's "The Other Dead Man" [Spring 1988] undeniably was), we *would* run a Lost Race/Lost Land adventure if a suitable, valid one came along.

We are certainly committed to scary stories. What do we mean by "scary"? Is this so subjective a reaction that there is no way we can qualify it?

No. Human beings have certain obvious fears, fear of death foremost among them.

Editors & Publishers:
Darrell Schweitzer
John Betancourt
George H. Scithers
Assistant Editors:
Leslie Smith
Dainis Bisenieks
Vincent Evangelisti
Diane Weinman
Circulation Manager:
Richard Kabakjian
Computer Consultant:
David J. Williams III
Of Counsel:
Yale F. Edeiken
Photographer:
Advanced Litho, Inc.
Typesetters:
The Twin Company, Inc.
Campus Copy Center
Printer:
Malloy Lithographing, Inc.
Hard-cover Binder
Hoster Bindery, Inc.

SUBMISSIONS?

Like most editors, we get unsolicited manuscripts, *lots* of them. We survive, as do other editors, only by imposing Rules.

Yes, we read unsolicited manuscripts — *if* they are in proper manuscript format. Each must arrive with a self-addressed, stamped return envelope big enough to take that manuscript back to you, or with a stamped, addressed, business-letter-sized envelope *and* instructions to dispose of the manuscript if not bought. And no, we will not read manuscripts in unacceptable format.

This proper format is described in numerous reference works. One of them is *On Writing Science Fiction: The Editors Strike Back!*, by George H. Scithers, Darrell Schweitzer, and John M. Ford — which also goes into the whole art and practice of writing and selling fantastic literature. *On Writing* is available for $19.50, postpaid, from Owlswick Press, PO Box 8243, Philadelphia, PA 19101 (if you live in Pennsylvania, add $1.17 for sales tax).

Most horror fiction somehow turns on this. The crude "slasher" films so popular with lowbrow audiences titillate and tease the viewer with death, mutilation, and menace.

More sophisticated audiences (such as those who read) have no objection to death, mutilation, and menace, but want it served up with a flavoring of *imagination*, the one element you surely will not encounter in *Hockey-Mask Killer Chops Teens, Round 46*.

H.P. Lovecraft's letters and essays are full of theorizing about the nature of the horror story. In fact he, more than any writer in the field in this century, worked out a complete critical theory and aesthetic. His famously quoted line (from *Supernatural Horror in Literature*) "The oldest and strongest emotion of mankind is fear, and the oldest and strongest kind of fear is fear of the unknown" is only the beginning of it. (And possibly not anthropologically sound. The oldest emotion may well be the desire to avoid starving.)

Lovecraft's horror fiction was aimed at more subtle, intellectual fears than merely dread of big, dripping things with teeth. "Cosmic" fear, as he put it, dealt with the seeming suspension of natural laws.

We can only agree. Surely the most frightening thing (and the most fruitful, for storytelling purposes) imaginable is, indeed, the *unimagined*, the discovery that we *don't know the rules* of existence, that there are vast and menacing (or just plain strange) forces in the universe which do not conform to our notions of how the laws of physics and biology work. Lovecraft, in working along these lines, was trying to arrive at a type of horror fiction which could convince a completely rational, materialistic person. New Age to the contrary, we are most convinced (and frightened) by horrors which don't rely on traditional, unchanged superstitions.

Horror for the rational person is the invasion of the irrational into our lives. It isn't so much the presence of the monster on the doorstep (frightening as that might be) but the implications of that monster's presence — that there *are* such things. At this point the protagonist must either conclude that he is going insane (another common topic for contemporary horror) or that the world is indeed out of control.

Many of us do feel that the world is out of control. Hence the popularity of such Stephen King stories as "The Mist," in which the old order of things completely vanishes and ordinary people must survive as best they can.

With the horror comes a dark *wonder*. The awe and mystery of the supernatural or strange should attract nearly as much as it terrifies. If we merely say "yuck" and run the other way, there isn't much story (or much reader involvement). But you'll notice the continued fascination with, say, vampires and the vampiric life. We want to see more of Dracula and understand the minutiae of his incredible existence, as the authors of later series-novels about vampires have long since discovered. We are tempted to peer into the unknown, even if it will surely destroy us.

Arthur Machen struck this balance perfectly in "The White People," in which a child is drawn deeper and deeper into witchcraft and tells of the experience in tantalizing, naïvely ambiguous language. Lovecraft did it again in "The Whisperer in Darkness," in which the protagonist, terribly afraid that the Old Ones are going carry his brain off into the depths of space, is also fascinated by the opportunity to explore the universe as a result, and to know the otherwise unknowable. In this sense, the archetypal horror story is the Faustus legend. We as readers follow in Dr. Faustus's footsteps, peering where we otherwise would not be able to, but, thankfully, paying for the privilege with a few dollars rather than our immortal souls.

A third element is most clearly demonstrated in the Machen story: *pathos*. If the story is merely about rotten, nasty people getting eaten by Things, then the reader's interest will soon wane. There has to be some form of sympathy. Boris Karloff realized this in his famous performance, when he made the Frankenstein monster pathetic even as it was terrible. In "The White People," the little girl remains completely innocent, even as she descends into the depths. Stephen King's stories are frequently about appalling things happening to good, decent people. That is also one of the strengths of *Dracula*, that the victims (Lucy in particular) are sympathetic people who are victimized by the Count about as randomly as

if they were hit by lightning.

All these elements come together in Alan Rodgers's "Emma's Daugther,"[Fall, 1988]. The story is about something which, if it happened in real life, would both terrify and appall. The events in the story would up-end our most established views of reality. Think: what if we discovered, truly, that the dead don't have to stay dead? Then there is the mystery, the plunge into the darkness of existence beyond life. And, at last, the pathos. This horrible thing (a small girl reanimated, living as a zombie) was brought about by a sense of perverted *love*. The story wrenches the emotions, lots of them, in many ways. That's what makes it scary.

Last issue brought numerous responses to Avram Davidson's article on the twentieth century's most spectacular occult charlatan and self-made legend, Aleister Crowley.

F. Gwynplaine MacIntyre writes:

Avram Davidson's "Adventures in Unhistory: The Great Rough Beast" was excellent overall, but it contained one factual error and several rather surprising omissions. First, the error: Aleister Crowley did not, as Davidson says (p.41), attend Trinity College, Oxford. In fact, Crowley was an alumnus of the slightly older and substantially larger Trinity College at Cambridge, which he left without taking a degree. I find this particular error slightly surprising, since Crowley was a textbook example of the Cantabrigian personality (cold, arrogant, acidulous) rather than the far more outgoing Oxonian prototype.

There are one or two spots in Davidson's article where he might have gone a bit farther. Fox example: he mentions Boleskine, the estate near Loch Ness where Crowley worked so much of his putative 'Magick,' yet Davidson says practically nothing about the place. Crowley maintained Boleskine as his base camp from August 1899 through February 1904 though he appears to have kept various bits of his Magickal apparatus there as late as June 1918. In recent years Jimmy Page, the guitarist for the rock band Led Zeppelin, bought the Boleskine estate solely for its association with Aleister Crowley. For several years, Page maintained Boleskine as a gathering place for people of allegedly 'Magickal' talents; the result of this was inevitable: Boleskine became the unofficial res-idence for all the layabouts, freeloaders, and leftover hippies of three continents. I visited Boleskine in the late 1970s, with Page's permission, and found nothing of Crowley there.

I am also utterly at a loss to understand why Davidson alludes, several times, to Crowley's alleged ability to make gold. The most cursory examination of Crowley's life shows that he was constantly in debt. Riches came to him frequently (usually through unsavory means, but surely never magical ones), yet Crowley invariably squandered the lolly as fast as it arrived . . . in fact, faster. Surely, if Crowley had possessed access to the Purse of Fortunatus, or any other sorcerous means of obtaining wealth, he would have availed himself of it. The fact that he never did so presents an obvious conclusion.

Edward Lee of Radford, Virginia is less happy with Davidson's article:

I must take issue with your inclusion in the Winter '88 issue of Avram Davidson's "Adventures in Unhistory: The Great Rough Beast." Davidson is an excellent fiction writer, I've enjoyed his work for years, but he should stick to subjects he knows when writing nonfiction. Particularly today, when so many young people are coming under the influence of cults and "religions," it is not responsible on your part to run an article about Aleister Crowley so filled with mistakes and misinformation.

Edward Alexander Crowley (not Alexander Edward) called himself Aleister for most of his life. Aleister was chosen, not because it was an antique spelling, but for numerological reasons. In numerology, each letter of the alphabet has a numerical value, and all the letters in the name are added together to produce a number. Some numbers have magical significance, others do not.

Crowley did meet Helena Blavatsky, and was initially much influenced by some of her ideas. Later he was to conclude that Theosophy was just so much hokum.

Prior to 1904, Crowley had only a passing interest in Egyptology. Because much of the Golden Dawn's ritual was supposedly derived from Egyptian sources, he knew that much, but not more. While visiting the Egyptian Museum in Cairo with his wife Rose, an event occurred which changed his direction and the rest of his life. Standing in front of an Egyptian stele (coincidentally exhibit #666 in the museum, and called the Stele of Revealing) Rose suddenly went into a trance and said to Crowley that "they" wanted to talk to him. She then gave him the details of a ritual which would allow this to happen. The ritual made no sense to Crowley, trained as he was in Golden Dawn ceremonial magic, but he was so interested in this happening that he performed the ritual as detailed a few days later. One point which has to be made about Crowley is that he was absolutely fearless in matters magical. He would literally try anything just to see what would happen.

On some specific points: Aleister Crowley was not called A.C. by close friends. His closest friends and his relatives called him Alec. I have seen many letters which refer to him thus, and have copies of letters from some of his relatives which complain about his scandalous behavior and his neglect of his daughter (who is probably alive today).

At the time that Crowley was jumping up the grade at the Golden Dawn, the head of that order was not William Butler Yeats, who never advanced very high in the order. The head, with whom Crowley had a tiff, was Samuel Liddell McGregor Mathers. Mathers knew that Crowley was going to take over the order from him if allowed to progress, so Mathers denied the advanced grade to Crowley. Shortly thereafter Mathers went into decline and the Golden Dawn as it then was fell apart.

On page 49 is the worst part of the article. Davidson says that Crowley is associated with the Black Mass. The Black Mass, which is of French origin, is an infantile attempt to be evil by perverting the superstitions of the Catholic Church. While it may be anti-Catholic or even anti-Christian, it has nothing to do with real evil, and nothing to do with magic. Crowley's rituals were never white or black. They were magic, or as I ought to say, Magick. Calling Magick good or evil, white or black, is just as ridiculous as saying the same about electricity. Magick is a source of power for personal change, and can be used to do good or evil as the disposition of the magician directs. Crowley was being truthful when he denied ever performing a Black Mass. He found the idea utterly

8

stupid.

Perhaps the greatest difference between Magick and electricity is that electricity is part of the physical world. It can be measured. It lights lightbulbs. If you use it badly, it has definite effects which can't be wished away, like electrocution. It is, in short, real. But no one can demonstrate that Magick is real, that it exists beyond the imagination of the magician. We must maintain a sense of perspective here. You betray yourself when you dismiss Catholicism as superstition, but seem to take Magick seriously. A Catholic would dismiss Magick as a superstition, and no "magician" could prove otherwise.

So the real subject under discussion here is the nature of belief, and the human mind's apparently infinite capacity for self-delusion. Did Crowley sincerely devote a lifetime chasing after shadows, or was he a fraud, in it for the money, power, and notoriety? Certainly he enjoyed the notoriety, which is why the incident in the Egyptian museum must be viewed very skeptically. Crowley went to great pains to develop and publicize his own legend. Isn't this the very sort of thing he would invent later on, both to give himself credibility and to thrill the faithful?

We recommend two books, neither specifically about Crowley, but both very revealing studies of occultism, cults, and the kinds of people who create and get involved with them: Sprague de Camp's Spirits, Stars, and Spells (available from Owlswick Press, $17.00) and Russell Miller's biography of L. Ron Hubbard, Bare-Faced Messiah (Holt). We suspect that Crowley and Hubbard had more in common than the admirers of either care to admit.

A final word on the subject of Magick and mysticism comes from poet and author **David Lunde**:

I very much enjoyed Avram Davidson's "The Odd Old Bird," with its ambiguously targeted title, and I was intrigued by Davidson's suggestion that Aleister Crowley might be the model for Yeats's "rough beast." I'm a great admirer of Yeats's poetry, but I had not run into this idea before. In regard to Yeats's mystical perceptions (e.g. the green elephants he saw following Crowley), Ezra Pound, who served as Yeats's secretary for *a while, tells an amusing story. Pound, of course, was a hard-headed American from Idaho and considered mysticism a load of horse-apples. On one occasion Yeats and Pound were seated at a sidewalk cafe with Yeats's back to the passing pedestrian traffic. A highly perfumed courtesan of the streets passed behind him, and suddenly Yeats's head lifted, his nose sampled the breeze, and he declared, "Ahhh, an odor from the other world!" upon which Pound collapsed giggling hysterically to the sidewalk.*

Peni R. Griffin writes:

As a new writer who intends to be an established writer if it takes her whole life, I would like to say that I am a little miffed at Alfonso D.J. Alfonso's suggestion to cut us some slack. If his hope and will to write can't outlast his rejection slips, he doesn't have what it takes to write anyway. The last thing a new writer needs is an editor who doesn't demand the very best. Nor do I mind seeing established authors get "Special" issues of magazines. I'm looking forward to my own too much! If a writer has been around long enough, producing enough good work for his name to improve magazine sales, then he deserves the recognition. It's no disgrace to be rejected in competition with a Gene Wolfe story; and I'm not afraid of being overlooked. After all, editors know that Gene Wolfe could die in a car crash tomorrow. It's always been my understanding that they liked to discover new authors; that this was how editors built their reputations and careers. If I give them something worth finding, they'll be glad to find it. Besides, how long would a magazine last that published slightly-under-par stories by unknowns in preference to polished tales by names?

Right you are. Your understanding is correct. Editors *are* always looking for talented newcomers, often for the more prosaic reason that they have to fill pages and the big names are often up to their ears in book contracts and can't write more than one or two short stories a year — certainly not enough to fill a magazine the size of *Weird Tales®* to the exclusion of everybody else!

Gene Wolfe sends corrections and comments:

The pulp paired with Secret Agent X *in my piece on Avram Davidson was* Operator

5, not plain Operator. *I should have caught that in galleys; obviously I didn't.*

Alfonso D.J. Alfonso says my roots aren't in Weird Tales. *I was a faithful reader when WT was one pulp among many. For what it may be worth, I believe it's reading, not selling, that provides roots. Roots are the things from which one's writing grows — if it does.*

You discussed cover letters; it seems to me that there is a sentence that ought to be in almost every such letter, though I doubt that you, or any other editors, see it very often: "I am a regular reader of your magazine."

Prolific correspondent and would-be author **Greg Koster** writes:

Looking through the letter column of #292, I find I have a letter in it! Evidently you have started an incentive plan: send a letter along with your MS., and even if we reject the manuscript, we'll publish the letter. Such a deal. If this is what getting published feels like, I'll probably expire with excitement after my first story acceptance.

Your comments on the nasty rejection of your rejection were good, but I have to speak my own piece on this subject:

The way to view unpublished authors is similar to the way you should view someone who has been diagnosed as having cancer. The treatment for cancer is long and arduous, can engulf the strongest character, and often has depressing side-effects. (Writing takes a sustained effort, can often seem endless and unprogressive, and there ain't no way rejections can be anything but dismaying.) Some patients give up and die. (Some writers stop writing and remain unpublished.) Some go off to laetrile clinics (they seek out vanity publishers and become something of a joke), and some persevere and triumph.

It is true that this struggle can induce something very much like paranoia, not that it excuses explosions at editors. In fact, editing probably ranks close to writing in ulcer-producing situations.

Thanks. We always appreciate sympathy. But your analogy to cancer patients is much too gloomy. Being a would-be writer is more like the would-be Olympic aquatics champion who is just learning how to swim. First you master the basic strokes. Then you can do laps to build up endurance. Then you get good at it. If you never make the Olympics,

9

at least you had a pleasant time in the pool. And you didn't *die*. While we think that anyone with any talent and education (including self-education) can be a writer if they try hard enough, there *is* life after rejection. Many people give up simply because writing is not central to their lives, and they are just as happy doing something else.

Author **Jefferson P. Swycaffer** offers a fine tribute to the late Hank Jankus:

Revealing though it may be of my naïveté in the publishing business, I'm writing to thank you for the art supporting my story in the Winter issue of Weird Tales®. *Hank Jankus's illustrations of my story — and the other stories! — were smooth, faithful to the action, stimulating to the imagination, and downright wonderful to see.*

His illustration for my story, specifically the picture of the multi-tentacled Lovecraftian horror moving unsteadily through the cavern of webs, was magnificent. He did a perfect job of showing what cannot truly be shown; he suggested things without making them visually explicit.

I was sorry to read of his recent death; it has always been my practice (again somewhat naïve, I fear) to write "thank-you" letters to the artists who have been selected to illustrate my stories. (I've seven books published, and I've been very fortunate in the results of the cover-art. Since I'm one of those people who buy books for the cover art, I know how effective it can be.)

Thank you, again, and condolences to us all for the loss of an accomplished and prolific artist.

We don't think you're being naïve at all. Illustrators, like anyone else, deserve to be commended for a job well done. Books *do* sell on the basis of covers, and magazines sell on the basis of both cover and interior artwork. So the artist is fully as important as any of the writers, and should be appreciated as such.

R. Scott Youmans of Virginia Beach, Virginia writes:

In my opinion, Weird Tales® #294 could quite possibly be the best issue to date. It had an excellent mixture of poetry (which I especially enjoy) and fiction which was well-balanced between the light and the dark. The stories which reached out and grabbed me were "Instrument of Allah" and "The Dimension Weasel." I enjoy stories where a character in the present is faced with something other-worldly. "Instrument" also leaves the reader hanging, asking questions. Will he tell anyone? Will he be believed? How has Williams been changed by the experience? Obviously, "Instrument of Allah" is my choice for best story, with "The Dimension Weasel" second, and "Kaeti and the Village," and "Magician in the Dark" tied for third.

I didn't take too well to Mr. Davidson's stories. "Nothing Like a Clean Weapon" seemed to be the best of the three, but the others . . . I couldn't warm up to them.

"When Jesus Comes Down the Chimney" was also a favorite of mine. It was a refreshing — even 'kinda neat' — look at tradition, religion, and Christmas. Other stories that were well taken include "The Frog . . ." and "The Ones Who Turn Invisible." The latter caused me to reflect on how I see the poor and homeless — very nice.

Keep up the GREAT work.

For our technologically inclined readers:

John Betancourt runs a computer BBS (bulletin board system) in Philadelphia. Phone number — modem only! — is 215–289–4144 (this number is PC Pursuit accessible), or 215–889–0997. 1200 or 2400 baud. You can leave messages for the editors of *Weird Tales®* there, get information on what's coming up in the magazine, or just discuss the latest in science fiction, fantasy, and horror.

The Most Popular Story

Results for issue #293 are in. First place goes to Avram Davidson for "The Odd Old Bird." Second goes to "When Jesus Comes Down the Chimney," by Ian Watson. For third place we seem to have a tie between "Instrument of Allah," by Robert Metzger, "The Tunnel," by Carl Jacobi, and "Message from Hell," by Robert Sheckley.

Keep those letters coming! We need to know what readers like — and dislike — in the magazine. Suggestions for Featured Authors and Featured Artists are also welcome.

THE DEN

by John Gregory Betancourt

People often wonder what the field will be like in ten or twenty years (and here I lump science fiction, fantasy, and horror all together). One recent article in *The New York Review of Science Fiction* ("The New Generation Gap," by Kathryn Cramer, July 1989) pointed out that the number of professional writers who sell work as teenagers has been steadily dropping. According to Cramer's research, 2.8% of the new writers between 1976 and 1986 made their first sale before age 20 (as compared to 28% making their first sale before age 20 from 1926–1935). She asks, "Will science fiction become a literature by 35-year-olds for 35-year-olds? Will this alienate our source of new readers, namely twelve-year-olds? Should science-fiction writers be trying to write for twelve-year-olds? . . . Is this new generation gap between new readers and new writers a good thing, or a problem to be solved? Is this a sign of the science-fiction field's maturity, or of its demise?"

As the field grows older and more respectable, of course it's going to have an increasing number of older readers and writers. You don't have to put away "that Buck Rogers stuff" after high school or college anymore: it's okay to read it. Science fiction, fantasy, and horror are respectable stuff — witness all the science-fiction bestsellers in recent years.

However, I would still doubt the accuracy of Cramer's figures from 1976–1986. Why? Because new writers tend to have a good deal of space between early sales, I've noticed. It takes time for someone to become known in the field; a few scattered short stories won't do it — unless they're something exceptional, which (let's face it) most early sales aren't. William Gibson — surely the quintessential 1980s science-fiction writer — sold his first short story in the mid-1970s. Had this survey been taken in 1980, he doubtless would have been skipped. Most writers publish their major works late in life. What Kathryn Cramer has counted are first sales by major authors. But who will be a major author in 10 years? And when did they sell their first short story? That's what counts.

Regarding "the disappearance of the teen-age writer" — nonsense. Any of the magazine editors will tell you there are plenty of young writers submitting material. And some of it is pretty close to publishable, if not actually so. Count the first sales George Scithers bought at *Asimov's*. One was even from a 15-year-old. (Ok, it was a pun story, but naytheless . . .) The problem (if you can call it a problem), lies more with marketing concerns and a plethora of professional writers. There are probably more science-fiction, fantasy, and horror writers alive and active now than ever before, and the number of genre magazines has slowly shrunk to the present 3 major and 3 minor ones. (I count *Aboriginal, Amazing,* and *Weird Tales*® as minor; *Analog, Asimov's,* and *F&SF* as major.) So established writers —

those with name-recognition value among readers — are of course taking the majority of available slots. That's just a publishing reality.

The problem may also be perception of markets. Kathryn Cramer asks, "What if an author's claimed first sale at age 15 was a fantasy story 'sold' to a newspaper which paid him in copies?" I would argue this isn't a professional sale: for it to be a professional sale, circulation must be at least 10,000 and you must be paid at least 3¢ per word. This is admittedly a combination of SFWA and Horror Writers of America standards, but I think it works.

However, it does still leave us with a matter to address: alternate markets. Namely the science-fiction/fantasy/horror small-press movement.

The small press has become the breeding ground for new writers, particularly young ones. Why? Because it's accessible. Where else can you get feedback on every submission you send out? Where else can you get bad or mediocre stories published, then commented on (in detail!) in the letters column? The SF/F/H small press has set itself up to train new writers better than the professional magazines ever could. In effect, the field now has its own minor league system.

Perhaps everyone won't understand what I mean by "small press." I don't mean the low-circulation SF/fantasy/horror fan magazine typified by William Crawford and *Marvel Tales* of the 1940s; Crawford's *Marvel Tales* really wanted to be a professional magazine, but wasn't. Instead, I mean the small-circulation magazines, usually desktop published these days, which are dedicated to finding and developing new talent: titles like *Space & Time, Grue, Eldritch Tales, Deathrealm, Weirdbook,* and *New Pathways* are a few of the ones with which I'm familiar. They generally have 2-color covers, are standard-sized or half standard-sized, and have circulations under 1000 — usually under 500. Most readers are also writers.

The new small-press magazines are a terrific place to get detailed feedback, get encouragement by selling a few stories (even if it sometimes is for less than a penny a word), and generally work on improving one's craft. I started there because I simply

wasn't good enough to sell to the professional markets — yet. They were an invaluable tool for improving my writing skills.

Looking back, I can pick out dozens of people who first appeared in small-press magazines. A few who have published novels within the last few years: Kevin J. Anderson, Jessica Amanda Salmonson, Mercedes Lackey, Phyllis Ann Karr, Charles di Lint, Charles Saunders (several of his DAW novels are cobbled together from work which appeared in *Space & Time*), and Gordon Linzner.

A step above *Space & Time* et al. are Dennis Mallonee's *Fantasy Book* and *Marion Zimmer Bradley's Fantasy Magazine,* both of which pay respectable amounts for fiction, but which don't have the circulation — yet — to be professional magazines. Why do I separate them from *Whispers*? Because they have the same openness toward new writers that small-press magazines show. *Aboriginal SF* should probably be lumped in here as well, for despite its circulation (20,000 at last count), it is pretty much a part of the same movement, and has the same openness toward new writers.

Looking at the Spring, 1989 issue of *MZB'sFM,* for instance, you see the following writers: George Barr, Deborah Wheeler, Mildred Perkins, Brad Strickland, Laurell Hamilton, Marina Fitch, I.F. Cole, and John Bunnell. The July-August, 1989 *Aboriginal SF* contains fiction by Patricia Anthony, R.P. Bird, Brooke Stauffer, Robert A. Metzger, and Kir Bulychev.

I recognize five names between the magazines: one because he's an artist, two because I've read their work, and two because we have bought from them for *Weird Tales®.* Who are the others? Where did they come from? Will they ever sell enough work to qualify as subjects for Kathryn's Cramer's survey?

Time will tell, I think.

And if it were true that there are fewer young SF writers these days, I would suggest that it may be a sign of the success of the school system. Writing seems to me to be the product of an imperfect socialization process. An unhappy childhood can turn a child to escapist literature — and in some cases, to writing escapist literature. As I see it, the U.S. school system serves two main purposes: keeping young people off the job market as long as possible, and socializing them so they won't create problems later in life. (There are few home-grown terrorists and revolutionaries in the U.S. for a reason.) What, you ask, about going to school for knowledge? If the government cared about schooling beyond token concerns, we would have an education system equal to that in France or Japan. But this a different problem, I think.

Necroscope, by Brian Lumley
TOR Books, 505 pp., $3.95
Necroscope II: Vamphyri!,, by Brian Lumley
TOR Books, 470 pp., $4.95

Of course all *Weird Tales*® readers are familiar with Brian Lumley's work, or will be soon enough (this being a special issue dedicated to him). So it seems only appropriate that we lead off with reviews of Lumley's two most recent novels in the U.S., which start off what will be a 5-book-long (or more!) series: *Necroscope* and *Necroscope II: Vamphyri!*.

They're great.

They're not horror, but they're great.

What are they if they're not horror? That's the hard part. I'd suggest Science Fictional Psychic Espionage Action-Adventure with Horror Overtones, but I doubt that would leave much room on the spine for the author's name. Whatever, the *Necroscope* books are certainly not horror as we know it, despite the presence of vampires (here, an alien creature which implants itself into a human and develops a symbiotic relationship).

The plot: Harry Keogh can talk to the souls of the dead, who linger at the places of their deaths. From them he gains much knowledge, and begins to increase his psychic gifts.

Meanwhile, in Romania, a long-dead vampire begins to exert its waning power. It wants to live again, and has found a willing pawn in Boris Dragosani, whose birth it engineered. Boris and Harry are roughly the same age, and by alternating between the two, many parallels are made. By the end, Harry is the force of ultimate good and Dragosani the force of ultimate evil.

Of course, the British and Soviet governments are involved. Both have ESPionage teams, and are researching the paranormal.

Telepaths, clairvoyants, telekinetics, and other psychic talents have all been harnessed to some degree. Both sides are engaged in a sort of psychic cold war. Dragosani signs up with the Soviets and begins working toward his own personal domination of the world. Harry is reluctant to join the British E-Branch, though, and has to be convinced of Dragosani's evil.

Necroscope II is about the origins of the vampires, and their destruction. While the threat is less great, it works as a mid-series book by progressing the action, introducing new characters, and generally fleshing out everything the first book only hinted at.

There is much action, adventure, and — indeed — horror here. Lumley has found a great formula, and seems to know it. I literally couldn't put the books down as I read them, they're that gripping.

Which is not to say the series is perfect. I do have several qualms: with Harry's powers increasing exponentially, where will they stop? He is godlike at the end of the second book. And, with the vampires dead, where can the series go? What can possibly top the first two books' climaxes?

I don't know. But I'm eager to find out.

Soft, by F. Paul Wilson
TOR Books, 306 pp., $17.95 (hc)

I was shocked to learn that *Soft* is F. Paul Wilson's first collection of short stories. It's certainly quite overdue. And, when I got to the dedication page, I was just as shocked to discover it dedicated to George Scithers, Darrell Schweitzer, and me, along with the other editors who had bought these short stories.

Collected here are 16 of his stories, including "Buckets," which is previously unpublished, spanning 20 years of his writing. Since they are arranged chronologically (by date of publication), the collection gives an interesting overview of Wilson's career. The earlier stories are science fiction, with minor horrific overtones ("Ratman," about a space-going exterminator and his intelligent rats, "The Cleaning Machine," which gets rid of dust, dirt — or people — who get too close). Then in later stories the horrors start taking center stage, many of them with medical themes ("Buckets" is an overly preachy story about the evils of abortion clinics; "Soft" is an AIDS parable, in which people's bones literally disintegrate in a most horrible fashion). The story reprinted from *Weird Tales*®, "Ménage à Trois," is in many ways a reworking of the formula for "The Cleaning Machine," and even has the same policemen in a similar framing device. But where the earlier story doesn't really come to life or involve the reader in characters — it exists to reveal its Great Wonder, that the machine is *real* — "Ménage à Trois" has meat on its bones, and succeeds on all levels. In fact, all the stories (with the exception of "Buckets") are gems.

F. Paul Wilson is one of the very best short-story writers in the field; this collection is long overdue. Don't miss it.

Book of the Dead, edited by John Skipp and Craig Spector
Bantam Books, 390 pp., $4.50

Book of the Dead is full of zombies. Not the Haitian kind, made by voodoo priests, but the George R. Romero sort — you know, like in *Night of the Living Dead,* with the dead suddenly risen everywhere across the planet, and boy are they hungry!

The foreword by George R. Romero gives the impression that these stories are based on his movies. Which isn't so — or, at least they're not based on the movies *I* saw. For instance, in "Saxophone," by Nicholas Royle, the dead are not only as intelligent as the living, but just as organized. These aren't the mindless creatures from *Night of the Living Dead* or *Dawn of the Dead,* or even the zombies with vestigial memories from *Day of the Dead.* They're something else.

The stories also offer conflicting reasons for the zombification of the world's dead. In Stephen King's "Home Delivery," aliens are at fault. In Joe R. Lansdale's "On the Far Side of the Cadillac Desert With Dead Folks," it's an experimental immortality virus that accidentally escaped from a scientist's laboratory. Which is it? Or is it something entirely different? In any series — whether it's short stories or books — I as a reader expect consistency.

But there is still much to like about *Book of the Dead.* The stories get stronger the deeper you get into the book, peaking with

Edward Bryant's wonderful "A Sad Last Love at the Diner of the Damned," which has impeccable characterization and manages to convince me that, no matter how bad the dead get, the living can still be worse. Other high points: Steve Rasnic Tem's "Bodies and Heads," which while not really a zombie story, is still so strange and eerie I won't forget it for some time; Brian Hodge's "Dead Giveaway," about a TV game show run by the dead *for* the dead; and David Schow's "Jerry's Kids Meet Wormboy," which is so excessive and disgusting that I loved it. Schow's was the only story in the collection I found even slightly nauseating — which says a lot for Schow as a writer. ("If you can't scare 'em," to quote someone famous, "go for the gross-out." Schow did.)

By all means pick up a copy. The Bryant story is worth the admission price all by itself.

East of Samarinda, by Carl Jacobi
Bowling Green State University Popular Press, $24.95 (trade pb)

Carl Jacobi, one of the more popular pulp writers, didn't just write horror and fantasy stories. His tales of the exotic corners of the world graced *Thrilling Adventure, Dime Mystery Magazine, Short Stories,* and many other pulp magazines. It's a shame more of his stories haven't been collected before now.

East of Samarinda will turn out, I fear, less of a success than it should be for a number of reasons. Primary among them is value for the money. As a reader, I would never have bought this book. First, it *looks* cheap: it has a 2-color cover, and the interior pages are photocopied from pulp magazines. Much as I like pulp magazines, when their type is reduced and copied, it gets hard to read. It would have been better to typeset the whole thing over again.

And $25 for a trade paperback? I don't care if the material isn't available elsewhere. You can get new hardcovers cheaper than that — like F. Paul Wilson's *Soft.*

Someone's making a lot of money off this book, and I'll bet it isn't Carl Jacobi. □

WEIRD TALES TALKS WITH

BRIAN LUMLEY

by Stephen Jones

Weird Tales: Can you remember when you first became interested in reading macabre fiction?

Brian Lumley: My mother always read a lot and liked the macabre stuff. We had these two huge collections of ghost stories and mysteries. My earliest memory of reading that kind of thing was when my parents had gone out one night and I was left alone. I got these books down from the high shelf, were they had been kept out of my reach, and I started to read them through. I still remember some of the stories: William Hope Hodgson's "The Voice in the Night" was in there, and A.E.D. Smith's "The Coat" was another one that grabbed my imagination at the time.

WT: As a child, did you ever try your hand at writing fiction?

Lumley: I wrote some "humorous" science fiction stories when I was fourteen, but luckily none of them have survived.

WT: You left your hometown of Horden, on England's northeast coast, when you were twenty-one to join the army . . .

Lumley: I had done what my parents wanted me to do — they had wanted me to have a proper job, so that for five years I'd been an apprentice woodcutting machinist and gained all the honors of the trade. But I didn't really want to do that for the rest of my life. I had all my qualifications, so I could always return to that trade whenever I wanted. I couldn't wait to get the Hell out of there, and on my twenty-first birthday I quit my job and four days later I joined the army.

WT: What was it like in the army?

Lumley: When I stepped into the Military Police barracks I knew I wasn't going to cause any trouble in that place — those guys were all nine feet tall. I was stationed in West Germany — Berlin — which I found fascinating and wonderful; I spent three years in Cyprus, then Malta, even parts of England — I was once the quartermaster of Edinburgh Castle — and I finished my time as a Sergeant Major training recruits.

WT: When did you first discover H. P. Lovecraft's stories?

Lumley: I had come across Lovecraft before I joined the army. When I was a kid, maybe as young as fourteen, I read Robert Bloch's "Notebook Found in a Deserted House," and I had possibly read one or two of Lovecraft's stories as well, although I hadn't recognised them as such. Then while I was in Germany I came across a copy of *Cry Horror!* This was a collection of Lovecraft's stories and I was fascinated. Around 1967 I contacted Arkham House and had a lot of Lovecraft material sent to me by August Derleth. He later suggested that I should try my hand at writing fiction.

WT: You began by contributing to *The Arkham Collector* . . .

Lumley: That's right. Derleth wrote me four or five consecutive letters praising my story "The Thing in the Moonlight II," which he particularly liked. Next, he was looking for stories for *Tales of the Cthulhu Mythos* and suggested that my story "The Sister City," which was very long, should be shorter. I personally cut it down, but

15

later I incorporated all the original material and built upon it for my first novel, *Beneath the Moors*.

WT: August Derleth had a reputation of often re-writing the work of new authors. Did this ever happen to you?

Lumley: Derleth hardly touched my stuff at all. He did, on several occasions, remove a bit of purple prose, but I would guess that he didn't change one percent of my work. For example, in *Beneath the Moors* there is only one word changed by Derleth.

WT: While Arkham House published *Beneath the Moors* and your short-story collections *The Caller of the Black* and *The Horror at Oakdeene* in hardcover, your first paperback success came with DAW Books' edition of *The Burrowers Beneath* in 1974 . . .

Lumley: In 1971 Derleth died. By that time I had started work on a new novel, and after his death I didn't really know what to do with the completed book. I had read quite a few DAW Books, so I thought I'd try it out on them. Donald Wollheim liked it and published it.

WT: *The Burrowers Beneath* introduced readers to your psychic detective Titus Crow, whose adventures you continued in a series of novels. Where did the inspiration for the character come from?

Lumley: I've always been impressed by the character of Van Helsing of *Dracula* fame. He was one of the psychic detectives I could really believe in — he was fully developed and I wanted to do the same thing with Titus Crow. So although I did not write the stories in any particular chronological order, I had a rough idea of the sequence in my mind and each story would add to his knowledge. This way the reader, hopefully, would eventually believe in him as well. People who regularly read my stuff always have a soft spot for the Titus Crow stories.

WT: Some of the books in the Crow series, such as *Spawn of the Winds* and *In the Moons of Borea*, contain some pretty outlandish concepts. Was this an attempt on your part to break out of the Lovecraft mould?

Lumley: I was experimenting. Remember I wasn't a writer, I was a soldier. What I was doing then I was doing as a hobby; I was writing it for no one except me. If it was published, then that was a bonus.

Now *The Burrowers Beneath* was horror; *The Transition of Titus Crow* was a science fantasy; the next one in the series was *The Clock of Dreams*, which was pure fantasy! It had the same characters but was set in Earth's Dreamland. The one after that, *Spawn of the Winds*, was science fiction, although it had macabre elements; and *In the Moons of Borea* was science fantasy. The last in the series, *Elysia*, is likewise science fantasy. Steve, you once said about a story of mine that it contained everything but the kitchen sink; well *Elysia* includes the kitchen sink as well! It spans Space and Time: the stars are right, the Old Ones return, and the "secret" we've known all along is revealed . . .

WT: One of your most offbeat books was *Khai of Ancient Khem*, which featured an Egyptian Pharaoh holding a television set on the cover of the 1981 edition . . .

Lumley: *Khai of Ancient Khem* was the only book of mine that was ever specifically commissioned. Berkley Books said this is the kind of story you should be writing — a story set in the Egypt of pre-history full of sex, mayhem, science fiction, fantasy, and horror. They said, "Do what the Hell you like, Brian, so long as it's full of everything." It turned out to be a rather long novel, although I did play it fairly seriously and tried to write it as best I could.

It was very successful despite that awful jacket, and a lot of people remember it. I still get letters asking where to get hold of copies. I have to say it's being re-published in England this year by Grafton with a much better cover this time! *Khai of Ancient Khem* is one book I can personally read again and still enjoy.

WT: Throughout the 1970s and early '80s your books were regularly appearing in American editions, while you remained virtually ignored in your native Britain. Were you bitter about this?

Lumley: Remember I was still a soldier. I didn't really give a damn: my wages were safe. Also, at that time my agent was American. Soon after August Derleth died, Kirby McCauley approached me and asked if I was looking for an agent. I never gave much thought to being published in England — I was never there! Apart from having a couple of stories in Richard Davis' original *Year's Best Horror Stories*, I didn't even consider a UK publisher at that time.

WT: Why did you decide to leave the army?

Lumley: I had done my time — twenty-two years. I could have stayed on, but by then I had decided to take up writing full time. It wasn't that I'd had enough — it was a wonderful life — but I could now turn my attention to writing and hopefully make a success of it.

WT: Why did you return to Lovecraft's concepts again with your trilogy *Hero of Dreams, Ship of Dreams,* and *Mad Moon of Dreams* ?

Lumley: They are not Lovecraft. Very few of my stories, except the very early ones, could be described as pastiches. They may have had some of Lovecraft's Mythos background, but they were not written in Lovecraft's style. I rarely emulated his writing — even I recognised at the time that it was a style which had gone. It was great, but you can't keep reading the same thing over and over again.

Now the Dreamlands, as in Lovecraft's *The Dream-Quest of Unknown Kadath,* were wide open: he'd created this wonderful, quite fantastic realm and done very little with it. I have always liked the idea of humorous adventuring, such as Fritz Leiber's Fafhrd and the Gray Mouser series. Now some people may say that Hero and Eldin are obviously derived from Leiber's characters, but they are not. In fact, Hero and Eldin are based on Bing Crosby and Bob Hope. That's absolutely true. Many of their wisecracks have the same flavor as Hope and Crosby in all the *Road* pictures. Those films were, in my opinion, absolutely fabulous pieces of farce, and my Hero and Eldin stories are the same. Occasionally they come up against real horror, just as Bob Hope would come up against a giant octopus. Those pictures fired my imagination when I was a kid, and although Hero and Eldin may not look like them or act like them, nevertheless their adventures derive greatly from the *Road* pictures of Bob Hope and Bing Crosby.

WT: In 1984 you published a substantial novel, *Psychomech,* blending elements of horror and science fiction. This was followed over the next three years by two sequels, *Psychamok* and *Psychosphere,* and another book, *Demogorgon.* What all these volumes have in common is a strength of writing, grounded in reality, that was missing from your earlier work . . .

Lumley: It is an interesting point. When I was living and working in the army I was writing fantasy. Having left the army and come to live in a world that is mainly escapist, my recent books more properly reflect real life.

WT: This is certainly true of your next two books, *Necroscope* and *Necroscope II: Vamphyri!,* where you take on the mantle of "The Robert Ludlum of horror," combining gritty spy fiction with the supernatural. How many titles are planned in the series?

Lumley: *Necroscope V* finishes the series with Armageddon! Then I want to go on to something really *big.* The people who have read *Necroscope* and *Vamphyri!* have said that they did so in one or two sittings. I have not yet spoken to anyone who said they were bored by them, and I've yet to read a bad review; I've read a couple of *grudgingly* good reviews by people who have always slammed my books before but now actually *like* these things!

People read these books in one or two sittings, which is precisely what I wanted them to do, but with the big book I'm planning it will have to be read in three or four sittings. Providing I can nail people's attention in that way, then I'm happy.

WT: Do you get much fan mail?

Lumley: I always get some fan mail, but never so much as now. With the *Necroscope* series I have been swamped with letters and I try to answer everyone at least once. People phone me up from America and Canada just to find out what's going to happen in the subsequent books.

WT: Are you still asked that perennial question, "Where do you get your ideas?"

Lumley: Oh yes. I suppose I'm just like every other writer, I can't answer it! When you've spent as many years as I have reading this kind of stuff, a lot of it has to sink in. There are many things you read where you think, "I could have done that better." Now whether you do it deliberately or entirely by accident, people will say that there are no new stories, and within certain limitations I think they are correct.

I believe that there are very few new stories in science fiction — you've got time travel, space travel, war stories, and love stories. And I suppose you must add to that alien stories. So whatever new stories you read in science fiction, they contain combinations of some of those elements and there is no escaping from it. Now horror is the same: there are certain basic themes which you can't escape from — you either have dead people walking about, or you have creatures invading the bodies of human beings. You have man's worst nightmares — that's what horror stories are all about — and any of those themes you explore have been explored before by another writer. Of course the way to overcome this problem is to not deliberately set out to find a type of story which has been done before and do it better, but to try and find something that frightens *you.*

WT: Do you think it's easier these days for a writer to break into print than it was when you started your career?

Lumley: I think it's easier now. The fanzines proliferate — there are a lot of Lovecraft-oriented fanzines and there are hundreds of others that are fantasy or science-fiction-oriented. Desk-top publishing has really opened the field up. Even if someone had talent, twenty or thirty years ago he would have to push really hard to get into print. But over the past few years we have seen good writers start out in fanzines and rapidly go on to be published in more permanent form. However, whereas it's easier to get into print nowadays, the standards have to be just a little higher as there are so many people trying to do it.

WT: You yourself have continued to support small-press publishers over the years, and a number of your more recent books have been published first by W. Paul Ganley . . .

Lumley: Maybe I wouldn't have been so supportive except that up until the early 1980s I was secure in the army — I didn't need the money, so I wasn't worried. However, I've enjoyed working with Paul Ganley; several of his Lumley books are now out of print and the prices being asked for them are ridiculous — if Paul and I had known, we might have kept some in reserve!

WT: Do you collect books yourself?

Lumley: I used to collect books — anything by Lovecraft, in all different shapes and sizes. I'm glad I did, because during a couple of traumatic years after I left the army I was short of money. Many of the books I had collected were valuable, so I sold most of them off.

WT: How do you see yourself as a writer?

Lumley: There is no hype or hyperbole on my covers. You will not find a single *one* of my books where sixty-five people on the back tell you how good the bloody thing is. I don't believe in it. If you have to have people telling you how good it is, then it isn't any good.

I really find no dividing line between what is called a "literary" writer and a "pulp" writer; I think success is what counts. I'd just like to be remembered as a guy whose books people enjoyed reading. I think it's quite obvious that there is no hidden meaning to my work — I'm not advocating anything. I'm just telling stories that I like and I want other people to like. □

MOVING?

Don't leave *Weird Tales*® behind! Send us your old address *(don't forget the zip code)* and your new one. We'll make sure you receive each issue without delay. Not a subscriber yet? Turn to the inside back cover for more information.

THE DISAPPROVAL OF JEREMY CLEAVE

by Brian Lumley

"My husband's eye," she said quite suddenly, peering over my shoulder in something of morbid fascination. "Watching us!" She was very calm about it, which ought to say quite a lot about her character. A very cool lady, Angela Cleave. But in view of the circumstances, a rather odd statement; for the fact was that I was making love to her at the time, and somewhat more alarming, her husband had been dead for six and a half weeks!

"What!?" I gasped, flopping over onto my back, my eyes following the direction of her pointing finger. She seemed to be aiming it at the dresser. But there was nothing to be seen, not anywhere in that huge, entirely extravagant bedroom. Or perhaps I anticipated too much, for while it's true that she had specified an "eye," for some reason *I* was looking for a complete person. This is perhaps readily understandable — the shock, and what all. But no such one was there. Thank God!

Then there came a rolling sound, like a marble down a gentle slope, and again I looked where she was pointing. Atop the dresser, a shape wobbled into view from the back to the front, being brought up short by the fancy gilt beading around the dresser's top. And she was right, it was an eye — a glass eye — its deep green pupil staring at us somehow morosely.

"Arthur," she said, in the same breathless, colourless voice, "this really makes me feel very peculiar." And

truth to tell it made me feel that way, too. Certainly it ruined my night.

But I got up, went to the dresser and brought the eye down. It was damp, or rather sticky, and several pieces of fluff had attached themselves to it. Also, I fancied it smelled rather, but in a bedroom perfumed as Angela Cleave's that was hard to say. And not something one *would* say, anyway.

"My dear, it's an eye," I said, "only a glass eye!" And I took it to the vanity basin and rinsed it thoroughly in cold water. "Jeremy's, of course. The . . . vibrations must have started it rolling."

She sat up in bed, covering herself modestly with the silk sheet (as if we weren't sufficiently acquainted) and brushed back a lock of damp, golden hair from her beautiful brow. And: "Arthur," she said, "Jeremy's eye was buried with him. He desired to be put to rest looking as perfectly natural as possible — *not* with a patch over that hideous hole in his face!"

"Then it's a spare," I reasoned, going back to the bed and handing it to her. She took it — an entirely unconscious act — and immediately snatched back her hand, so that the thing fell to the floor and rolled under the bed. And:

"Ugh!" she said. "But I didn't *want* it, Arthur! And anyway, I never knew he had a spare."

"Well, he obviously did," I sighed, trying to get back into bed with her. But she held the covers close and

19

wouldn't have me.

"This has quite put me off," she said. "I'm afraid I shall have a headache." And suddenly, for all that she was a cool one, it dawned on me how badly this silly episode had jolted her. I sat on the bed and patted her hand, and said: "Why don't you tell me about it, my dear?"

"It?" she looked at me curiously, frowning.

"Well, it has to be something more than just a silly old glass eye, now doesn't it? I mean, I've never seen you so shaken." And so she told me.

"It's just something he said to me," she explained, "one night when I was late home after the opera. In fact, I believe I'd spent a little time with you that night? Anyway, in that perfectly *vulgar* way of his he said: 'Angela, you must be more discreet. Discretion, my girl! I mean, I know we don't have it off as often as you'd possibly like — but you can't accuse me of holding too tight a rein, now can you? I mean — har! har! — I don't keep too close an eye on you — eh? Eh? Not *both* of 'em anyway, har! har!'

"So I asked him what on earth he meant? And he answered, 'Well, those damned *boyfriends,* my dear! Only right you should have an escort, me being incapacitated and all, but I've a position to maintain and scandal's something I won't hear of. So you just watch your step!'"

"Is that all?" I said, when it appeared she'd finished. "But I've always understood that Jeremy was perfectly reasonable about . . . well, your *affairs* in general." I shrugged. "It strikes me he was simply trying to protect his good name — and yours!"

"Sometimes, Arthur," she pouted then, "you sound just like him! I'd hate to think you were going to turn out just like *him!*"

"Not at all!" I answered at once. "Why, I'm not at all like him! I do

. . . everything he didn't do, don't I? And I'm, well, entire? I just can't understand why a fairly civil warning should upset you so — especially now that he's dead. And I certainly can't see the connection between that and . . . and this," and I kicked the eye back under the bed, for at that moment it had chosen to trundle out again.

"A civil warning?" she looked at me, slowly nodded her agreement. "Well, I suppose it was, really." But then, with a degree more animation: "But he wasn't very civil the next time!"

"He caught you out again?"

"No," she lifted her chin and tossed back her hair, peevishly, I thought, "in fact it was *you* who caught me out!"

"Me?" I was astonished.

"Yes," she was pouting again, "because it was that night after the ball, when you drove me home and we stopped off at your place for a drink and . . . and slept late."

"Ah!" I said. "I suspected there might be trouble that time. But you never *told* me!"

"Because I didn't want to put you off; us being so good together, and you being his closest friend and all. Anyway, when I got in he was waiting up for me, stamping round the place on that pot leg of his, blinking his one good eye furiously at me. I mean he really was raging! 'Half past three in the morning?' he snorted. 'What? *What?* By God, but if the neighbours saw you coming in, I'll . . . I'll —'"

"Yes," I prompted her. "'I'll — ?'"

"And then he threatened me," she said.

"Angela, darling, I'd already guessed that!" I told her. "But *how* did he threaten you — and what has it to do with this damned eye?"

"Arthur, you know how I dislike language," her tone was disapproving. But on the other hand she could see that I was getting a bit ruffled and impatient. "Well, he reminded me how much older

he was than I, and how he probably only had a few years left, and that when he was gone everything would be mine. *But,* he also pointed out how it wouldn't be very difficult to change his will — which he would if there should be any sort of scandal. Well of course there wasn't a scandal and he didn't change his will. He didn't get the chance, for it was . . . all so very sudden!" And likewise, she was suddenly sniffling into the hankie she keeps under the pillow. "Poor Jeremy," she sobbed, "over the cliff like that." And just as quickly she dried up and put the hankie away again. It helps to have a little cry now and then.

"But there you go!" I said, triumphantly. "You've said it yourself: he *didn't* change the will! So . . . not much of a threat in that!"

"But that's not all," she said, looking at me straight in the eye now. "I mean, you know how Jeremy had spent all of that time with those *awful* people up those *awful* rivers? Well, and he told me he'd learned something of their jojo."

"Their juju," I felt obliged to correct her.

"Oh, jojo, juju!" She tossed her hair. "He said that they set spells when they're about to die, and that if their last wishes aren't carried out to the letter, then that they send, well, *parts* of themselves back to punish the ones they held to trust!"

"Parts of them— ?" I began to repeat her, then tilted my head on one side and frowned at her very seriously. "Angela, I —"

But off she went, sobbing again, face down in the pillows. And this time doing it properly. Well, obviously the night was ruined. Getting dressed, I told her: "But of course that silly glass eye *isn't* one of Jeremy's parts; it's artificial, so I'm sure it wouldn't count — *if* we believed in such rubbish in the first place. Which we don't. But I do

understand how you must have felt, my darling, when you saw it wobbling about up there on the dresser."

She looked up and brushed away her tears. "Will I see you tomorrow night?" And she was anxious, poor thing.

"Of course you will," I told her, "tomorrow and every night! But I've a busy day in the morning, and so it's best if I go home now. As for you: you're to take a sleeping draft and get a good night's sleep. And meanwhile —" I got down on my knees and fished about under the bed for the eye, "— did Jeremy have the box that this came in?"

"In that drawer over there," she pointed. "What on earth do you want with that?"

"I'm simply putting it away," I told her, "so that it won't bother us again." But as I placed the eye in its velvet-lined box I glanced at the name of the suppliers — Brackett and Sanders, Jewellers, Brighton — and committed their telephone number to memory. . . .

The next day in the City, I gave Brackett and Sanders a ring and asked a question or two, and finished by saying: "Are you absolutely sure? No mistake? Just the one? I see. Well . . . thank you very much. And I'm sorry to have troubled you. . . ." But that night I didn't tell Angela about it. I mean, so what? So he'd used two different jewellers. Well, nothing strange about that; he got about a fair bit in his time, old Jeremy Cleave.

I took her flowers and chocolates, as usual, and she was looking quite her old self again. We dined by candlelight, with a background of soft music and the moon coming up over the garden, and eventually it was time for bed.

Taking the open, somewhat depleted box of chocolates with us, we climbed the stairs and commenced a ritual which was ever fresh and exciting despite its growing familiarity. The romantic preliminaries, sweet prelude to boy and girl togetherness. These were broken only once when she said:

"Arthur, darling, just before I took my draft last night I tried to open the windows a little. It had got very hot and sticky in here. But that one —" and she pointed to one of a pair of large, pivot windows, "— wouldn't open. It's jammed or something. Do be a dear and do something with it, will you?"

I tried but couldn't; the thing was immovable. And fearing that it might very well become hot and sticky again, I then tried the other window, which grudgingly pivoted. "We shall have them seen to," I promised.

Then I went to her where she lay; and in the next moment, as I held her in my arms and bent my head to kiss the very tip of a brown, delicious . . .

Bump!

It was perfectly audible — a dull thud from within the wardrobe — and both of us had heard it. Angela looked at me, her darling eyes startled, and mine no less; we both jerked bolt upright in the bed. And:

"What . . . ?" she said, her mouth staying open a very little, breathing lightly and quickly.

"A garment, falling from its hanger," I told her.

"Nevertheless, go and see," she said, very breathlessly. "I'll not be at ease if I think there's something trapped in there."

Trapped in there? In a wardrobe in her bedroom? What could possibly be trapped in there? She kept no cats. But I got out of bed and went to see anyway.

The thing fell out into view as soon as I opened the door. Part of a manikin? A limb from some window-dresser's storeroom? An anatomical specimen from some poor unfortunate's murdered, dismembered torso? At first glance it might have been any of these things. And indeed, with the latter in mind, I jumped a foot — before I saw that it was none of those things. By which time

Angela was out of bed, into her dressing-gown and haring for the door — which wouldn't open. For she had seen it, too, and unlike me she'd known exactly what it was.

"His leg!" she cried, battering furiously at the door and fighting with its ornate, gold-plated handle. "His bloody *awful* leg!"

And of course it was: Jeremy Cleave's pot left leg, leather straps and hinged knee-joint and all. It had been standing in there on its foot, and a shoe carton had gradually tilted against it, and finally the force of gravity had won. But at such an inopportune moment. "Darling," I said, turning to her with the thing under my arm, "but it's only Jeremy's pot leg!"

"Oh, of *course* it is!" she sobbed, finally wrenching the door open and rushing out onto the landing. "But what's it doing there? It should be buried with him in the cemetery in Denholme!" And then she rushed downstairs.

Well, I scratched my head a little, then sat down on the bed with the limb in my hands. I worked its joint to and fro for a while, and peered down into its hollow interior. Pot, of one sort or another, but tough, quite heavy, and utterly inanimate. A bit smelly, though, but not unnaturally. I mean, it probably smelled of Jeremy's thigh. And there was a smear of mud in the arch of the foot and on the heel, too. . . .

By the time I'd given it a thorough bath in the vanity basin Angela was back, swaying in the doorway, a glass of bubbly in her trembling little hands. And she looked like she'd consumed a fair old bit of the rest of the bottle, too. But at least she'd recovered something of her former control. "His leg," she said, not entering the room while I dried the thing with a fluffy towel.

"Certainly," I said, "Jeremy's *spare* pot leg." And seeing her mouth about to form words: "Now don't say it, Angela. Of *course* he had a spare, and this is it. I mean, can you imagine if he'd somehow broken one? What then? Do you have spare reading glasses? Do I have spare car keys? Naturally Jeremy had spare . . . things. It's just that he was sensitive enough not to let you see them, that's all."

"Jeremy, sensitive!" she laughed, albeit hysterically. "But very well — you must be right. And anyway, I've never been in that wardrobe in a donkey's years. Now do put it away — no, not there, but in the cupboard under the stairs — and come to bed and love me."

And so I did. Champagne has that effect on her.

But afterwards — sitting up in bed in the darkness, while she lay huddled close, asleep, breathing across my chest — I thought about him, the "Old Boy," Jeremy.

Adventurer, explorer, wanderer in distant lands. That was him. Jeremy Johnson Cleave, who might have been a Sir, a Lord, a Minister, but chose to be himself. Cantankerous old (old-*fashioned*) bugger! And yet in many ways quite modern, too. Naïve about certain things — the way he'd always trusted me, for instance, to push his chair along the airy heights of the cliff tops when he didn't much feel like hobbling — but in others shrewd as a fox, and nobody's fool. Never for very long, anyway.

He'd lost his eye to an N'haqui dart somewhere up the Orinoco or some such, and his leg to a croc in the Amazon. But he'd always made it back home, and healed himself up, and then let his wanderlust take him off again. As for juju: well, a man is liable to see and hear and touch upon some funny things in the far-flung places of the world, and almost certainly he's like to go a bit native, too. . . .

The next day (today, in fact, or yesterday, since it's now past midnight) was Friday, and I had business which took me past Denholme. Now don't ask

me why, but I bought a mixed posy from the florist's in the village and stopped off at the old graveyard, and made my way to Jeremy's simple grave. Perhaps the flowers were for his memory; there again they could have been an alibi, a reason for my being there. As if I needed one. I mean I had been his friend, after all! Everyone said so. But it's also a fact that murderers do, occasionally, visit their victims.

The marble headstone gave his name and dates, and a little of the Cleave history, then said:

> Distant lands ever called him;
> he ever ventured,
> and ever returned.
> Rest in Peace.

Or pieces? I couldn't resist a wry chuckle as I placed my flowers on his hollow plot.

But . . . hollow?

"Subsidence, sir," said a voice directly behind me as a hand fell on my arm. Lord, how I jumped!

"What?" I turned my head to see a gaunt, ragged man leaning on his shovel: the local gravedigger.

"Subsidence," he said again, his voice full of dialect and undisguised disgust, gravelly as the path he stood on. "Oh, they likes to blame me for it — saying as 'ow I don't pack 'em down tight enough, an' all — but the fact is it's the subsidence. One in every 'alf-dozen or so sinks a little, just like Old J.J.'s 'ere. This was 'is family seat, y'know: Denholme. Last of the line, 'e were — *and* a rum un'! But I suppose you knows all that."

"Er, yes," I said. "Quite." And, looking at the concave plot: "Er, a little more soil, d'you think? Before they start blaming it on you again?"

He winked and said, "I'll see to 'er right this minute, sir, so I will! Good day to you." And I left him scratching his head and frowning at the grave, and finally trundling his barrow away, doubtless to fetch a little soil.

And all of this was the second thing I wasn't going to report to Angela, but as it happens I don't suppose it would have made much difference anyway. . . .

So tonight at fall of dark I arrived here at their (hers, now) country home, and from the moment I let myself in I knew that things weren't right. So would anyone have known, the way her shriek came knifing down the stairs:

"Arthur! *Arthur!*" her voice was piercing, penetrating, very nearly unhinged. "Is that you? Oh, for *God's sake* say it's you!"

"But of course it's me, darling, who else would it be?" I shouted up to her. "Now what on earth's the matter?"

"The matter? The matter?" She came flying down the stairs in a towelling robe, rushed straight into my arms. "I'll tell you what's the matter. . . ." But out of breath, she couldn't. Her hair was wet and a mess, and her face wasn't done yet, and . . . well, she looked rather floppy all over.

So that after a moment or so, rather brusquely, I said: "So tell me!"

"It's *him!*" she gasped then, a shudder in her voice. "Oh, it's him!" And bursting into tears she collapsed against me, so that I had to drop my chocolates and flowers in order to hold her up.

"Him?" I repeated her, rather stupidly, for by then I believe I'd begun to suspect that it might indeed be "him" after all — or at least something of his doing.

"Him!" she cried aloud, beating on my chest. "Him, you fool — *Jeremy!*"

Well, "let reason prevail" has always been my family motto, and I think it's to my merit that I didn't break down and start gibbering right there and then, along with Angela. . . . Or on the other hand, perhaps I'm simply stupid. Anyway I didn't, but picked up my flowers and chocolates — yes, and Angela,

too — and carried them all upstairs. I put her down on the bed but she jumped up at once, and commenced striding to and fro, to and fro, wringing her hands.

"Now what *is* it?," I said, determined to be reasonable.

"*Not* in that tone of voice!" she snarled at me, coming to a halt in front of me with her hands clenched into tight little knots and her face all twisted up. "Not in that 'oh, Angela's being a silly again' voice! I said it's him, and I *mean* it's him!"

But now I was angry, too. "You mean he's here?" I scowled at her.

"I mean he's *near*, certainly!" she answered, wide-, wild-eyed. "His bloody bits, anyway!" But then, a moment later, she was sobbing again, those deep racking sobs I just can't put up with; and so once more I carried her to the bed.

"Darling," I said, "just tell me all about it and I'll sort it out from there. And that's a promise."

"Is it, Arthur? Is it? Oh, I do hope so!"

So I gave her a kiss and tried one last time, urging: "Now come on, do tell me about it."

"I . . . I was in the bath," she started, "making myself nice for you, hoping that for once we could have a lovely quiet evening and night together. So there I am soaping myself down, and all of a sudden I feel that someone is watching me. And he was, he was! Sitting there on the end of the bath! Jeremy!"

"Jeremy," I said, flatly, concentrating my frown on her. "Jeremy . . . the man?"

"No, you fool — *the bloody eye!*" And she ripped the wrapper from the chocolates (her favourite liqueurs, as it happens) and distractedly began stuffing her mouth full of them. Which was when the thought first struck me: *maybe she's cracked up!*

But: "Very well," I said, standing up, striding over to the chest of drawers

25

and yanking open the one with the velvet-lined box, "in that case —"

The box lay there, open and quite empty, gaping at me. And at that very moment there came a well-remembered rolling sound, and damned if the hideous thing didn't come bowling out of the bathroom and onto the pile of the carpet, coming to a halt there with its malefic gaze directed right at me!

And: **Bump!** — **bump!** from the wardrobe, and **BUMP!** again: a final kick so hard that it slammed the door back on its hinges. And there was Jeremy's pot leg, jerking about on the carpet like a claw freshly wrenched from a live crab! I mean not just lying there but . . . active! Lashing about on its knee-hinge like a wild thing!

Disbelieving, jaw hanging slack, I backed away from it — backed right into the bed and sat down there, with all the wind flown right out of me. Angela had seen everything and her eyes were threatening to pop out of her head; she dribbled chocolate and juice from one corner of her twitching mouth, but still her hand automatically picked up another liqueur. Except it wasn't a liqueur.

I waved a fluttery hand, croaked something unintelligible, tried to warn her. But my tongue was stuck to the roof of my mouth and the words wouldn't come. *"Gurk!"* was the only thing I managed to get out. And that too late, for already she'd popped the thing into her mouth. Jeremy's eye — but *not* his glass eye!

Oh, and what a horror and a madness and an asylum then as she bit into it! Her throat full of chocolate, face turning blue, eyes bulging as she clawed at the bedclothes going "Ak — ak — *ak!*" And me trying to massage her throat, and the damned pot leg kicking its way across the floor towards me, and that bloody nightmare glass eye wobbling there for all the world as if its owner were laughing!

26

Then . . . Angela clawed at me one last time and tore my shirt right down the front as she toppled off the bed. Her eyes were standing out like organ stops and her face was purple, and her dragging nails opened up the shallow skin of my chest in five long red bleeding lines, but I scarcely noticed. For Jeremy's leg was still crashing about on the floor and his eye was still laughing.

I started laughing, too, as I kicked the leg into the wardrobe and locked it, and chased the eye across the floor and under Angela's dressing-table. I laughed and I laughed — laughed until I cried — and perhaps wouldn't have sobered yet, except . . .

What was that?

That bumping, out there on the landing!

And it — he — Jeremy, is still out there, bumping about even now. He's jammed the windows again so that I can't get out, but I've barricaded the door so that *he* can't get in; and now we're both stuck. I've a slight advantage, though, for I can see, while he's quite blind! I mean, I *know* he's blind, for his glass eye is in here with me and his real eye is in Angela! And his leg will come right through the panelling of the wardrobe eventually I suppose but when it does I'll jump on it and pound the thing to pieces.

And he's out there blind as a bat, hopping around on the landing, going *gurgle, gurgle, gurgle* and stinking like all Hell! Well sod you Jeremy Johnson Cleave for I'm not coming out. I'm just going to stay here always. I won't come out for you or for the maid when she comes in the morning or for the cook or the police or anybody.

I'll just stay here with my pillows and my blankets and my thumb where it's nice and safe and warm. Here under the bed.

Do you hear me, Jeremy?

Do you hear me?

I'm — not —— coming —— out! □

THE DISAPPROVAL OF JEREMY CLEAVE

VDF

MAGIC'S PRICE

by Larry Walker

VDF

When the troll came out of the black trees, the snow screaming under his heavy feet, the horse reared and tried to turn about. The troll was a large one, slope-browed and shaggy and long-nosed, hulked over by his own weight. In one hand he carried a club. "Halt there. Tell your name," he said, in a voice deeper than a man's.

The rider reined the horse's head down. Cloaked and hooded in black, he bore a spear in his right hand, and an axe hung at one knee. His rein-hand grasped a halter rope, by which he led a young, pale bull. The bull was making no trouble, for it had been blindfolded.

Deep in the night forest, a wolf howled.

"My name is Jorulf Ospaksson," the rider said. "I go to Ygg-Fafnir." His breath made a mist-cloud before his face.

The troll frowned. "Those who seek Ygg-Fafnir must answer three riddles," he said, halting a little, as if the words had been learned by rote. When he opened his mouth he showed tusks the size of a man's thumb.

"I know the rules," said Jorulf.

"First," said the troll, scratching his head and sing-songing like a child reciting, "if the world was born out of . . . of . . ."

"Ginungagap."

"Right, Ginungagap, the great abyss. If the world was born out of Ginungagap, where did Ginungagap come from?"

"I don't know."

"Second. Frey gave up his sword to win the love of Gerd, so he will be swordless at . . . don't tell me . . . Ragnarok. Ragnarok, right. Why doesn't he just buy another sword?"

"I have no idea."

"Third. If Odin knows everything that will happen, why is he always running about seeking the counsel of witches and giants? Does he think he can do anything about Doom?"

"I couldn't tell you."

"You have failed the test," said the troll, hefting his club. "Now I get to crush your head."

"No," said Jorulf.

"No?" asked the troll, closing one eye.

"No."

"Why not?"

"Because I know the master-word."

"Master-word?"

"The word to unmake you, troll. This is it — *seeming*. You are a seeming, sent out by Ygg-Fafnir to frighten trespassers and ward him from a world-full of enemies. You are nothing. Go away."

The troll vanished, looking to the end just an inch or two out of his depth.

Jorulf found himself in a pool of light cast by torches above him, held by men who looked down from the wall of a circular stockade. He heard his name whispered, and whispered again.

"You heard who I am," he said to them. "Tell Ygg-Fafnir I've come."

One guard disappeared. The gate opened and two armed men crunched out and stood facing him, spears in hand. "Get down and take off the cloak, Jorulf Ospaksson," one said. No one enters unsearched. It's the same for all."

"Of course," said Jorulf. Alighting, he handed the bull's rope to the second guard, who looked at it, and at the placid bull, doubtfully. "He won't hurt you if you don't call him names," said Jorulf. The bull tossed its head. Jorulf dropped his cloak. The torchlight showed him as a man of middle height and middle age, strong-bodied, with thinning fair hair — or was it silver?

Carefully, the first guard patted down Jorulf's clothing. He checked his hands closely, studied his rings and buckles, even searched his hair.

"I bear no charms," said Jorulf, smoothing the hair again. "No rune-sticks in my shirt, no animal bones in my breeches."

"And no steel," said the guard. "Ygg-Fafnir brooks no steel in his house — it crosses the magic. We'll hold your weapons for you."

"I know how it works."

The guard picked up Jorulf's cloak, studied it on both sides, shook it out, and handed it back to him. Jorulf slung it over one shoulder.

A head appeared from behind the gate. "The master says to let him in."

Creaking on frozen hinges, the gate opened wider.

"See the horse and the bull warmly stabled," said Jorulf. He gave over his arms and went in.

He made his way along a trodden path to the center of the compound, where the queer, round hall stood. He stopped for a moment before the door of its built-on entryway and ran a hand over his frosty beard.

Then he squared his shoulders and strode in, through to the main hall, smelling smoke and boiled beef and manure. There was a central hearth-fire, and there were golden lamps hung on chains from the rafters, and silver-gilt shields hung around the walls, but their brightness was weak and shy, except where it reflected in the eyes of four-and-twenty berserkers, who sat on the benches in a circle. Jorulf knew them for berserkers by their filth, and by the nervous darting eyes and the restless hands. He recognized none of them. Few of that brotherhood stayed long in a place.

Across from the doorway he saw, through the smoke, a huge, graying man, heavy with his own strength, in the high seat between the carven pillars.

"You have changed, Jorulf," rumbled Ygg-Fafnir, "but there's wolf in you yet, I'll wager. How many years has it been?" As he spoke, he fiddled with a set of polished, carved sticks strung on a thong.

"Eight."

"I've missed you. Berserkers can be hired for a ring and a throat-full of mead. But friends are rare for a man like me."

"For a man like me as well," said Jorulf. "I had good days in this house. A berserker needs others of his kind to get pissing drunk with him, and to tell him what a devil of a fellow he is, else the memories grow too heavy." He felt the eight-and-forty eyes on him, sharp as knife points.

"Sit, eat," said Ygg-Fafnir. "The guest seat here beside me. I always trusted you, Jorulf, and trust is a sweet I taste less and less. Thralls! Set up a table! Bring the best for Ygg-Fafnir's last friend!"

In a minute Jorulf was seated behind a trestle-table. Thralls brought water and a towel for washing and set before him mead and cheese and barley cakes and boiled beef. An ivory knife was laid by his hand. Jorulf fell to with a long road's appetite, but he had the wit to notice the thrall woman who filled his horn. Red-haired and green-eyed, she carried herself proudly, despite the iron thrall's collar around her neck, and she looked him fair in the eye.

"Beware that one," said Ygg-Fafnir with a crooked smile. "She's my prize — a true witch out of Ireland. Daughter of kings."

Jorulf watched as she moved out through the kitchen-door. "I wonder you keep such a woman. You were never one to trifle with powers."

"A special matter. We matched spells, she and I, in Orkney, and set our freedoms on the outcome. I beat her fairly, and she is bound by the direst oaths. You may have her tonight, if you wish." As he spoke, Ygg-Fafnir leaned back in his seat and cocked an eyebrow at the berserker on Jorulf's right.

Silently, the berserker drew a flint knife from his belt and, holding it in his left hand, inched it behind Jorulf's back.

A second later the man was lying in the wreck of the dinner atop the table, one of Jorulf's hands on his throat and the ivory knife at his belly. Jorulf roared, *"Is this your hospitality, Ygg-Fafnir?"*

Ygg-Fafnir leaned back and laughed, a booming sound like the cracking of lake-ice in bitterest winter. "The wolf abides, Jorulf — I knew it! You looked so honest and farmer-respectable coming in, I had to see your heart again. Forgive me a jest."

Jorulf pushed the berserker off the table, and the man rolled and came up on his feet, then darted out the door, laughing. Jorulf kicked the table off its trestles and stood with his hands clenched. "I did not come here for jests."

"And why did you come?"

Jorulf sat and looked at his hands. They trembled. He covered his face with them a second, took them away, and said, "Ulvig is dead."

Ygg-Fafnir gasped and jerked up, standing braced for a moment with his hands on the pillars, his rune-string dangling from one wrist. He breathed in starts, as if elf-shot, then fell back into his seat.

Eyes closed, he asked, "How did it happen?"

"A sickness went through our neighborhood the last month. Cramps, vomiting, fever. She was gone in a night."

Ygg-Fafnir passed a hand over his forehead. "She gave you how many children?"

"Four sons, two daughters."

"And now she's gone. So strong she was. She could shelter a man in a North Sea gale."

"Less and less with the years. She was the best of wives, but she bore a sorrow, and I had no help for it."

"I thought — I hoped — that with a good man to husband, she might learn to be happy. Wise as she was, she should have learned to prize you."

"We were great friends. But she loved another."

Ygg-Fafnir waved a helpless hand, and the rune-sticks clattered. "The magic," he said.

"Yes. The magic."

"The magic is a mistress who brooks no rival. A warlock can have thrall-women, and whores, but never a wife. One eye in his head, and that ever on the runes.

"Oh, I've seen the young ones, the postulants, trying to claw up from the shallow mysteries. They are like children. They won't pay the price. They think they can master the runes without curbing themselves more cruelly than any Christian monk."

"And is the magic worth the price?" Jorulf whispered.

"Look at my hall, Jorulf! The richness of the woodwork, the splendor of the gold and silver! Look at my house-carles! Do you know of any man in the world who can manage four-and-twenty berserkers, and keep them from murder? And it's not only berserkers I rule! Kings have brought their prayers to my footstool, and paid well for my wisdom and my arts. Who is greater in the north than Ygg-Fafnir? You, of all men, know whence I come. We've seen the day, you and I, when we stole a rabbit's carcass from a wolf, and sheltered in the hollow of a snowdrift, and thought ourselves lucky."

"And now your world has shriveled to the size of this house, and you dare never go out for fear of steel, and runes, and spells, and the unaccountable elves. And the only men you trust are berserkers, who have no ambition beyond their lusts, and you lie at night with a woman who would gladly cut your throat."

Ygg-Fafnir swung to face Jorulf, one arm crooked around the high-seat post. "I will not be judged by you," he hissed, teeth bared. "I will not be judged by a berserker, half a beast — I who am half a god! Remember, Jorulf, I know you of old! I know what is in your heart!

"You say Ulvig had a sorrow! Had you no blame in that?"

Jorulf sat and watched his fists quivering on his knees. "What husband does all he might?" he said through clenched teeth. "I tried. For her I sold my manhood. You called me a good man, but I knew it shamed her to have a berserker to husband." He looked at the men on the benches, crouching or lying restless, watching his every move, ready to spring if he showed their master any threat. "She used to say berserkers are like cats, only filthy." One of the berserkers rolled backwards and hooted.

"We went to my farm in the mountains, and there I studied to live in utter peace. I worked my fields and kept to myself, and with time my mind grew quieter. When my neighbor came to me and said, 'Bring your axe and support my suit before the Thing,' I said, 'No, it's no affair of mine.' When a man cheated me on a horse, and another over boundaries, I swallowed my anger and kept my axe tied to my belt. For I knew my wife lived in fear that one day things might come to blows, and the blood would flow up behind my eyes again, and the wolf take my mind. I have the name of a coward at home.

"So do not think I judge you for trading your manhood for power. I traded mine for love of a woman who could not love me. I only wonder which of us got the better bargain."

Ygg-Fafnir sat back. "So you came back to my house at the last to tell me of her death. That was kind of you."

"No. I came because of the bull."

"The bull?" Ygg-Fafnir looked at him sideways.

"Two years since you changed Einar Brusasson, Ulvig's brother, into a bull."

Ygg-Fafnir frowned. "So I did," he said. "The boy wanted me to pay a settlement for breaking my betrothal to his sister. It was an old matter by then, and he was ill-spoken. I wearied of his voice, and silenced it."

"Ulvig was fond of him. His brothers sent him to us to keep, when he grew

uncurbable, and like me he lost his wildness with her. She asked me many times to come to you on his part. I refused, knowing well that you never unmake a spell, and afraid, I suppose, of this house and company. But she begged me dying, and now I have nothing to lose.

"So I ask you — for old friendship's sake, for the sake of the woman who should have been yours — will you bend your rule? Make Einar a man again?"

Ygg-Fafnir slouched in the high-seat, his chin on his chest, beard flowing down to his belt. "It's no trifle you ask," he said. "When a man has been a beast a while, he can never be quite a man again. Two years is a long time."

"Still I ask. A berserker too is not quite a man, but I live in my fashion, and choose it over dying."

Ygg-Fafnir looked around at his mad house-carles. "I've often wondered," he said, "what would happen if all my berserkers went wolf at once. We'd have broken heads then, not so?"

"It would be bare-handed slaughter, each against all. In the end there'd be one man left, perhaps, sick and wounded and choked with self-loathing."

"Then suppose you'd been berserk all of two years. Would it not be best to let be?"

"She bade me ask."

Ygg-Fafnir straightened. "You know I cannot refuse. Odd, that the wishes of the dead have more weight than those of the living." He called out, "Witch!" and clapped his hands twice. The Irishwoman appeared without a sound.

Ygg-Fafnir took up a flat stick of birchwood from the bench. He drew his belt-knife (bronze) and said, "Give me blood," while he set to carving a figure in the stick.

Dead-faced, the woman picked up the ivory knife Jorulf had dropped and cut her forearm. She held the arm out to Ygg-Fafnir, who dabbed in the blood with his finger and stained the carving, whispering a tune to himself. He blew on the rune to dry it and dismissed her with a wave.

He handed the rune-stave to the berserker on his left and said, "Take this to the stable and lay it between the horns of Jorulf's bull. Then bring the beast here."

The two men found little to talk of as they waited. Jorulf sat clenching and unclenching his fists. His eyes met those of one of the berserkers across the hall, who winked at him, then laughed when he turned his face away.

When the berserker returned from the stable, he supported in his arms a younger man, fair and shaggy-bearded, who stumbled with each step and stared about with mindless round eyes. A cloak had been flung over him, for he was naked.

"For pity's sake, give him clothes," said Jorulf.

"He wouldn't wear them," said Ygg-Fafnir. "His thoughts are still a beast's thoughts." He said to the berserker, "Let him stand alone."

The man stepped away, and Einar swayed for a moment, then tipped, moaning, to the floor.

Jorulf rose. "What's wrong with him?"

"He's forgotten how to walk on two legs," said Ygg-Fafnir. "Don't fret over that — walking is the easy part."

Jorulf went to kneel by the young man. "Einar," he said. "Einar — are you all right?"

Einar looked up at him and smiled, drooling from one corner of his mouth. He knit his brows, then said, "Jo— Jo— Jolf?"

"Jorulf. Yes, Einar."

"Ei— Einar!" He caught the name like a ladder rung, and Jorulf thought he saw a spark of understanding in the dull eyes.

"Einar. Einar." The young man said his name over and over. He scrambled up on all fours, looking down in puzzlement at his hands.

"Come, Einar. We'll walk. Soon you'll remember all, and I'll take you back to your father's house."

Jorulf lifted Einar by main strength, draped the cloak and one of his arms over his shoulders, and began to walk him around the hearth. And around again.

"Einar, Einar," the young man said. "Einar, Einar . . . Jorulf."

He jerked suddenly, looking towards Ygg-Fafnir, who watched, slumped in the high-seat.

"YOU!" he bellowed, eyes rolling.

"All in good time," said Jorulf, tugging at his arm.

They walked some more, Einar craning his neck now and again to stare at Ygg-Fafnir, and shaking his head. Jorulf could feel the muscles in his back twitching, as cattle's do. At last Einar stopped and tore loose (his strength was shocking). Leaning on a pillar, he stared at the warlock.

"Ulvig!" he said at last, eyes lighting.

Ygg-Fafnir recoiled as if struck.

Einar turned on Jorulf and grasped his shoulder with one powerful hand. *"ULVIG!"* he roared. The cloak dropped.

"Yes, Ulvig. Your sister."

"Ulvig?"

"She's not here. Walk now." Jorulf tried to move him.

But Einar stayed. He looked wildly about and cried, "Ulvig dead!" The berserkers were up on hands and knees now, eyes wide, nostrils flared.

"You'd best take him away now, Jorulf," said Ygg-Fafnir, his face pale. "Tell him, if he comes to some kind of mind again — tell him it was the magic. Nothing less than the magic."

Jorulf wondered how Einar could have guessed Ulvig's death (though beasts have ways). He bent to pick up the cloak to cover his wife's brother. Straightening, he saw Einar staring at Ygg-Fafnir, mouth open, and he turned to see what the matter was.

He caught just a flash of it — a shining of horns, the wave of a tufted tail — then he was clutching at the boy, who ran, bellowing, for the high-seat.

The berserkers were on him in a second, leaping and howling.

Jorulf threw himself at the pack of them, his only thought to protect Einar. A blow struck his cheek. A hand clutched at his leg. A man blocked his way, and he lifted the fellow bodily and threw him aside. Another he felled with a fist to the head. He struggled and clawed, and as he strove he felt the blood rising behind his eyes, and there came something like peace as the wolf ran away with his mind in its teeth.

The blood cooled and drained away at last, and Jorulf drifted slowly back. He seemed to hear, far off, a hoarse voice shouting the same words over and over. At last he recognized the voice as his own, screaming through his ragged throat a song of blood and revenge. He had forgotten how good it felt while it lasted.

He found himself sprawled on the floor, a bench at his back. He could not see from one eye, he was scratched and bitten everywhere, there was a large gash in his right leg, his head ached damnably, and he thought some ribs were broken. All around him the smoky hall was piled with the bodies of Ygg-Fafnir's berserkers, all bloody, all dead. One lay with his head in the hearth, sending up a stink of burning hair. Jorulf crawled over and pulled him away from it.

He looked over at the high-seat, where Ygg-Fafnir yet sat, motionless, his face purple and his eyes staring. The fingers of what was left of Einar still clutched his neck.

Jorulf tensed at the sounds of footsteps behind him, and he twisted to see the Irish witch.

"They're all dead," she whispered. "Even the guards from the stockade, who came in with their spears. You were a wonder! Never have I seen a man fight as you fought. All berserkers have a devil, but yours must be father to them all! I see why they made songs about you!"

Jorulf shook his head. "I can't have slain them all," he croaked.

"They mostly slew each other, once Ygg-Fafnir's death unbound them. And I cut the throats of those who breathed yet when all was done." She brought out from behind her back a flint knife. "All but you."

"Get me water," said Jorulf, dragging himself up on the bench and holding his head in both hands.

"I'm no thrall any longer, Northman," said the witch, and as she spoke her iron collar parted of itself and fell to the floor. "Ygg-Fafnir's death unbound me as well. I can be mistress here or I can go home to Ireland.

"Yet I'll get you water, as a kindness." She went to a cask and ladled some out in a bowl. She brought it to him, with a towel. Jorulf drank most of it, then splashed the rest on his face and groaned.

"Let me," she said, and began to gently clean his wounds. "I do not forget those who do me good, even by chance."

"I thought — I thought you were bound to use no spell against Ygg-Fafnir."

"Nor did I. I cast a seeming against your bull-boy."

"I see," Jorulf said. "You showed him what seemed to be a cow behind the high-seat. His bull-thoughts for the cow, and his man-thoughts for his sister, got scrambled, and he did what any bull would do."

"Ygg-Fafnir spoke the truth. He could never have had a man's life. Still, I cannot deny I owe you somewhat for him. Northman, I'll make you a gift."

"I want nothing from you."

"Come back with me to Ireland. I'll make you a great man. I'll teach you the magic. You've seen what the magic can do."

Jorulf sputtered, then fell backward, laughing while tears rolled into his ears.

When the fit had passed, he shook his head and said, "I have children waiting for me at home."

"Any beast can breed children. I myself bore a child once. I ate her flesh in a secret place, and gained great power thereby."

Jorulf dragged himself to his feet. He showed her his back and lurched out the door.

It seemed as if the cold air carried her screams for miles as he rode away — *"How dare you judge us, who are half gods, you who are half a beast? How dare you despise the price we pay?"* □

A DOLL'S TALE

by John Peyton Cooke

I used to get angry whenever Cindy's mommie came home from the supermarket with yet another "demon doll" horror novel. But that was a long time ago, when I was newer, when my dress was clean and Cindy kept my hair brushed, when she spent more time playing with me than with any of the others.

It all started about a year ago, one day when Cindy was sitting on the couch in the family room, burping me over her shoulder. I was looking out the picture window, waiting for her to finish.

Cindy patted me on the back and pretended I was through burping. "There, there," she said, in that high-pitched, squeaky voice of hers. "That's a good baby. Does Huggums feel better?"

She pulled my string. "Mommie," I said flatly as my string retracted. But even at that time I already knew she wasn't really my mommie; I had read the brand on the bottom of my foot: *Made in Taiwan.* I was nobody's fool.

Cindy leapt from the couch and suddenly I was hanging for dear life from her dainty fingers as she ran to the kitchen table. Cindy's mommie was there, taking groceries out of several bags and sorting them out.

"Whad'ja get, Mommie?" asked Cindy. She dropped me on the table and I lay there on my back, no longer able to see because my eyes had closed.

"I didn't get any candy, if that's what you're looking for."

Apparently because there was no candy to be eaten, Cindy picked me

back up and held me upright under her arm. My eyelids popped open, and since Cindy was standing on a chair, I could see the whole table and kitchen before me. Cindy's big brother Rob was there, and I felt embarrassed because my dress had slid up over my waist. I caught him staring at me lasciviously in his Ozzy Ozbourne T-shirt, and quickly averted my gaze.

But what I saw next was even worse. There, among the groceries strewn about the table, was a new horror novel. In red, bleeding, raised lettering, the title was *Die, Dolly, Die!* The cover was black, with a painting of a doll's baby face with green, glowing eyes and fangs protruding over its chubby little lips. I stared at the book in shock, my eyes stuck open.

As the groceries got shuffled around, the book fell on its face. Although I tried to resist, I couldn't help myself, and I read the copy on the back cover:

In the terrifying tradition of The Playpen *comes a novel of un-stoppable, heart-wrenching horror:* Die, Dolly, Die!

Todd and Samantha Morgan had the perfect family and a beautiful house in the quiet town of Badger Prairie. Their pride and joy was their youngest daughter, Tammy, who was "gifted," bright, intelligent, and pretty. The Morgans had not a single worry in the world. . . .

Until they bought Tammy an antique porcelain doll named Lucy. Tammy said that Lucy "told" her things in the night . . . that she "made" her do things. And when the Morgans' neighbors

37

started to die, and the school children who teased and taunted Tammy started to die, they realized they *were next. . . .*

Because Lucy was short for Lucifer, and there was no way to stop her. . . .

Die, Dolly, Die!

I was mortified! How could anyone write something so horrible about a harmless doll? And how could people like Cindy's mommie pay *money* for it and *read* it?

But I didn't let it get to me. I figured I could forgive Cindy's mommie this once. As far as I could tell, she harbored no particular hatred toward dolls, so I assumed her interest in the book fell into the category of "guilty pleasures."

But in the months that ensued, I managed to catch glimpses of other books she had bought: *Witch Doll, Baby Satan,* and *The Dolly Upstairs,* to name a few. I began to wonder if there were more to this than met the eye.

During this time, I was treated well. Cindy burped me, fed me, changed me, and dressed me up nearly every day. Often she would invite me to tea parties and jungle safaris with the stuffed animals, and I always got to sleep with her at night, too. Life was easy.

That is, until the beast moved in.

Cindy's parents gave her big brother a dog for Christmas. Not a puppy, but a large, energetic, curious, hungry *dog*. I was in Cindy's closet with the other toys while Christmas was going on in the living room, but I could hear Rob playing with the beast, Cindy's mommie giving him a lecture on its care and feeding, and Cindy saying "What's his name? What's his name?"

"Ozzy," said Rob.

A little while later, when the family was eating breakfast, I heard Ozzy making his way down the hall. The door to Cindy's room was open, and he lumbered right in, a fat, full-grown, fluffy collie with a tongue a mile long and razor-sharp teeth. Even if I could have

moved of my own volition, I wouldn't have; I was petrified. Ozzy sniffed the red shag carpet of the room and then headed for the trash can next to Cindy's dresser. He buried his head in the can, and when he pulled it out he had the wrapper to an ice-cream sandwich in his mouth. Within seconds, he chewed it and swallowed it, and licked his jowls. He seemed hungry for more, and continued his search, sniffing every inch of the room.

Somebody call the doggie, please, I thought.

I could hear, from the dining room, dishes clinking and kids talking with food in their mouths — breakfast was far from over. Nor was it over for Ozzy. Shortly, his long nose appeared in the closet, then his whole hairy head and ruff. He cocked his head and stared at me with his dark, watery eyes, perhaps sensing my complete state of panic.

He bent down his head and clamped his jaws on my delicate, pink plastic body, and strutted out of the closet. He shook me violently — as if I were some dirty dust rag he could just throw around. With each swift shake, my eyes opened and closed rapidly. I became dizzy and disoriented. The next thing I knew, Ozzy was prancing down the hall with me in his mouth, slobbering and panting as he approached the breakfast table.

"Oh!" Cindy's mommie gasped. Then she laughed, and quickly tried to suppress it, probably for Cindy's sake, not mine. *I knew it,* I thought, *She's a doll-hater.*

But Rob and Cindy's daddie didn't care what anyone thought. They laughed away, unashamed. "Get her, Ozzy!" Rob yelled excitedly. "Hey, Mom, can Huggums be his new toy?"

"No!" Cindy screamed. "No, Mommie, no!" Nestled in her lap was one of those soft, cute, fat, expensive dolls with puckered faces.

"But you don't need Huggums any-

more," Rob said. "You just got that nice new doll, and Ozzy doesn't have anything to play with. Or maybe you want to keep Huggums and let Ozzy have your new one, huh?"

"No!" she screamed again, much louder, and began to cry. "Mommie, tell him Ozzy can't have Huggums or Krystle!"

Cindy was hanging tightly onto Krystle, acting as if the world were coming to an end.

"I don't see anything wrong with Rob's idea," said Cindy's daddie. He wanted to see me torn to shreds!

But Cindy's mommie demurred. "No, absolutely not. I simply will not have it. Huggums and Krystle both stay with Cindy, and that's final."

"Hooray!" Cindy cheered, and kissed Krystle's nose.

Ozzy's teeth, meanwhile, were sunk deep in my plastic flesh. I was so frightened I wet my panties.

Rob got up and said, "Here, Ozzy, give it up." Then he grabbed me by the legs and ripped me from the dog's mouth. Cindy shrieked. The beast still had my right arm, which he promptly chewed and gulped down before anyone could take it from him.

But that was just the beginning.

On New Year's Eve, Cindy's parents spent the night out of town at a friend's party, leaving Rob in charge of taking care of both the house and his sister. He took care of Cindy by locking her in her room and invited his friends over for a party. All the kids at the party got excessively drunk and stoned, and the police came twice to tell them they were being too loud. Somehow, Rob managed to clean up the house before his parents returned.

But Cindy threatened to tell.

To keep her quiet, Rob took me from her closet and forcer her to watch as he threw me in the clothes dryer and turned it on. He left the door open and kept the machine running by holding

40

the door sensor button with his finger. I was hurled to and fro, tumbling head over heels, my head pounding against the metal walls of the revolving barrel. All the while Cindy screamed, tears streaming down her face. Rob didn't turn off the dryer until she got down on her knees and promised she would never tell their parents about the party.

But did the child learn from this? Of course not. She kept finding ways to get Rob in trouble, and in turn, he kept torturing me to keep her in line.

When Cindy said she was going to tell their parents about the stack of *Hustler* magazines in his closet, he took a black magic marker and drew a beard on my face and a swastika on the front of my dress. When she was going to tell about the "funny cigarettes" he smoked, he took his lighter and set my hair on fire, partially melting my scalp. When she was going to tell about what he and his girlfriend had been doing one afternoon when she had barged into his room, he popped out one of my eyeballs with his switchblade and ran over me with his motorcycle.

After that, whenever Cindy pulled my string, something inside me skipped and I simply said, "Me, me, me, me. . . ."

Cindy didn't love me anymore from that point on. She left me out of all the fun things, keeping me hidden away in the darkest corner of her closet, with the spiders. Krystle, who never spoke to me, was now the center of attention at all the tea parties, and got to lead the jungle safaris. I wasn't even invited to them. In fact, the only reason I was still around had nothing to do with Cindy caring about me; she was just too selfish to let anything go.

Then one day, Cindy and her mommie were cleaning out the closet when her mommie said, "Oh, Cindy! You really ought to let me throw this thing away." She held me up and looked at me with disgust. "You never play with it anymore, and look at the shape it's in! Tire tracks! How on earth did it ever get this way? You had better not treat Krystle like this."

"Oh, I don't, Mommie. Krystle's nice."

"So can I throw it away or not, dear?"

"Sure, Mommie, you can throw Huggums away."

"Good."

Throw Huggums away? Good? I couldn't believe my little plastic ears. Cindy was going to let her mommie kick me out of her life, just like that? What was to become of me?

I was thrown into the kitchen trash, were I landed headfirst in a pile of refried beans. A few hours later, Cindy's daddie carried the trash sack out to the front lawn for pick-up. By then I had resigned myself to my fate. I decided that dolls were all destined to come to tragic ends, and enjoyed a little consolation by thinking Krystle would someday be thrown onto a pile of refried beans as well. I waited, hoping the garbage truck would arrive soon, but knowing it would not come until morning.

Sometime later that evening, I heard Rob and Ozzy on the front lawn. "C'mon, Oz, hurry up!" I could hear Ozzy relieving himself on a nearby bush. Then Rob said, "No, Ozzy, you dunderhead. Get out of the trash."

But it was too late. Ozzy plunged his head in the sack and sniffed around. Suddenly, he grabbed me in his jaws and took me out of the garbage. He pranced towards his master across the moonlit lawn, drooling all over me. I was glad to be saved from the trash, but as Ozzy came closer to Rob, I wondered which would be worse — to be at the mercy of a garbage compactor or of this metal-head.

"What've you got there, boy? Well, look at that! What was sweet little Huggums doing in the trash, huh?" He leered down at me from above, the bright orb of the full moon reflecting in his black eyes. Ozzy's breathing was quick, his breath hot; he stood still.

"Hand it over, Oz," Rob said sternly.

Ozzy's jaws clenched down tighter.

"I said, hand it over!"

Rob tried to pull me from the dog's mouth, but Ozzy was too strong for him and darted off, through the open front door of the house. He carried me into Cindy's bedroom and set me down on the chair by her bed. (It made me wonder if dogs can actually *think*, like people and dolls.) Ozzy left and went into the living room to wrestle with Rob.

Cindy was sleeping soundly beneath a quilted bedspread, every now and then letting out a little, dainty snore. Krystle, the bitch, was tucked lovingly under the child's arm.

Ozzy's act had been brave and noble, but how far would it get me? The next day, Cindy's mommie would probably throw me away again, for good. There would be little Ozzy could do against *her*.

I sat there for a long time, just thinking. I wondered what I had done to deserve all the misfortunes I had met with. I had been treated unjustly, even *cruelly* by the whole family, except for Ozzy, who had redeemed himself. But what, being a doll, could *I* do about it? It seemed hopeless, and I became very depressed.

Then the whole house became quiet. I heard the wind picking up outside and the feeble tapping of tiny raindrops against the windowpane. The full moon was lower in the sky than before and now cast a brilliant ray right into my single remaining eye.

It was then I came up with my plan.

I wondered then if I could speak to Cindy without the use of my string, and say what I wanted to say, and get her to do what I wanted her to do.

"Cindy," I said. I repeated it softly, over and over, until she woke. "Cindy."

Yes, I could do it!

When she saw who was talking to

her, she bolted upright in her bed and clutched her quilt tightly up to her neck, her eyes wide and staring in horror. She gasped, and just barely managed to say, "Huggums?"

"Yes, it's me — Huggums!" I must have looked awful, with refried beans on my bald head, beard, swastika, tire tracks, and an arm and eyeball missing. But I knew what to say; I had watched TV. "So you thought you'd gotten rid of me, eh?"

She swallowed hard, speechless, terrified.

I tried to make the moonlight reflect in my eye. I wanted to look at menacing as Rob had seemed to me. I had to be convincing, because my life depended on it. It was either them or me.

"Cindy, do you know the big knife your mommie has told you never to touch? Now listen to me very carefully. There's something I want you to do. . . ." I proceeded to tell her my plan, in which she would slit the throats of her parents, and chop her brother up into tiny pieces, and then go after the neighbors just for the Hell of it.

She heard me out, stricken dumb. I think I had her in my power for a few seconds, but then, from under her arm rose Krystle.

Krystle looked at me and said, "Huggums, darling, that is so cliché!"

Krystle told Cindy she was just having a very bad dream, to go back to sleep, and everything would be fine when she woke up the next morning; Huggums would be gone.

And that's how it turned out. Cindy's mommie discovered me before the child woke and personally delivered me into the hands of the greasy garbage collectors.

It was then I realized those "demon doll" horror novels were entirely works of fiction.

Krystle, you'll get yours! □

ICED ON ARAN

by Brian Lumley

King Kuranes's Questers, called Hero and Eldin for short — though neither one of them was short, for being ex-waking worlders they were much taller than the average dreamlander, or *Homo ephemerens,* as Eldin was wont to call them — were labouring up the slopes of Mount Aran above the trees and toward the snow line.

Hero was rangy, springy of step, younger than his friend; Eldin was stocky, gangling, somehow apish in his length of arm and massive strength, and yet not unattractive. They loved each other like brothers but would deny it almost to the death, while defending each other to that same grave limit; they loved as well adventuring, girls, booze, and especially their travels and travails as the Lord of Ooth-Nargai and the Skies Around Serannian's special emissaries, agents, and trouble-shooters in general — though the latter was something they'd also deny, except when they were broke and needed the work. Like now.

King Kuranes (or "Lord," he made no special distinction and only rarely stood on ceremony) was cooking something up for them right now, a job in far Inquanok; for which reason he kept the pair waiting in timeless Celephais on the Southern Sea while he made his various arrangements from his manorhouse seat in that city. Alas, but sitting still on their backsides was something that Hero and Eldin didn't do too well; a day or two of total inactivity was normally sufficient to drive them to drink, and from that to other diversions. They'd been drinking last night, had started in boasting, and a boozing companion (one Tatter Nees, a wandering balladeer from Nir) had found himself filling the role of adjudicator.

Their bragging had ungallantly covered women, though never referred to individually by name; deeds of derring-do in various far-flung places; fantastic feats of physical prowess which, if true, would have made the pair the greatest athletes in all the dreamlands! (They weren't, as it happens, though neither were they slouches.) And finally they'd started in on their climbing skills:

"Who was it," Hero noisily demanded, slopping muth-dew in his enthusiasm, "climbed a Great Keep of the First Ones alone and unaided?"

"And who," Eldin thumbed himself in the chest, "scaled the Great Bleak Range, even to the topmost ridge?"

"We were together on that!" Hero at once protested. "I did it too!"

"Aye, and stubbed your toe on the top," Eldin reminded, *"and* damned near crashed down the other side to your death. You would have, too, if a friendly little crevice-grown bush hadn't taken pity on you!"

"I was *knocked* over the rim fighting with Yib-Tstll's vast stone idol avatar, as you well know!" Hero was affronted. "And that's something else I do better than you — fight!" He jumped up, rotated his fists menacingly, leaped nimbly up and down and hither and thither like a frenetic boxer — until his head crashed against a low beam, which brought him to an abrupt, shuddering standstill. Then, staggering a little and grimacing a great deal, he collapsed back into his seat.

The Wanderer (as Eldin was also named) and Tatter Nees laughed till they cried, and Hero too dizzy and dazed even to protest.

"Well," said Tatter eventually, "fight and climb all you like, just as long as you don't go climbing Hatheg-Kla or Mount Aran. They're forbidden to mortal men, those two peaks, and the strange old gods who decree such things are pretty unforgiving."

"Eh?" Eldin raised a shaggy eyebrow. "Aran, forbidden? I mean, I know Hatheg-Kla's a bit hairy — old Atal of Ulthar's an authority on that, if ever there was one — but snowy old Mount Aran? A mere hill by comparison with some mountains! What, Aran of the ginkgoes and the eternal snows, whose frosty old crown's forever white? Aran, where he rises from ocean's rim to look down on Celephais and all the southern coast? Aran, that most benevolent of crests, forbidden? I didn't know that!"

"Aran?" Hero mumbled, still recovering from self-inflicted clout and gingerly fingering the lump he could almost feel rising on his head. "That molehill! *Hah!* I'd climb it in a trice!"

"Then I'd climb it twice in a trice!" growled Eldin, and more cautiously, "Except it's forbidden. According to Tatter here, anyway."

"Tittle-Tatter!" cried Hero. "I'd run up Aran before breakfast, just to keep myself in trim!"

"And I'd be on top waiting for you," returned Eldin, "having gone up ahead for a breath of fresh air!"

"Now *that's* climbing talk!" Hero declared, sticking out his jaw. "In the morning, then?"

"Tonight, if you like!"

"No, morning's soon enough — and anyway, I've a headache."

"What? What?" cried Tatter. "Mad-

ness, and I'm party to it! Only climb Mount Aran — or race to the top, if you will — and tomorrow here's me composing a lyric farewell to two of my dearest friends, which I shall call 'Quest No More, My Fair Brave Lads.'"

"One fair brave lad," said Hero, "and one old ratbag!"

"More muth!" cried Eldin to the somewhat troubled taverner, who knew their reputation. "I want to drink a last toast to a gallant loser, before he burns himself out on the slopes of Mount Aran."

And so it went. . . .

Neither one of the questers remembered Tatter tottering them up ricketty stairs to their respective ricketty beds in a cheap, tiny, ricketty garret room. But both of them remembered their oath. Perhaps they regretted it, too, but things didn't work out that way.

Across the distance of the single pace separating them where they lay, as the sun's first rays crept in through a small-paned window, they blinked crusted eyes and tasted mouths like old shoes with dead rat tongues, and Eldin said: "Hero — *ugh!* — about Aran . . ."

"Forget it — *yechhh!*" Hero had answered, wondering why muth wasn't called moth. "I won't hold you to it. What would it prove?"

"Exactly."

"I mean, you're all those years older than me . . ."

And after a moment, in a somewhat harsher tone: "Exactly — and that much more experienced! So get up, pup! The sun's up and Aran's snows are sweet and cool and waiting."

Which was how they came to be here now.

During the climb they'd been pretty quiet, heads clearing, thoughts their own, probably wondering what madness had prompted this contest. The only good thing about it was that it was burning the muth out of their systems. A hangover which might normally last

two whole days should be gone by the time they hit the snow line. . . .

Mount Aran *was* a mountain, one of the ocean-fringing range of mountains whose roots lay in the Tanarian Hills beyond Ooth-Nargai, but it was not one of those sheer-sided monster mountains like Ngranek or (worse far) Hatheg-Kla. Its lower slopes were green, gentling up through palms and shrubs and ginkgoes, then gradually shifting to scree and bare rock, finally crossing the permanent snow line to rise more steeply, but not frighteningly so, to a white rounded peak. In the waking world it would not have the height to support permanent snow and ice — relatively few mountains do — but these were the dreamlands and things were different here.

Perhaps the questers thought of these differences as they struggled higher across slopes of loose, sliding shale, using the roots and springy branches of the few remaining mountain shrubs for leverage. Differences like the "timelessness" of Aran and Celephais, where the seasons never seemed to change and people led inordinately long, almost interminable lives. Hero, considering this, thought: *I'd be bored to death if I thought I was going to live, or dream, forever!* And he grinned at the apparent contradiction in his thoughts.

Eldin saw that infectious grin; it signified the younger quester's emergence from muth-fume, also the resurgence of his natural good-humour. What's more, it might indicate that he was actually enjoying this balmy scramble, which Eldin frankly was not. The Wanderer scowled. "Funny, is it?" he asked. "This foolish contest you've goaded me into?"

"Funny?" Hero parked himself on a boulder, drank deep of the crisp air. "Daft, more like! Actually, I wasn't smiling at your discomfort; I've more than enough of my own. No, it was something else I was thinking of, far

removed from the scaling of Aran. As for goading: we goaded each other, I reckon."

Eldin sat down beside him, said: "You see no point in this, then?"

Hero shook his head. "None at all! Let's face it, we've climbed, you and I, in previously undreamed places. And what's Aran but a big hill, eh? Hardly a climb to tax our talents."

Eldin shrugged. "That's true enough — why, we're half-way up already, and not even noon! So why do we do these things, tell me that?"

Hero grinned again. "With nothing to test our mettle, we test each other. Or maybe it's the forbidden fruit syndrome, eh?"

"Because Tatter said we mustn't? You mean like naughty children? Is that all there is to us, Hero?" He nodded, considering it quite possible, gazed down on Celephais with its glittering minarets and caught flashes of Naraxa water where that river cascaded down to join the sea.

Before they'd sat down the Wanderer, too, had been dwelling a little on the timelessness of things: chiefly on Aran's snowy crest, which was the same now as the first time he'd seen it, oh, how long ago? What kept the ice going? he wondered. Why didn't it melt away? Or, on the other hand, why didn't it get so thick it formed a glacier down to the sea? Had it been this way immemorially? And if so, would it be the same a thousand years from now?

"Sometimes," said Hero, breaking in on his thoughts, "I feel weary."

"That's my line, surely?" Eldin snorted. But it pleased him anyway. What? Hero tired? Ridiculous! He was like a workhorse! But if he really was tired . . . well didn't that say something for Eldin's stamina, who must always keep apace of him?

Hero turned up the collar of his jacket. Fine when you were on the move, but at this altitude it quickly got cold when you sat still. *"Brrr!"* said the younger quester, and: "Tell you what, let's go up to the snow and find a block of ice, and ride it down to Celephais. That should satisfy Tatter. And we'll tell him we climbed opposite sides and clashed heads at the very top!"

"Suits me, if you say so," Eldin agreed. "But who cares what Tatter thinks?"

Hero sighed. "That's what makes me tired. Not Tatter especially but people in general. These reputations of ours, *they're* what really keep us going. And that's the answer to your question why do we do it. What are rogues if they quit their roguish ways, answer me that? Brawlers, boozers, adventurers: if we stop doing those things, what's left? 'Hey, look! There go Hero and Eldin. They were a couple of bad old boys — in their time . . .' See what I mean?"

Eldin thought about that for a moment, said: "Now I really *do* feel weary! Let's go and collect that ice and get down out of here; we break the mood of the place, change what shouldn't be changed."

They stood up, started climbing, crossed from scree and riven rock to snow and ice. And there, more than two-thirds of the way to the top —

"Ho, there, you lads! Lost your way, have you?"

Startled, the questers scanned about. The thin snow was dazzling in morning sunshine where it coated Aran's ice, so that they must shield their eyes from its glare. But up there, fifty yards onto the ice, a thin small figure, pick in hand, staring at them apparently in some surprise. They moved toward him, saw that he was old, gave each other sour glances.

"A right pair of adventurers, we are!" Eldin muttered under his breath, which plumed now in the frozen air. "What? Come to climb a 'forbidden' mountain — and granddads leaping about all over its peak?"

As they drew closer, so the old man studied them minutely; they could feel his eyes on them, going from faces to forms, taking in every aspect, comparing Hero's bark-brown garb to Eldin's night-black, the former's curved blade of Kled to the latter's great straight sword. And finally: "David Hero," he said. "Or Hero of Dreams, as they call you. And Eldin the Wanderer. Well, now — and it seems you really have lost your way!"

While the oldster had examined and spoken to them, they in turn had given him the once-over. There seemed no requirement for a detailed scrutiny: what was he but an old man? In no way threatening. Still . . .

He was dressed in baggy grey breeks tied at the ankles, his large feet tucked into fur-lined boots that went up under the cuffs of the breeks. His grey jacket was fur-lined, too, and buttoned to his neck. Upon his head he wore a woollen cap with a pompon, beneath which his hair and beard and droopy moustache were white as snow. All in all, his attire looking so grotesquely large and loose on him, it seemed to the questers he must be the merest bundle of sticks inside. Certainly his hands were pale and thin, as the petals of some winter-blooming flowers; blue-veined, they were, and very nearly translucent. Likewise his face, framed in curling locks of wintry hair: all pale and shiny as if waxed, or covered perhaps in a thin skim of clear ice. Icy, too, his eyes; indeed, grey and cold as snow-laden clouds, but not unfriendly for all that. And not without curiosity.

"What brings you here?" he finally asked the pair, his voice almost a chime. "Why do you climb Aran?"

"Because it's here!" growled Eldin at once. And: "Do we need a reason?"

The old man held up placating hands. "I wasn't prying," he said. "I've no authority one way or the other. Just making conversation, that's all."

Hero spoke up. "No motive to our

being here," he said, "except we thought we'd climb Aran, that's all. But what's in it for you? You'll pardon my saying so, but it seems to me you're a bit long in the tooth for shinning up mountains."

The old man gave them a gummy grin. "A man's as old as he feels," he said. "And who's to say who feels the younger, you or I? Looks to me like you two are feeling old as the hills themselves right now — if you'll forgive *me* saying so. As to why I'm here: why, I cut the ice for the fishmongers and butchers and vintners in Celephais! The ice of Aran provides my living, you see, as it did for my grandfather and father before me. Cutting it, and carving it, too — though the latter's more properly a hobby, a small self-indulgence, with nothing of profit in it. Obviously I can't take my carvings into town, for they'd quickly melt. Up here, however, why, they last forever!"

"Carvings?" Eldin looked all about. "I see no carvings . . ." Perhaps the old lad was an idiot.

The icemonger grinned again. "Only brush the snow away where you stand," he said.

The ice-slope had been simplicity itself in the climbing, for here and there it went up in uniform ripples, almost like steps, with only a thin crisp covering of snow to round off their sharp angular shapes. Eldin scuffed at some of these flat, regular surfaces with his boots, saw that in fact they *were* steps, cut with infinite care into the ice of Aran. And, narrowing his eyes toward the peak, now the Wanderer saw that indeed the steps would seem to go all the way to the top.

"Steps!" said Hero, following Eldin's gaze, and at once felt foolish. Of course they were steps!

The old man nodded. "To make the climbing of Aran easier, aye."

"But who'd want to make the climbing of a forbidden mountain easy?" El-

48

din was puzzled.

The old man laughed. "An icemonger, of course! My grandfather first cut steps on Aran's frozen slopes, and after him my father, and now I cut them. You see, the mountain is not forbidden to me. But ice-steps are not the carvings I was talking about, Wanderer. You brushed snow from the wrong place."

The questers looked again.

Between the rippling stairways where they ascended, large expanses of the slope showed columnar, lumpy, or nodal structures beneath a thin snow sheath. Eldin got down on his knees to one edge of the steps and brushed away snow with his hands. Hero likewise on the opposite side of the steps. And now an amazing thing, far beneath the snow —

"Wonderful!" said Hero, his voice full of admiration.

A figure reclined there, laid bare by the quester's hands. The figure of a man carved in ice. He sat (or seemed to) on the slope, his back against an ice boulder, hands in his lap, and gazed out through ice eyes far across all the lands of dream. He was middling old, but yet looked ages-weary, and his downward sloping shoulders seemed to bear all the weight of entire worlds. His ice-robes were those of a king, which the ice-crown upon his head confirmed beyond a doubt. But even without the royal robes and ice-jewelled headgear, still the figure was unmistakable.

"Kuranes!" Hero whispered, seeing in the ice an image almost of life itself, yet at the same time a Kuranes utterly unknown to him.

"The Lord of Ooth-Nargai, aye," the old ice carver whispered. "My father sculpted this in a time when Kuranes dwelled in the rose-crystal Palace of the Seventy Delights, before he dreamed himself his manorhouse and built his Cornish village on the coast. As you can see, the king was weary in those days and jaded of the dreamlands; see how clearly it shows in his mien? But once he'd builded a little bit of Cornwall here —" he shrugged. "— his weariness fell off him. My father had thought he might visit this place, come up and see himself shaped in ice, but he never came. Still, time yet."

Hero was astounded. "The king didn't sit for this?"

The old man gave a curious, brittle little laugh. "No, it was done from memory. My father's skill was great!"

Hero scuffed at a flat, snow-layered area next to the ice-carved king. It was empty, just a flat space cut out of Aran's ice. "Well, if Kuranes ever does come up here," he said, "and if he sits here, why, then he'll be beside himself!" He grinned.

"That was a joke," Eldin drily explained, but the old ice cutter only narrowed his eyes. The Wanderer had meanwhile cleared away snow from half a dozen ice-carvings. In doing so he'd brought a curious thing to light. While Kuranes's figure was carved only once, the rest — and the slope, as far as the eye could see, was literally covered with snow-humped shapes — appeared all to be duplicated. They sat, kneeled or reclined, or occasionally stood there on the slopes of Aran, in perfect pairs like glassy twins cut from the mountain. Two of each, almost exactly identical, strange twinned stalagmites of ice in human form.

Eldin uncovered more figures, Hero too. "I recognize a few of them," the Wanderer mused. "Here's old Cuff the fisherman. He never married, stayed alone all his days. Most people keep young in Celephaïs, but Cuff grew old. Toward the end he didn't even speak to people, stopped fishing, just sat around on the wharves staring out to sea. People said he was tired of life."

The cold was starting to get into Hero's bones. "I don't know how you can work up here," he told the old man. "It's so cold here even Zura's zombies would last forever!" Snow was beginning to fall: light flakes like confetti cut from finest white gossamer drifting down near-vertically out of the sky. "As for your work," Hero went on, "I can't fault it. But don't your fingers freeze up? These things must take days in the carving! And there are thousands of them . . ."

The old man smiled his thin, cold smile. "I wrap up warm," he said, "as you can see. Also, I'm used to the cold. What's more, I work very quickly and accurately. It's in my blood, come down from my grandfather, through my father to me. And sometimes I have advance knowledge. I get to know that someone else desires to be carved in ice. Come over here and I'll show you something." He led the way nimbly across the snow-slope, knowing every step intimately. Hero and Eldin followed.

As they went, Hero asked the Wanderer: "So what happened to old Cuff the fisherman? Did he die?"

Eldin shrugged. "Drowned, they say. After a storm they found his boat wrecked on Kuranes's Cornish rocks. They didn't find Cuff, though, and he was never washed up. The sea keeps its secrets. Actually, I'd forgotten all about him till I saw him — both of him — up here."

"How about that?" Hero asked the old ice cutter. "Why do you carve two likenesses of your subjects? And why, pray, only one of Kuranes?"

"Here we are," the old man might not have heard him. "There — what do you think of that?"

"Why, I . . . I'm floored!" Hero gasped.

"Or, maybe, 'flowed?' " said Eldin. "You know: ice-flowed?"

Hero groaned and rolled his eyes, but the old man said, "Flawed, yes! Kuranes, I mean. You asked why only one of him. Because the ice was flawed. When my father set to work on the second image, it shattered. And so there's only an empty space beside him."

49

The questers said nothing, merely gazed in astonishment at ice-sculptures — of themselves! The carvings were far from complete; indeed, they were the crudest of representations, the merest gouges and slashes in blocks of ice; but just as a great artist captures the essence of his subject with the first strokes of his brush, so were the essences of Hero and Eldin here caught. Perhaps in more ways than one . . .

Hero's gape turned to a frown, then an expression of some puzzlement. "Two things," he said. "Yet again you've only represented us once apiece. But weirder far, why are we here at all? We didn't ask to be sculpted in Aran's ice; and as for your being forewarned, why, you couldn't have been! We only knew ourselves last night, and even then we weren't sure."

By way of answer, the old man asked questions of his own. "I'd like to be certain on that point," he said. "About your coming up here, I mean. You told me you climbed Aran 'because it was here.' By that do you mean that you automatically do things you should not? Which in this case is to say, because the climbing of Aran is forbidden? Or was it simply that you were bored, tired of mundane dreaming?"

Hero looked at him a little askance. "Mundane dreamers? Us? Hardly!"

Eldin's ice-statue sat, elbow on knee, chin in palm, gazing frostily on Celephais. The Wanderer got down beside it, put his real elbow on the empty knee, adopted the same pose more or less and stared into the statue's roughly-angled face. "You keep asking us our reason for climbing Aran," he said. "Because we shouldn't, you ask, or because we were bored? Well, actually — if it's that important to you — it was a bit of both. See, we've been a little out of sorts, Hero and I."

"No, no!" cried the sculptor at once. "Don't sit there but here, right alongside. That's right. Good! Good!" Simi-

larly, he positioned Hero beside his carving, which sat straight-armed, hands on knees, staring bleakly ahead. Then he took out tools from his pockets, began to chip away. First at Eldin's unfinished sculpture, then at Hero's and so on back and forth.

"You didn't answer my questions," said Hero, watching him out of the corner of his eye. "How come you've already started work on us? And why only one piece apiece?"

"My friends," said the old man, "you see the work of long, lonely years here. Here are represented years before I was born, and years before my father was born. There are a number of celebrities carved here — like Lord Kuranes himself — but mainly the works are of ordinary men. Now, the carving of ordinary men is all very well, but it is unrewarding. I mean, in another century or so, who will know or remember them, eh? But men such as you two, destined to become legends in the dreamlands . . ."

"You carved us because we're famous!" cried Eldin, beaming.

"Or infamous!" Hero's frown persisted.

"What better reasons?" Again, the old man smiled his thin, cold smile.

"Something here," said Hero, hearing warning bells in the back of his head (or maybe the tinkling of warning ice-crystals), "isn't quite right. I can't put my finger on it, but it's wrong." And talking about fingers: the old man had just put the finishing touch to Hero's right hand — which even now promptly fell asleep upon his knee, as dead as if hard-bitten by frost. Hero made to rise, stir himself up, but —

"No, no, no!" the old man chided. "Now that you are here, at least do me the courtesy of sitting still. Fifteen or twenty minutes at most, and the job's done. And while I work, so I'll tell you my story."

"Story?" Eldin repeated him, watching how he carefully molded his boot from ice — and feeling his real foot go suddenly cold inside the real boot, with a numbness that gradually climbed into his calf. "Is there a story, then?"

"Ooth-Nargai," the sculptor appeared to ignore him, his fingers and tools alive with activity, "is said to be timeless. For most people it is, but for some it isn't. If all a man wants is a place that never changes, then Celephais in Ooth-Nargai's the spot. But there are those who want more than that, who *must* have change, restless souls whose hearts forever reach beyond the horizons we know. Alas, not all are fortunate enough to be far-travelled questers such as you two."

"Don't get to believing that all quests are fun and games, old man," Hero cautioned. "Me, sometimes I get heartily sick of them!"

"And me!" said Eldin. "Sometimes I think, wouldn't it be grand just to sit absolutely still for a thousand years."

"Exactly!" said the iceman. "And if such as you can become bored, jaded, dissatisfied, how then the little fisherman —"

"Like Cuff?" said Hero.

"— and the potter and the quarrier, who've never seen beyond a patch of ocean or the hot walls of a kiln or the steep sides of a hole in the ground? And so, in the far dim olden times, every now and then a man would climb Aran." He fell silent, concentrated on his work, shaped Eldin's elbow where it joined his knee.

"Eh?" said the Wanderer at length. "I don't think I follow." He felt an unaccustomed stiffness in his arm, the one that propped up his chin, and grunted his discomfort. But other than that he kept still.

"Maybe," the sculptor continued, "in the beginning, they came to broaden their horizons, to gaze across the dreamlands on lands afar, which they'd never see except from up here. Anyway,

that's how it started . . .

"Now, my grandfather was no ordinary ice cutter. He was a passionate man with a passionate skill. And yet he was compassionate, too. And he knew his talent was magical. He could not bear the loneliness, the boredom, the utter ennui of certain of his fellow men, men who grew old and withered despite the timelessness of Ooth-Nargai. Aye, and he could spot such men at once, for sooner or later they'd invariably enquire of him: 'What's it like, up on Aran?' "

"Is there a point to this story?" Hero suddenly asked, his teeth beginning to chatter. "Lord, I'm freezing! Are we daft, sitting here in the snow like this?"

The old man, working on Hero's sculpture, put a final touch to the jaw — and at once Hero's teeth grew still, almost as if they were frozen in position. "A point? Of course! For when he was asked about Aran, my grandfather would say: 'Aran is forbidden! Don't ask about it. It's not for you to know. No one climbs Aran except me, to cut the ice.' "

"Ah!" said Eldin. "It was him started the myth, then?"

"Because of his consuming compassion," answered the sculptor, "yes. He must be sure, you see, that only the most bitter men climbed Aran — only the ones in whom life's animation was dying! The ones without ambition, without aspiration, in whom nothing was left worth dreaming! Those for whom timelessness and changelessness had grown fused into one vast and dull and slothlike anathema! What matter to them if Aran were forbidden? What matter anything? They'd climb anyway, and damn the consequences! But did you say myth? No myth, my friend. Aran *is* forbidden — except to such as you!"

Eldin's feet and legs were finished, his thighs, too, also the arm and hand which cupped his chin. The Wanderer would now extend a finger to scratch an itch on his cheek, made so to do — discovered he could not! It seemed the blood had run out of his hand and arm, leaving only a cold numbness there.

The old man now returned to working on Hero, rapidly finished arms and shoulders and neck, also hands where they clasped knees. Following which Hero could only watch him from swivelling eyes, for his neck had suddenly stiffened into a cramp, doubtless from holding the same position too long. Except that now . . . now the alarm bells were clamouring that much louder and faster in the young quester's mind. He'd seen, heard and felt much here, so that that which he'd begun to suspect must at least be better than a guess.

He made a real effort to stand up then and couldn't; only odd parts of him had feeling, remained in his control at all. And even those parts were rapidly succumbing to a cold, unfeeling rigidity. Here he sat beside his image, twinned, one of him carved in ice and the other human — *for the moment!*

And it was then, like a bright flash of lightning in his mind, that all became known to him. "You're making a big mistake," he started to blurt the words out, but stiffly, from one side of his half-frozen mouth. "Eldin and I, we're not bored with anything! Why, we've got more go in us than . . ."

But what they had more go in them than remained unboasted, for the iceman quickly touched Hero's statue on the lips and brought them to a perfect image of life — and simultaneously froze his actual mouth into complete immobility!

Eldin had been watching from the corner of his eye; he'd recognized the panic, now shut off, in Hero's voice. "What *is* going on?" he now demanded, thoroughly alarmed. "What in the name of all that's — ?"

The sculptor touched the Wanderer's statue's hair, Hero's statue, too, and

etched their locks into icy replicas of life. And oh, the *cold* that seeped down from the roots of their hair into their brains then, and what sudden, frozen horror as they knew for a certainty their fate!

Tears flowed freely from the old man's eyes, freezing like pearls and rolling from his cheeks as hail. He knew they had not come here like the others, tired of an endless, changeless existence and more than ready to accept any alternative. But he also knew he couldn't let them go down again. Only turn these two loose, with tales of fabulous ice sculptures on the slopes of Aran, and tomorrow the people would come in their thousands! Of course, that would be the end of it: the selfless services of three generations of master icemen terminated. Services, yes — for surely it were better —

"Hero!" came a distant cry, soft on the tingly, downy air, startling the sculptor like the crack of a whip. "Eldin!"

What? The old iceman looked down the slope, saw a king's courier waving his arms at the edge of the ice. Looking up here, he'd see nothing of the ice statues, just snow and dazzle and the pair of seated questers, dark figures against a glaring background. He would not see the sculptor, not unless he stepped onto the ice, and he was not likely to do that because the snow-slopes of Aran were forbidden.

Gasping, the old man turned back to the questers. But too late, they were stirring! And anyway, the courier had seen them, for as yet they were not turned to ice. Not quite. Another touch here, a stroke there . . . it had been *that* close! But too late now, too late . . .

And: *Too late!* — the old man's thoughts were imaged in Hero's mind, for he also had heard the courier's cry. Through ears of cold crystal he'd heard it, and his brittle brain had taken it in, and his faltering, freezing heart had given a lurch. Part of him said: *go away, whoever you are. I've done with all that. I'm ice now, part of the permafrost, a glassy pimple on Aran's frosty face. I'm at peace with everything!*

But another part had been galvanized into a great start, had gasped and drawn air, had shouted (however silently), *no! I am* NOT *ice! I'm David Hero — Hero of Dreams!* And that part of him had won.

The snow went out of Hero's eyes, Eldin's too, and they creakingly lowered their heads and their gaze, staring down the slope. There the courier capered and waved. "Hero! Eldin! Are you two going to sit around all day? My master has a mission for you. You're to report to him at once."

Hero stood up. Or rather, he slowly straightened his knees until his backside lifted and his body tilted forward, then straightened his waist until his hands slid from his knees along his thighs. Thin sheaths of ice cracked and fell from his various joints and limbs as he moved them, and the first tinglings of returning life told him all would be well.

"I said —" the courier shouted.

"We heard what you said!" Hero shouted back, which came out as a series of croaks.

"Eh?" the courier cocked his head on one side.

Hero cleared his throat, tried again. "You go on ahead. Tell him we're coming." And as the courier shrugged and turned back down toward the tree line: "How'd you know we were here, anyway?"

"I've been looking for you all morning," the messenger called over his shoulder. "Tatter Nees told me where you'd be. But I don't think I'd better report that to my master!"

"Thanks!" Hero yelled.

"Good old Tatter!" Eldin grunted. He'd struggled to his feet and clumsily brushed himself down, sending thin

splinters of ice flying as he shook his massive frame. This proved effective but not a little painful, too. *"Ow!"* said the Wanderer, and several other things which don't need recording. Then he glanced down the slope at the courier. "Do you know what the king wants with us?" he shouted.

"Something about a job in Inquanok. You'd better hurry . . ." And with that the courier departed, scrambling away down the slope. The echoes of their shouting slowly trembled into silence; it stopped snowing; the questers looked first at each other, then all about at the frozen humps under the snow.

"Inquanok?" said the Wanderer presently. "That's a drab, bleak sort of place to go a-questing, isn't it?"

"You'll hear no complaint from me," said Hero. "Not this time. But first —"

It took them only a few minutes to find what they were looking for. The other statues on the slope were under an inch or so of snow. This one, however, carried only the finest dusting. They clambered over the slope toward him and saw that he was three. Then, when they'd brushed snow from the other two, they understood. The three were dressed all alike, and they were obviously blood-related, but there were differences which made each one an individual. Grandfather, father, and son. "Son" was the one with only a film of snow. There'd been no time for any more.

Eldin growled low in his throat, began to draw his straight sword — and Hero stopped him. "Vandal!" the younger quester softly accused. "What? You'd deface a work of art such as this?"

"Deface?" the Wanderer glared. "I'd destroy 'em, all three! Especially him. Why, he looks half-way pleased with himself!"

"No need, old friend," Hero shook his head. "He's destroyed himself. His time had come and he knew it. He'd probably wanted to do it for a long time, and we were the one small push he needed to send him over the edge. He must have known we weren't right for this place. When he sensed we were coming he tried to carve our images and got only the roughest outlines; but he'd done much better with Kuranes, which shows how close the king came at one time!"

Eldin caught on. "We weren't right for this place . . ." he mused. "But the old iceman himself, he was."

Hero nodded. "As for the look on his face: pleased with himself, did you say? Looks more to me like he's just sighed a long, last grateful sigh — and it's frozen there forever."

They made their way back to the ice steps. "And this one?" the Wanderer stood, sword in hand, beside the image of the Lord of Ooth-Nargai.

"Leave it be," said Hero. "If there's a sort of sympathetic magic in these things . . . I'd hate to think we were the ones brought some sort of doom down on old Kuranes. And who are we to decide a man's destiny, anyway? You never know, p'raps he *will* want to come up here one day — and maybe the old iceman has a son of his own, eh? You know: to carry on the line, and the work?"

Frustrated, Eldin returned to his own ice sculpture. "Well this at least is one destiny I can decide!" he declared.

"That I'll grant you," said Hero, coming up behind. "These really don't belong here at all." With great grunting heaves they wrested their images from their bases and threw them flat.

And with a great deal more courage than skill, the pair steered their amazing sledges down across the ice, less rapidly across scree and rock faces, shudderingly into the heart of the trees on Aran's lower slopes. From there they went on foot, and as the statues melted behind them, so their steps grew lighter along the leafy way. . . . □

THE LADY OF BELEC

by Phyllis Ann Karr

Until after the birth of their third child, her lord had locked her into a chastity belt each morning, hanging the key around his neck before opening the door of their bedchamber. At night, he would relock the door with a large key and hide the key somewhere about the chamber while she undressed by rushlight, with her back to him, her eyes seeing only his shadow moving on the tapestry. When all was ready, he would summon her to the bed, unlock the chastity belt, and pull her under the linen sheets and the covers of animal furs to him.

The Lady of Belec did not complain. The chastity belt was a symbol of his love for her. She was his jewel, to be guarded as carefully as a soft, white pearl from the depth of the sea, or the golden amber that hyenas emitted from their bodies and buried jealously in the sand to keep it from mankind, or a great ruby like the Heart's Blood of Jesu, crystallized in the holy chalice. She might have asked to wear the belt on top of her gown, as she heard some of the high ladies did at court, especially when it became fashionable after the goblet of Queen Morgan le Fay showed the unfaithfulness of womankind in the courts of King Mark and King Arthur. But the Lady of Belec was not quite clever enough with her fingers to make the slits that would be needed in order to fit the metal through her skirt, nor quite bold enough to have worn a gown so perforated. Sufficient that the Lord of Belec wore the small iron key in plain sight against the murrey brown cloth of his surcoat.

Nevertheless, the symbol of his love was not comfortable, and she was glad each time he laid the belt aside for a few months in consideration of a child swelling within her.

The first two babes were daughters, coming little more than a year apart; and, after the birth and the churching, the chastity belt. The third child was, at last, a boy; and, after his birth, the Lord of Belec brought out the belt no more, except when he left the castle to hunt or to visit some old friend or kinsman. It was as if by giving him a son she had at last proven her faithfulness, as if only now did the Lord of Belec consider their marriage fully sealed.

She rejoiced in the freedom with which she could now move by day — freedom all but forgotten since her girlhood years. And yet, conversely, now that he seemed satisfied with their union, she felt less secure, and thought wistfully sometimes of the old nightly rituals . . . as she thought wistfully of so many things in her past.

Once, when she was a girl not quite fifteen, Sir Gawaine had visited this castle of Belec, her father's castle then. Sir Gawaine of Orkney, Sir Gawaine of the golden tongue, Sir Gawaine the favorite nephew of the King himself, Sir Gawaine with the golden pentangle, the symbol of perfection, on the crimson of his shield and surcoat. The great Sir Gawaine, in his early manhood then, looking to her mature, strong, ageless, and, with his fine golden hair falling to his shoulders, his fine golden beard,

VDF

his kind brown eyes and ready smile, seeming to her much as she thought sweet Jesu must have been when He walked among the unbelieving Jews of the Holy Land. Gawaine's voice seemed to her like Jesu's, also — or at least, since Gawaine spoke in pleasantries instead of holy parables, like the voice of an angel fay.

The Damsel of Belec waited on her father and Sir Gawaine as they sat at table and talked of things she could not understand, things she could partly understand, and things she might have understood if she had not had to pour ale or replenish a platter of meat and bread. Often enough to nourish her, though not enough to sate her, Sir Gawaine had looked in her direction, either full in her face or with a soft, sliding glance that showed his awareness of her and appreciation of her efforts, and spoken of matters she could perfectly understand, comparing the flow of life to the flow of the seasons . . . or telling short tales of the bravery, fellowship, and love at court . . . or likening glory to the sun and the sun to the King, love to the moon and the moon to the Queen and the Queen to all good and beautiful womankind.

The old minstrel of Belec had been sick that week with the beginnings of the fever that was to kill him, but Sir Gawaine had shown her a few new bransle steps as well as he could without music. Afterwards, they sat together by the fire in her father's chamber (a rare honor for her, to be allowed to sit here with a guest). Sir Gawaine had drawn out Excalibur to show them, holding him up full in the firelight, hilt flashing like the sun and blade gleaming like the moon, and told them the tale of how Arthur had received the great sword from the old Lady of the Lake and later given it in trust to his nephew.

Before the Damsel of Belec left them, Sir Gawaine had taken her in his arms,

in sight of her father, and kissed her gently on the forehead. For a few moments, her hands felt the beat of his heart beneath the crimson silk of his surcoat; for half a heartbeat, his lips touched her skin.

He had left the next morning before daylight; but often, during the months that followed, she pressed her fingers to her forehead and then to her own heart until she seemed to feel him again, as clearly as when it had truly happened. And, indeed, those few heartbeats had never truly ended for her.

A few years later, feeling his end draw near, her father arranged her marriage with the third son of an old friend. Thus she would gain a lord and protector, and her husband would gain a wife and the castle and lands of Belec. So far as she knew, only one obstacle had threatened the union.

Her father used to boast of the occasion when they of Belec had entertained the greatest knight of the land and favorite nephew of the King. Her bridegroom-to-be seemed to find displeasure rather than satisfaction in the account. Once the Damsel had heard angry words between her father and her future lord, the younger man hotly demanding proof that his bride was unstained, the older as hotly protesting her honor and his own. This happened in the garden, and they seemed not to be aware she sat in her arbor, enjoying the thick green of summer.

"If any other," she heard her bridegroom say, "*any* other — even the King himself — were to touch . . ."

Her father began to interrupt with a shout, but it turned into choking. Hearing another fit in his cough, the Damsel rushed from the arbor where she had sat innocently concealed. Her future bridegroom did not seem embarrassed.

Her father recovered. The marriage was read and sealed. The next morning her new lord pronounced himself satisfied of her virginity on the bridal night. Yet quarrels continued, long and heated, between her husband and her father. Those which she overheard seemed to be of foolish matters, and she tried to beg her husband not to cause her father more fits. Her husband seemed sincerely to repent of his hot temper; but he could not control it. Some of the folk of Belec whispered that the new lord's temper hastened the old lord's death, and perhaps it was so. But her father was old and ill, and would have died soon in any case.

Once, shortly after the birth of their first son, she ventured to ask her lord, "What would you have done, that first night, had you not found me . . . to your taste?"

"Had I not found you to my taste," he replied, kissing her and trying in his way to make a pleasantry, "I would still have done my duty and given you children, but I would also have taken a paramour."

She suspected he had a paramour already, in the castle of one of those old friends he visited thrice or four times yearly; but all men could not be like holy priests or knights of the King's court, sworn to perfection. "If I had been otherwise to your taste, but not a virgin, my Lord? Would you have abandoned me?"

"I would have taken a burning brand from the fire," he said, "and thrust it through your foul body."

She did not mention such things again. Nor did she ever give him cause to quarrel with her. When he sought to quarrel, she was silent, or answered him only with agreement, even when he abused her. Sometimes he would stalk out and quarrel with another; several times over the years there were servants with cracked heads to mend, and three or four times there were dead knights to bury, after her lord indulged his temper. But never did he beat her,

as she heard some lords beat their wives. And if sometimes, in temper, he put sword or spear through a retainer or a passing knight-errant, that was less than she heard of other knights doing in sport and honor.

On the whole, she did not regret her marriage. She was practical enough to realize that not everyone could go to court, and that not all loves were for wedding, nor even for bedding. Her lord seemed a good husband to her, in most ways; and even if he were not, he would still have been her father's bequest to her, and precious on that account. She was ever faithful to him in body and intent; and, when she noticed that those servants and retainers to whom she spoke most often were those with whom her husband was most like to quarrel violently, she learned to keep her eyes lowered at all times except when alone with her husband and children, and to give what few orders she issued through the lips of one of her two damsels.

Always, however, she kept just below the skin of her breast, where he could not see it, a thin line in the shape of the golden pentangle that Sir Gawaine of Orkney wore on shield and surcoat. The five-pointed star was to her more than the symbol of all perfection and all true love, as the memory of the sword Excalibur shining silver and brilliant summed up more than beauty and honor. Together, the sword, the pentangle, and especially the man reflected a glory too bright for the world, a perfection that, being too noble to remain on earth, must rise to Heaven of itself, and in rising draw all the rest of mankind up with it, at least partway. She thought of the other knights, of Sir Gawaine's brother Sir Gareth Beaumains, of his favorite cousin Sir Ywaine of the Lion, of the great Sir Lamorak de Galis, or of Sir Lancelot, of whom Sir Gawaine had spoken as his special friend, giving Lancelot praise that in the opinion of the Damsel of Belec could belong only to Gawaine himself. All other great knights, the King himself, even Jesu in her prayers, all had Sir Gawaine's face, above their various shields and surcoats which her imagination could not quite fill in from the descriptions she had heard.

For thirty-five years, the feel of Sir Gawaine's lips upon her forehead and Sir Gawaine's heartbeat beneath the silk of his surcoat never faded, though the skin that remembered was growing wrinkled and mottled.

From the time of his visit until the time of her marriage, she had counted the days and months, hoping he would come again. Even after marriage, though her mind willed him to stay away — for her husband's sake, not for Sir Gawaine's, who could have defended himself at need against any three other knights who dared attack him in enmity — her heart raced and her hands trembled when she heard of his being anywhere within two days' ride of Belec. But the King's knights must do the King's good work; and the greater the knight, the more he must do. It had been a priceless gift that he came even once, all the more precious in that he came so early in her life, leaving her so many years to cherish the memory.

Belec lay on the way between London and Dover. Surely, she thought, the King's work must bring one of his knights past them here again sooner or later. Whenever, from crenel or thin, deep-set window, she glimpsed some strange knight or party of knights ride by, the blood throbbed in her neck. Even a visit from some lesser companion of the Round Table or the Queen's Knights would be a thing to savor, a second glimpse of the great, noble world beyond the walls and fields of Belec.

No other knight was Gawaine, but another knight could, perhaps, tell her news of him. She was old enough now to sit as mistress, helping entertain visitors; and surely not even the Lord of

Belec could grow jealous of hospitality offered to one of Arthur's own good knights.

The Lady of Belec realized unbelievingly that she had been old enough for most of her life, now, to sit as mistress in her father's hall, and never another knight from Arthur's court had she helped to entertain, nor any strange knight at all — only, from time to time, a minstrel, or a wandering holy man, or an old friend of her husband's. Her children, those who had survived childhood, were grown and gone, the last daughter married at an earlier age than her mother had been, the last son killed in the great tournament at Winchester. Unlike their mother, the daughters had left Belec for the castles and manors of their own husbands, where, perhaps, some of them might entertain knights from Arthur's court, or see tournaments. The Lady of Belec had never seen a true tournament, only a small one her father staged at his own castle even before the visit of Sir Gawaine. The thought that her sons had died in the exercise of glory somewhat eased the pain of their deaths. She had never, in any event, felt as close to her sons as to her daughters.

She thought, sometimes, of holding another tournament at Belec. Perhaps it would bring back Sir Gawaine for a day or two. But her lord would never have permitted so many strange knights so close to her; and, moreover, a tournament at Belec could only be a tawdry mockery of such great tournaments as those of Winchester, Lonazep, Surluse, or the Castle of Maidens. Better not to lime the twig for Sir Gawaine at all, than to lime it with such bait!

And then, too — she looked at herself in the water of her small garden pond — she was growing old. If he came now, he would be disappointed in her. Then she remembered that he would have grown old, too . . . ten years older than she. Perhaps it was best that he never return, best to keep the memory of him always as he was thirty-five years ago.

But no. He could never grow old, any more than Jesu in her book of hours could grow old. Or, if he did grow older, it could only ennoble him still more.

The Lady of Belec heard rumors sometimes, news that was months or years old and distorted beyond measure. There was talk that King Arthur's great court was not as it should be, that adultery was more common than faithfulness, that the Queen herself had taken a lover, or several. Now love, now jealousy of the Queen was said to have driven Sir Lancelot mad more times than once. An angel, or several angels, had appeared in the guise of knights and led the companions of the Round Table in search of the Holy Grail; only half these knights had returned to the King, but none had come past Belec.

Then Lancelot had actually been found with the Queen, in her chamber. The Queen had been burned at the stake and Lancelot driven into exile across the sea. Then the Queen had not been burned, but cast off and put into a convent. Then the King himself had crossed the sea, shipping with his host from Cardiff or another port far to the north, to make war on Lancelot for stealing the Queen from him. Then the Queen had not been put into a convent, nor carried over the sea with Lancelot, but was to marry the King's nephew, Prince Mordred, in London; and folk said that Prince Mordred was trying to raise the country to his own banner and soon would be here in the south.

The Lady of Belec sat in her small garden, enclosed by the walls of her father's castle, watching the spring herbs turning into summer herbs and the summer ones into fall, and trying to reconcile the reality of Sir Gawaine's visit thirty-five years ago with the impossibility of what was said to be happening now. All her life she had lived within an area of land that she could

have walked across in half a day. One time only had the greatness of King Arthur come into her life. Sir Gawaine's visit was truth to her, and all the rest was falsehood.

Then a great host passed by on its way south to Dover, and folk said it was the new King, Prince Mordred, and that he would have come aside to claim more men from the Lord of Belec, but was in too great haste.

Three days went by, then four, and there came rumors of a great battle at Dover, half on the land and half in the sea, with ships sinking for the weight of the blood that was spilled within them.

Close on the heels of these newest rumors, Sir Gawaine came again to Belec.

He came in the night, and he came with thirty men around him, knights, squires, and yeomen. He came with a crowd of country folk following him. The Lady of Belec heard their voices and woke before her husband. She rose, climbed to the narrow window, looked down and saw their torches on the other side of the moat. She did not see Sir Gawaine. She only saw six men carrying a long litter, and a throng of men and torchlights surrounding them. She woke her husband.

The Lord of Belec would not permit her to come down to greet the party of knights. He shut her in the bedchamber, and she heard the heavy bolt fall on the other side of the door.

She could not return to bed. With great care, she dressed herself in her best gown. It was more than twenty years old, older than her youngest daughter, who was not three years away from home; but she rarely had occasion to wear it, and it was still unfrayed, though somewhat faded, like her hair. She plaited her hair slowly, noticing by the firelight that there were still a few strands of black among the long, gray ones. She twined it up on top of her head, and she rubbed her face and neck with the precious, perfumed ointment she used only on the highest feast-days. Then she sat beside the fire and waited.

Soon she heard the bolt withdrawn. She stood, her blood throbbing, wondering what she would say, how she would persuade her lord to allow her to descend to the hall, why it even seemed important that she go.

There was knocking on the door. The Lord of Belec would not have knocked for permission to come in to his lady. She called out that whoever was without should enter.

He entered, a strange knight, almost as old as her lord, with an animal she thought might be a lion or a gryffon embroidered on his surcoat. Its colors were hardly visible for the dust. "My Lady?" he said.

"I am the Lady of Belec."

"My cousin visited your castle once, my Lady. He spoke highly of it. Perhaps that was before you came here . . ."

"I have always been here." She would not ask who this knight was, nor who was his cousin; but she thought she could trace a faint resemblance, through the years and the shadows. "Is your cousin below?"

He nodded and stepped aside. She crossed to the open door, and the strange knight, the cousin, escorted her down. Was this, she wondered, the courtesy that fine ladies enjoyed at court? No, it was the poor shred of an ancient garment that the last wearers were trying vainly to hold together in the face of a freezing wind. The spirit . . . aye, she could feel what must have been the old spirit of the cousin knight, struggling to walk steadily beneath grief and weariness. But the grace was lacking.

He led her into her own hall as if she, and not he, were the stranger. She knew her husband must be here, frowning at her. She wondered, very briefly, how the strange knights had persuaded

him to allow her presence, to permit her to be brought down by one stranger. Then she forgot the Lord of Belec. For the table was raised on the trestles, and on the table lay a tall man in a crimson surcoat.

She stepped forward. His hands were folded in prayer, the fingertips partially covering the golden pentangle on his breast. No man, how saintly whatsoever, slept with his hands folded in such rigid, motionless prayer. She moved her gaze slowly up to his face.

The silver did not show so clearly in golden hair as in black, but the face was sunken and withered with more than age, the lips were beginning to pull back despite a cloth tied round the jaws, and a gold coin weighed down each eyelid. The Lady of Belec screamed.

Then she stood for several moments, panting, listening to the echoes of her shriek die away in the high beams of her hall. Sir Gawaine of the golden tongue had returned to her at last, and brought with him the reality of all the rumors of these later years.

"Where is the sword Excalibur?" she said. "He should be holding the cross of the sword Excalibur."

"He gave the great sword back to the King when he was dying," said the cousin of Sir Gawaine. "During the battle at Dover, a wound he had from fighting Sir Lancelot reopened."

"Sir Lancelot? He would not have fought with Sir Lancelot." That much remained of the old vision, a memory of how Sir Gawaine had praised Lancelot as his truest friend. They could not have fought, unless in friendship and mere testing of arms.

"Lancelot had killed Gawaine's brothers, rescuing the Queen from the stake."

She screamed again, a longer scream, and fell to her knees, clutching the table, not quite daring to reach farther and touch his hands.

Footsteps approached her. Her hus-

band's voice came down from somewhere above her, angry, but low —
unusually low, for his anger. "Stand up.
You disgrace my hall."

She stood, but she did not turn to face
the Lord of Belec. She gripped the edge
of the table and stared down at her
other lord, the lord of thirty-five years
of hope and trust. "Ah, my lord Sir Gawaine!" She reached out at last and
seized his folded hands. "Ah, my Lord,
my noble Lord, the only Lord I have
ever loved in all my life!"

It was not only for the death of one
man alone that she cried, but for the
death of honor and glory and nobility,
for the decay of every true and good
ideal from within, for the loss of the
calm center of her soul.

The sudden shuddering pain in her
neck seemed for an instant merely the
natural extension of the storm within
her. But the strange, dizzy angles at
which her eyes met the whirling walls
and floor — Mercifully, her consciousness was extinguished before she fully
realized what had happened.

Gawaine's cousin, Sir Ywaine of the
Lion, and his companions had among
them some of the finest of those few who
remained to Arthur and all of the
Round Table. They cut down the Lord
of Belec with immediate justice.

Then they carefully bound the head
of the Lady of Belec back to her body.
The top bandage was a band of crimson
velvet, tied with threads of slightly tarnished gold. They carried her body back
with that of Sir Gawaine. Thus, at last,
the Lady of Belec came to court with
the lord of her true soul, to be buried
beside him in the same tomb. □

LOVE SONG FROM THE STARS

by Robert Sheckley

Lollia was a small, pine-clad cone of rock in the eastern Aegean. It was uninhabited, a difficult place to get to, but not quite impossible. Kinkaid rented an aluminum boat with outboard in Chios, packed in his camping equipment and, with a fair wind and a flat sea, got there in six hours, arriving just before sunset.

Kinkaid was tall and thin, with snubby features and fair, freckled skin, blotchy now in the fierce Greek summer sun. He wore a wrinkled white suit and canvas boat shoes. He was thirty-two years old. His hair was blondish-red, curly, and he was going bald on top. He was a member of an almost vanished species, the independently wealthy amateur archaeologist. He had heard of Lollia on Mykonos. A fisherman told him that the island was still visited from time to time by the old gods, and that people with any prudence stayed away. That was all Kinkaid needed to want to go there at once. He was in need of a respite from Mykonos's café amusements.

And there was always the chance he'd find antiquities. Many discoveries

have been made in the open, or under an inch or two of soil. Not in the well-known places, Mycenae, Tiryns, Delphi, where scientists and tourists have been studying for hundreds of years. It was the less likely sites that yielded the lucky finds nowadays, places on the edge of a great culture. Like Lollia, perhaps.

And even if he didn't find anything, it would be fun to camp out for a night or two before flying on to meet his friends in Venice for the film festival. And there was always the chance he'd find something no one else had ever come across.

As for the fisherman's talk of the old gods, he didn't know whether to put that down to Greek love of exaggeration or Greek superstition.

Kinkaid arrived at Lollia just before sunset, when the sky of the Aegean darkens swiftly through the shades of violet into a deepening transparent blue. A light breeze ruffled the waters and the air was lucid. It was a day fit for the gods.

Kinkaid circled the little island looking for the best place to land. He found a spit of land just off the northern point. He pulled his boat ashore through light surf and tied it to a tree. Then he climbed the rugged cliff, through luxuriant underbrush scented with rosemary and thyme.

At the summit there was a small plateau. On it he found the remains of an old shrine. The altar stones were weathered and tumbled around, but he could make out the fine carving.

There was a cave nearby, slanting down into the hillside. Kinkaid walked toward it, then stopped. A human figure had appeared in the cave mouth. A girl. She was young, very pretty, red-haired, dressed in a simple linen dress. She had been watching him.

"Where did you come from?" Kinkaid asked.

"The spaceship dropped me off," she told him. Although her English was flawless, she had a faint foreign accent which he could not place, but which he found charming. And he liked her sense of humor.

He couldn't imagine how she had gotten there. Not in a spaceship, of course; that was a joke. But how *had* she come? There had been no sign of another boat. She was unlikely to have swum the seventy miles from Chios. Could she have been dropped off by helicopter? Possible but unlikely. She looked as though she was ready for a lawn party. There wasn't a mark of dirt on her, and her makeup was fresh. Whereas Kinkaid was aware that he looked sweaty and rumpled, like a man who has just finished a difficult technical rock climb.

"I don't want to seem inquisitive," Kinkaid said, "but would you mind telling me how you got here, really?"

"I told you. The spaceship dropped me off."

"Spaceship?"

"Yes. I am not a human. I am an Andar. The ship will return for me tonight."

"Well, that's really something." Kinkaid said, humoring her. "Did you come a long way?"

"Oh, I suppose it must be hundreds of millions of miles to our planet of Andar. We have ways of getting around the speed of light, of course."

"Sure, that figures," Kinkaid said. Either the girl was carrying a joke a long way or she was a loony. The latter, most likely. Her story was so ridiculous he wanted to laugh. But she was so heartbreakingly beautiful he knew he'd break down and cry if he didn't get her.

He decided to play along. "What's your name? Why did you come here?" he asked.

"You can call me Alia. This is one of the planets the Andar decided to look into, after the Disappearance forced us to leave our home planet and go out into space. But I'm not supposed to talk about the Disappearance."

She was crazy all right, but Kinkaid was so charmed by her that he didn't care.

"You wouldn't happen to be one of the old gods, would you?" he asked.

"Oh, no, I'm not one of the Olympians," she told him. "But there were stories about them in the old days, when my people visited this planet."

Kinkaid didn't care what she said or where she was from. He wanted her. He'd never made it with an extraterrestrial. It would be an important first for him. Aliens as pretty as this didn't come along every day. And who knows, maybe she *was* from another planet. It was OK with him.

Whatever she was and however she got here, she was a beautiful woman. Suddenly he wanted her desperately.

And she seemed to feel something for him, too. He considered the shy yet provocative way she kept on glancing at him, then looking away. There was a glow of color in her cheeks. Perhaps unconsciously, she moved closer to him as they talked.

He decided it was time for action. Masterful Kinkaid took her in his arms.

At first she responded to his embrace, then pushed him away.

"You are very attractive," she said. "I'm surprised at the strength of my feelings toward you. But love between us is impossible. I am not of your race or planet. I am of the Andar."

The alien thing again. "Do you mean that you are not a woman in the sense we would mean on Earth?" Kinkaid asked.

"No, it isn't that. It's a matter of psychology. We women of the Andar do not love lightly. For us, the act of mating means marriage and a lifetime commitment. We do not divorce. And we *do* intend to have children."

Kinkaid smiled at that. He had heard it before, from the Catholic girls he used to date back in Short Hills, New Jersey. He knew how to handle the situation.

"I really do love you," he said. For the moment, at least, it was true.

"I have — certain feelings toward you, too," she admitted. "But you can't imagine what is involved when you love an Andar woman."

"Tell me about it," Kinkaid said, slipping an arm around her waist and drawing her to him.

"I cannot," she said. "It is our sacred mystery. We are not allowed to reveal it to men. Perhaps you should leave me now, while there's still time."

Kinkaid knew it was good advice: there was something spooky about her and the way she had appeared on the island. He really ought to leave. But he couldn't. As far as women were concerned he was a danger junkie, and this lady represented an all-time high in female challenges. He was no painter or writer. His amateur archaeology would never gain him any recognition. The one thing he could leave behind was his record of sexual conquests. Let them carve it on his tombstone: Kinkaid had the best, and he took it where he found it.

He kissed her, a kiss that went on and on, a kiss that continued as they dissolved to the ground in a montage of floating clothing and the bright flash of flesh. The ecstasy he experienced as they came together went right off the scale of his ability to express it. So intense was the feeling that he barely noticed the six sharp punctures, three on either side, neatly spaced between his ribs.

It was only later, lying back, spent and contented, that he looked at the six small, clean puncture wounds in his skin. He sat up and looked at Alia. She was naked, impossibly lovely, her dark red hair a shimmering cloud around her heart-shaped face. She did have one unusual feature which he had not noticed in the passion of lovemaking.

67

There were six small erectile structures, three on each side of her rib cage, each armed with a slender hollow fang. He thought of certain female insects on the Earth who bite off the heads of their mates during the act of love. He still didn't really believe she was an extraterrestrial. But he didn't disbelieve it quite as strongly as before. He thought of different species of insect on the Earth which resemble other species — katydids that look like dry twigs, flies that imitate wasps. Is that it? Was she about to take off her body?

He said, "It was terrific, baby, even if it *is* going to cost me my life."

She stared at him. "What are you saying?" she cried. "Do you actually think I will kill you? Impossible! I am an Andar female; you are my mate for life, and life for us lasts a very long time."

"Then what did you do to me?" Kinkaid asked.

"I've simply injected the children into you," Alia said. "They're going to be so lovely, darling. I hope they have your coloring."

Kinkaid couldn't quite grasp it at first. "Are you sure you haven't poisoned me?" he asked. "I feel very strange."

"That's just the hibernation serum. I injected it along with the babies. You'll sleep now, my sweet, here in this nice dry cave, and our children will grow safely between your ribs. In a year I'll come back and take them out of you and put them into their cocoons and take them home to Andar. That's the next stage of their development."

"And what about me?" Kinkaid asked, fighting the desire to sleep that had come powerfully over him.

"You'll be fine," Alia said. "Hibernation is perfectly safe, and I'll be back in plenty of time for the birth. Then you'll need to rest for a while. Perhaps a week. I'll be here to take care of you. And then we can make love again."

"And then?"

"Then it'll be hibernation time again, my sweet, until the next year."

Kinkaid wanted to tell her that this wasn't how he'd planned to spend his life — an hour of love, a year of sleep, then giving birth and starting all over again. He wanted to tell her that, all things considered, he'd prefer that she bite his head off. But he couldn't talk, could barely stay awake. And Alia was getting ready to leave.

"You're really cute," he managed to tell her. "But I wish you'd stayed on Andar and married your hometown sweetheart."

"I would have, darling," she said, "but something went wrong back home. The men must have been spying on our sacred mysteries. Suddenly we couldn't find them anymore. That's what we call the Great Disappearance. They went away, all of them, completely off the planet."

"It figures they'd catch on sooner or later." Kinkaid said.

"It was very wrong of them," Alia said. "I know that childbearing makes great demands on the men, but it can't be helped; the race must go on. And we Andar women can be relied upon to keep it going, no matter what lengths we must go to. I *did* give you a sporting chance to get away. Goodbye, my darling, until next year."

□

Take a walk with us.

There are nightmare worlds, worlds of exploded suns, worlds of magic, and worlds forgotten by time. There are worlds without end, and we visit them all.
Join us.

THE DEMON CAT

by Keith Taylor

A hideous waul tore the forest's nighted silence to shreds. Felimid's horse shied violently. Brush crackled against her plunging flanks. The twenty bronze acorns in golden cups which hung from the reins swung together, chiming.

The young bard controlled his mount with the skill of one born to horsemanship. Above him, thick summer leaves made it impossible to see the sky, or glimpse even one star. He had been careless, he knew, and in strange country like this he would certainly not find his way again until daylight.

"Wildcats mating," he murmured soothingly. "Large ones, surely — enormous — but just wildcats, you foolish beast."

Screams filled the dark. Felimid's neat-boned grey mare trembled, and might have shied again had he allowed it. He did not. A winding trail in the heart of a dark wood was no place to indulge her tricks.

The shattering racket went on, and Felimid wondered. Maybe it was nothing so ordinary as wildcats mating, after all. It sounded avid, with a note of dreadful eagerness. The youth fan-

VDF

cied he could almost hear words in the yowling. No sort of animal whelped on the ridge of the earth made noises quite like that.

He loosened his sword in its sheath, suddenly feeling that there might be work for it before sunrise. His foster-father had given it to him when he turned fifteen, and it was a noble weapon, forged by the master smith Donchad.

Riding warily along the trail between huge oaks, Felimid began to hear human voices. They ranted and yelled in response to the feline cries as if at a gathering of madmen. The grey mare stopped, quivering, and would go no farther for any kind of urging.

Felimid tethered her to a limb and went forward, walking softly.

He came to a wide clear space, roughly circular. The trees around it stood barely three times the bard's height, and they had grown one-sided and misshapen, seeming to flinch from that area where no trees grew.

In the centre of it rose a dark ceremonial mound. People capered about its base, bounding, mowing, tossing their arms high. Save that they *were* people, Felimid could tell nothing about them in the dark, not age, condition, or sex. There was no moon, and clouds obscured even the stars.

Something moved on the mound's terraced sides. Leaping to the crest, it gave a new series of demoniacal screams. Eyes like green beryl shone in a furred head white as the snow of one night. From nose-tip to tail-tip it was the same colour without a dissenting hair, and plainly visible as if it had been washed in pure light. It sprang and lashed its tail and batted the air with taloned paws in vicious playfulness, never ceasing its racket.

As he listened, sweating, Felimid became sure the sounds boiling from its throat were words. The impression he had ignored as fancy had been right.

He beheld a demon from the Otherworld.

From the distance, he could only guess its size. Belike it weighed as much as he did, and could break a stag's neck with malefic ease. The bard felt entranced, or fey.

He became aware that the raving humans were howling the cat's words like a slogan. From their mouths it was intelligible, though just as free of meaning. They shrieked it time after time.

"Never let Sadba know!"

The bard had ceased breathing, and his hand was clenched hard on the ivory, gold, and sapphire hilt of Donchad's work. When he noticed it, he sighed after air and slid blade from scabbard. Then he retreated down the winding path. He did not doubt that if his horse whinnied in fear he was a dead man. Having a fence of swords all around him would be no help. The hilt felt comforting, though, in spite of what his mind believed.

Holding the mare's mouth, he cut her tether and mounted. As he rode back the way he had come, a many-throated yell rang after him, filtered through the leaves.

"Never let Sadba know!"

The first time the trail forked, he took the other turning. By dawn he was out of the forest.

"Did I dream it?" he wondered aloud, and he knew he had not. He, Felimid mac Fal, was a poet of the third rank, qualified and initiated in that degree barely a month before. The bardic sight which cannot be deceived by magical glamours was now his. He knew what dreams were like, even waking dreams.

The demon cat had been real.

Felimid rode on through the morning, a lithe young man muscled smoothly as an otter, his brown hair intricately coiled and knotted. Wide green eyes and a snub nose gave him a guileless look. Nor did his appearance quite lie.

At fifteen, he was very nearly as innocent as he seemed.

He wore a purple cloak over a sky-blue tunic bordered with gold. The studs and clasps of his sandals were bronze with blue enamel, like his buckle, his two brooches, his triskele cloak-pin, and the plates of his scabbard. His grey mare's trappings were eye-catching as well, from the golden sunburst on her brow-band to the spiral ring encircling her tail. Felimid liked to make a pleasing show.

Before noon he came to his destination, the fort of the local king. A broad well-kept avenue led to its gates, and stone-faced earthworks surrounded it, ring within ring. A timber stockade formed the innermost defence.

As Felimid approached the hill, he heard someone sobbing. Out of curiosity, he dismounted, The sobs rose to howls of childish agony, then died in sniffles and gulps. Parting some bushes, Felimid found a dark-haired girl of seven curled in their shelter, womb-fashion. Despite staining and disarray, her clothes showed high rank.

She sat up, glaring at him hatefully. Swollen, blotched, running at the nose, her face was not prepossessing, and clearly she did not like his intrusion.

"Go away!" she commanded.

"Pardon me for disturbing you," Felimid said, "but I'm a stranger in this tuath, and you look like a woman of knowledge. Can you be telling me whose fort it is on the hill there?"

She sniffled some more. "It's my grandfather's," she said at last. "He's King Augaire, and he's lord of this tuath and the three around it."

"Then I'm where I should be, after all. I missed my path in the forest, but I suppose I could not avoid such a great kingdom unless I turned around entirely and went the other way. Now what can bring sorrow to you?"

"My sister!" the girl wailed. "They will give her to the demon to eat!"

For a moment Felimid saw not the girl but the macabre *ceilidh* of the night before, so vivid was the memory.

"So, ho," he murmured, focussing his gaze on her wet grubby face anew. "What is this demon like?"

"It's a horrible white cat big as a mountain. It kills sheep by the hundred, cattle by dozens. It kills men and women and children, too." She gulped. "It killed my uncles when they went to fight it. Now they are drawing lots in the royal clan for sacrifice. The Druids say there is nothing else to do."

A number of ideas fitted themselves together behind the bard's limpid eyes. He offered no words of empty sympathy. Instead, he asked one more question.

"Tell me, royal person . . . who is Sadba?"

"My grandfather's best wolfhound."

Because she was seven years old, she did not find his question irrelevant or callous. Children live in the moment and move from topic to topic like butterflies. She wiped her nose with dirty knuckles.

From the king's avenue a voice called out, "Mellal!"

The girl's head turned. Plainly, she heard her name. She said urgently, "Pretend you haven't seen me!"

Felimid lowered his voice. "Lady Mellal, it's a deal you are asking, so. The king your grandfather might punish me, did he know I helped you to hide. I'll chance it, though. Give me your royal promise to go no further from the dun, and my tongue shall have fetters on it. And pretend you have not seen *me*."

She nodded gravely, a princess bestowing a favour. The state of her face spoiled the effect a little.

As Felimid left the thicket, he met a young woman noticeably big with child. She turned at the sound of the foliage parting, exasperation and relief mixed in her expression — until she saw a stranger. Two fully armed warriors accompanied her.

"Oh, young sir, have you seen a seven years' child?"

"Never in days, lady," Felimid said, all candour and innocence. He looked at the two fighting men. "What sort of child is it you're looking for, that you must have such protectors, and you no more than a pebble's toss from the royal dun? Does he spit molten lead and strangle wolves with his hands?"

In the bushes, Mellal covered her mouth lest she betray herself with a giggle.

The young woman did not smile. "No, this is a girl, granddaughter to the king."

"And guards are needed these days within the very ramparts," added one of the fighting men. "The land is under a curse, haunted by a demon!"

"Be silent," growled the other. "That's whimpering . . . you, stranger. What is your name and what do you here?"

"I'm Felimid mac Fal, and my people are the Corco Baiscinn. For the rest, I would rather account once to your door-keepers in the right way, not twenty times to all the men who take a whim to question me."

Flushing with anger, the warrior leveled his spear. "You impudent pup!"

"Let be, Cichol." The young woman's voice held amusement. "Can you not see that he's a bard? Of two colours only, but a bard. Besides, it's Mellal we're seeking."

"Aye, true," the warrior Cichol said slowly. "But be careful of your words, Felimid mac Fal. This dun has come upon bad days. Not alone the dun, but the kingdom entire. There's grief and anger over it like a storm, and you'll find tempers sudden, though you be fifty times a bard."

"Then thanks for the caution," Felimid said.

He rode up the grassy royal avenue, thinking that he must see the king at once. Hadn't he news which might save Mellal's sister from a terrible fate? He saw visions of the whole dun listening enspelled as he spoke, despair and baffled fury changing to hope because of his words. He loved plaudits and attention as much as any youth of fifteen.

They did not come his way at once. His newly-won status as a bard of the third rank brought him within the dun, while his grandfather's name and a hint that he could aid against the demon took Felimid as far as the *aithech fortha*, the king's proxy in legal matters. It was no position for a man simple or easily impressed. This one had the tough mind of a survivor and awls for eyes.

"Young sir, I'll be blunt," he said. "We have had soothsayers and visionaries and fortune-hunting liars in rows, all claiming power to rid the kingdom of this demon cat. None has made his big words good. This newest horror, that the lady Carina must be given to the monster, has made the king implacable. He will listen to a man or woman with a scheme to save her, yes. However, he has sworn to have any who waste time with self-serving nonsense sawn apart living between two planks."

Felimid wondered if he would not have done better to mind his own business. Seeing his indecision, the *aithech fortha* smiled flintily.

"Do you prefer to turn around and ride away?" he asked.

Felimid remained silent for some time, considering the seamed, experienced face of the *aithech fortha*. Nothing he saw there reassured him.

"It's nothing I claim," he said at last, "and no promises I make. Where such forfeits are demanded, I'd never come hunting a fortune, what's more — even had I the stomach to profit from a king's pain. But I know what I saw yesternight." He drew a risk-drunken breath. "I'll not turn around, wise though it may be. I believe I'll see the king."

King Augaire received him in the

open, his royal chair set up before a triple row of pear trees. Eyes sunken, expression harsh, he gazed at the bard. Because he was young and not particularly wise, Felimid saw only the harshness. It did not occur to him that perhaps Augaire would rather not hope, lest he be disappointed again.

A woman sat on a round leather cushion to one side of the king's chair. Felimid's heart stumbled as he guessed who she was.

Carina.

The lot-chosen sacrifice to the demon cat.

She wore a white linen gown embroidered with blue silk, and a cincture and fillet of gold. Her black hair hung somewhat dishevelled. She was fighting the fear that shadowed her eyes with a cup of drugged wine, and appeared no more than eighteen — thought the bard, who was younger yet.

Behind the king's chair stood four of his mercenaries, tough-handed killers who would not be restrained by respect for a bard if Augaire ordered them to slay. Behind Felimid stood only the *aithech fortha.*

"Well, stranger?"

"My name is Felimid mac Fal, lord. My people are the Corco Baiscinn, and my father's father Fergus is nothing less than the Chief Bard of Erin. He proclaimed you king at your inauguration."

"Aye, before you were born." Augaire's face did not soften. "Before you were born, and before he was Chief Bard. A fine man. I hope you his grandson are worthy of him. You saw this demon, you say?"

Felimid chose not to complain that the king was brusque. "True for you, lord. I beheld him by chance, as I rode through the forest. . . ."

He told the story stylishly, though with no extravagance or digression. The king listened grimly, a man who had heard many things in his time and knew too well all the foolish, fearful, careless, or grasping reasons why folk lied. A man more difficult to impress or convince the bard could hardly have faced, unless it was the *aithech fortha.*

King Augaire listened until the end, and was only once moved to exclaim.

"Men and women, worshipping this monster? In my kingdom, where it has taloned two sons of mine who died fighting it? If I find them, if this is true, all shall die!" He shuddered with rage and his hands clenched. Mastering himself, he said after a harsh breath, "Speak on."

Felimid told the rest. Augaire leaned forward, his grey-bearded chin on his hand, pondering.

"Never let Sadba know," he repeated. "There is but the one Sadba in these four tuatha that I call to mind — my own great wolfhound bitch, and she's beyond compare. This demon cat is immune to weapon-steel. Brave men have died proving it, time after time, Fiacc and Murcharta among them." Grief darkened the king's eyes and drew down the corners of his mouth. "Might Sadba succeed, where they failed?"

The young woman had been gazing at Felimid as if he might, for her, be saviour or tormentor, but at any rate brought with him relief from the inexorability of a settled fate.

"Grandfather, there seems no other hope for me," she said.

"Nor is there, any longer." Augaire rested a hand on her shoulder. "My girl, I would raise a war-host and fight a battle to save you, if a war-host could do it. Here, that is no answer, though if the demon were slain, I'll take oath ten trusty men could do what else is needed. Yet the Druids say there is no way to abate this scourge but by sacrifice. You are royal; what would you have me do?"

Carina grew red, then pale. "Gods, oh gods, grandfather! I know the lot fell to me! I'd not have the kingdom suffer more, but I wish to live! It's not even death, so much as this way of dying. It's vile."

She bent her black head. Her teeth sank into her lip, drawing blood, and of the seven men present, not one found it easy to look another in the face. Words died even in Felimid's mouth.

The scream of a strong man in his death agony shocked the air. They all partly welcomed it in their secret hearts, for it broke the tension and freed them from helplessness. The scream was repeated. Then came a choking, a gurgle, and a bubbling moan that trailed into silence.

"Cenn Cruaich!" one of the mercenaries grunted. "That was someone's last noise."

"I believe you are right." Augaire made a sharp gesture. "Garrchú, Pirmin! Go swiftly and see what caused it. Bring me word at once. You others, remain."

With salutes, the two men designated left on their errand. The king sank into preoccupied brooding; from time to time he struck the arm of his chair with his fist. The Lady Carina smiled faintly, and placed a hand over his sinewy wrist.

"Grandfather, I'd guess there has been a quarrel, some old grudge revived. All in the dun feel raw as burned men. It takes nothing to set one at another, these days. Yes?"

"How well I know!" Augaire cursed fiercely, a prey to the same baffled anger. He loved his granddaughter, yet was helpless to save her.

His mercenaries returned swiftly, as he had commanded. Leashed snarling between them was the greatest wolfhound bitch Felimid had seen. Her head, lifted, reached his chest. Gore dripped from her lips and fangs.

"It was the Lord Samildan, sire," panted the man named Garrchú, bracing himself as the bitch lunged against her leash. "Sadba attacked him. He's

76

dead meat."

His companion, Pirmin, laughed harshly. "By the gods, yes. He could not be deader."

"Samildan!" the king said. "Slain? And by my dog? His family will demand that she be destroyed."

"She'd have been destroyed at the time, belike, had we not interfered. We almost went the way Samildan did, getting her leashed."

"She attacked him unprovoked? Not easy to believe. I do *not* believe it. Be still, Sadba."

"I heard four different stories, sire," Garrchú said. "One is that Samildan attacked *her*, with a spear. Sure it is that he carried one. Not that it did him good at all."

"If you'll allow me, lord?" Felimid was perhaps over-confident in his new status as a bard of two colours, but his deferential manner disarmed anger. "I know nothing of your dun or its ways, but is this not too much for chance? I appear, with news that your bitch Sadba can maybe end the demon's devastation — and at once, this occurs."

"You have a thought?"

"I've a suspicion, just . . . it is ugly."

King Augaire laughed harshly. "Then, by earth and sky and sea, it's apt to be right! Little that's pretty has happened here of late. Tell what you suspect, son of Fergus's son."

"The folk who did homage to the demon shouted over and over, 'Never let Sadba know!' Why should they fear that? How could there be any danger of one of them betraying the secret to her, unless he was coming here?"

"Ha!" Augaire rose from his chair. "Samildan? And maybe others . . . wait. Let me think upon this."

He looked behind him, at the small grove of pear trees. In a little while he turned back.

"A man hidden there might have heard all we said. Then, if he went at once to kill Sadba — he'd have had to go swiftly indeed, for us to hear his death-cry so soon after — I can make sense of it. And it may be. I recall that Samildan's clan has lost four head of cattle only to the demon, and not one man, woman, or child."

"Here are my orders," he said. "None of you will say a word of this. It's to be secret even from your own shadows.

"Garrchú, Pirmin! Take Sadba to my chamber and hide her there. Oengus Nic, my friend," — this to the *aithech fortha* — "go before them, send away the present guards, and have these men replace them. Give it out that I slew Sadba myself. Have a goat's carcass wrapped in linen and buried beneath a cairn, for show. If Samildan was indeed a false man, and there are others, let's be lulling them. Swiftly!"

"Yes, lord; at once."

They went. King Augaire looked speculatively at the two mercenaries who remained, then at Felimid. "You will all attend me closely until this thing is settled. By tomorrow night, it will be. You see, Felimid, that is — it *was* to be — the night Carina must be offered to the demon cat. Will you be one of the men who goes to prevent it? You brought the news."

The sudden demand startled Felimid. Standing by, admiring Augaire's decisiveness and craft, he had begun to feel less than closely involved; to think that he had played his part and that whatever action might follow concerned others. Now he was called upon to decide and act.

He did not see at once that he was being tested, or that by refusing he would harm such belief as he had won. Nor was he sure if it was courage or cowardice, but he did know that to refuse this challenge with Carina's grey eyes watching him was a thing he would not do.

He acceded with panache. "You honour me, lord!" Bowing to Carina, he added, "I could not strive to a better

end, lady. The day after tomorrow will be a brighter one."

"I am hoping so."

Her words rustled like dead leaves in the wind. Carina's world had felt strange to her since the Druids spoke their augury. She heard without hearing, saw without seeing, and most of the time could not believe in what was to happen. The rest of the time, she did. Then she had to strangle screams of terror, because she knew that once she let them begin she would never stop screaming.

She was not inclined to make a graceful, smiling speech of thanks to a stranger who might be just one more charlatan.

The same thought had struck the king and Oengus Nic. Now it struck someone else. One of the king's mercenaries, a large-jawed fellow with a surly, jealous eye and an accent from beyond the sea, drew Felimid aside.

"Hear me, bard," he said. "It's in my mind that you are a glib-tongued sniffer after reward. Your pretence that you knew nothing of this demon cat before you entered the kingdom . . . why, it's unlikely."

Felimid's temper was not ruffled. "It would be unlikely in the highest degree," he said, "had I come here with any set purpose. I did not. See you, I spent most of the winter in study and feats of memory to attain the third rank of bard, and the rest in fasting alone to attain the true sight through visions. After all that, I had a wish to be free of discipline for a while, so I wandered at random for days and nights, not caring where I might be. When I realised I had come to this part of the land, I had the whim to visit King Augaire. My grandsire and he were friends of old. But as I'd never been here before, I lost my way in the forest."

The mercenary scowled. "I'll watch

you, nonetheless. And take the head from your shoulders if you have lied, no matter if you are fifty times a bard."

"Thrice only, at present," Felimid said lightly. "I think my head will stay where it is. You may come and ask my pardon when all's done."

That night he told stories for the king and Carina, in the king's own chamber which had been barred from others. He accompanied the tales with harp music. Sadba the wolfhound paced the chamber, not liking her confinement. Her jaws had long since been cleansed of blood in sweet water. White-toothed, pink-tongued, she stretched in her brindled power and licked the king's hand.

A strong man with a spear had not been able to withstand her. Felimid knew it, and yet when he thought of the silken malignity of the creature he'd seen in the forest, he doubted that even Sadba could battle it and win.

He played fidchell with Carina, and kept his doubts to himself. He won easily — not because of skill alone, for Carina was reckoned a fine player. She played for a distraction, for something to do. Her mind was not on the game.

Watching her by lamplight, Felimid wished strongly to see her with her eyes unshadowed by threatened horror. Of his own desperate situation he thought little. No youth of fifteen fully believes he can die.

Drinking potent birch wine, the king spoke seldom and briefly. He knew what death was. He had seen battles, fought in feuds and arbitrated them, only to see them flame to life again no matter what judgement he gave. Two sons of his had recently died. *My nephew is tanist heir. He will survive me. I'm old. If I cannot protect my kingdom and my granddaughter from this demon, it's time I went the way of the useless. Besides . . . this way I may strike hard blows in vengeance before I go.*

He turned his gaze to the young pair setting up the board for another game. Sadba nuzzled his hand.

The next night, a small procession entered the forest. Carina rode in a canopied litter. It oppressed her suffocatingly. Far rather would she have been open to the air and sky than endure this grim privacy. She had ample time for that. If things went amiss, she would be as private and enclosed by dawn as anyone could be.

A second, more secret party raced for the ceremonial mound by other paths. King Augaire led it, clad in plain linen and leather, a sword slung across his back and a round targe on his arm, with Sadba loping beside him. Felimid came next, in leather tunic and buskins, armed like the king. The four mercenaries who had known the king's plan since he conceived it trod close behind. Six other fighting men, chosen for courage and trustworthiness, followed last.

It occurred to Felimid that perhaps they had orders to slay him if he behaved suspiciously or tried to drop back, for he was learning.

He was right; they had.

The thirteen reached the mound an hour before Carina's party. They settled down to wait in the circle of trees about the clearing, hidden in the undergrowth.

Someone muttered, "I'm eager to be slaying."

King Augaire said in a low, matter-of-fact voice, "I will kill the next man who opens his mouth with nothing necessary to say."

No one else spoke.

They saw Carina's party arrive and carry her to the top of the mound. In an outburst of fury and grief, one man placed himself before her, swearing to remain and defend her while he possessed life. Carina, steady-voiced, thanked him but ordered him to leave with the rest. More passionately than before, he refused. He might have inflamed the whole party with his purpose, but the lady's calm insistence and the terror the demon cat had spread through four *tuatha* proved stronger in the end. They departed, leaving her chained to the frame of her litter. The dissenter among them was carried by force when Carina ordered it.

She sat, her legs trembling. The shaking spread throughout her body.

Her escort had scarcely left when three loud owl-hoots sounded from the nearby forest, a pre-arranged signal. Tears ran from Carina's eyes. Her grandfather and his men were there. She wasn't alone. Her kinsmen were prepared to fight for her, however long the chances.

I can bear anything now, she thought.

Her fetters jingled as she moved. They were false; she could free herself whenever she wished. Her escort had not known that. Even the smith who had made the fetters did not know. The king's mercenaries had tampered with them in secret, while the king watched. He was a careful man.

They all waited some time. A warning hiss from the warrior nearest the path brought them all to readiness. Folk had come into the clearing; in ones and twos, more continued to arrive. Some even passed along the same trail Augaire's band had used.

The night was less dark than the first one Felimid had known in this place. A sickle moon rose above the trees, and the young bard saw better in the dark than most. Some details of bearing and gesture made him think these cultists were well born.

Like Samildan . . . how can they do it?

He knew a fight was coming. He had been trained in weapon-use, and ridden on cattle raids with other high-spirited young men, and once fought clear of an ambush with others of his clan. He knew something of action, and folk he held worthy to judge had called his sword-skill exceptional. Still, he had never slain. Nor did he crave to.

On this night he might have to take death or give it. Against these cultists, he did not mind greatly. Once more he thought, *How can they do it?*

King Augaire, with a reign of five-and-thirty years behind him, could have answered that. They paid homage to the demon in the hope that it would slay or ruin their rivals, bringing them power. The sheer wild joy of cruelty the demon embodied belike drew some.

New arrivals emerged from the forest. Felimid judged their numbers at fifteen or eighteen by now.

"Welcome, sacrifice!" someone shouted to the lady.

She deigned no reply. A cousin of hers, crouched beside Felimid, said between his teeth, "Scum!"

Suddenly, the demon cat was there.

It sprang into the clearing from a gnarled tree branch. Beautiful, deadly, and assured, it paced across the grass. Its fur gleamed whiter than Carina's gown.

"There is your kill, my darling," King Augaire said urgently to Sadba. "There! Take it! Go!"

The mighty bitch obeyed. Her long brindled coat rippled in the wind she made as she rushed across the clearing. Taller and heavier than the demon, she struck it with her shoulder as it flowed about to face her, bowling it over. It came yowling to its feet in an explosion of rage.

Raising a war-shout of *"Sadba is here!"* the king charged from concealment. Eleven men followed, repeating his cry. Felimid's rush was as swift and his shout as fierce as anybody's.

Sadba struck at the back of the demon's neck. Lithe as no creature she had ever attacked before, it twisted from beneath her jaws and bounded to the base of the terraced mound. Sadba sprang after it, the one natural beast in the kingdom swift enough to catch the thing she pursued. Half-way up the mound, she caught it once more.

Sadba's teeth went in to the bone at the demon's shoulder joint. Earth sprayed from under her blunt-nailed feet as she tossed the cat through a shrieking somersault. That foreleg was torn out of joint.

The demon slid its sound foreleg over Sadba's neck in a loathsome parody of embrace. Its claws came out. Its back legs rammed against Sadba's belly, raking. The feline teeth sank home.

Sadba screamed. Destroyed, turned in a heartbeat's space to gory wreckage by a thing whose like she had never encountered, she nonetheless found the grip she had been seeking. Her jaws closed on the back of the demon's neck.

"Sadba is here!" yelled King Augaire's men.

Spears flashed, sinking into flesh, spilling red. Shields broke bones. Payment was taken in one hot indulgence of slaughter for all the demon had made Augaire's kingdom suffer. The demon's adherents were also armed; they sold their lives at a price, but they fought against men fiercely determined to buy.

A dark shape in a flapping cloak ran at Felimid. Edged metal flashed. Felimid caught the stroke on his targe, and his arm was jarred to the shoulder. His own sword sprang down. Because the bard was left-handed, his enemy could not interpose his shield in time and had to parry, blade against blade. He did so clumsily. Felimid's cut drove the flat of the man's own weapon down on his brow, dazing him. He staggered, and struck desperately with his small round shield.

The targes boomed together like the heads of fighting stags. Felimid slid the edge of his own behind his adversary's, and brought the effort up from his braced ankles to lever the other man's

shield aside. He sent his sword forth, angling the thrust for the guts. His point found the pad of muscle over his foe's hip instead. The man went down.

"Yield!"

It was a foolish demand. The fellow had nothing to gain by surrender. He slashed scythe-like at the bard's feet. Felimid sprang back to save himself from being crippled.

His foe turned to bolt. In the murk beneath the trees, he stumbled, and as he lurched up from his hands and knees, Felimid caught him. The bard's sword flashed. Roaring, the fellow vanished down a pitch-dark forest path at a hopping, staggering run. He carried with him a stab wound in one hip and a diagonal slash across his right buttock.

After hesitating a moment, the bard decided not to follow.

Someone rushed at him, bawling *"Sadba is here!"* Their swords rang. Felimid held him in play while sidling out from under the dark, twisted shadows into the moonlight, such as it was.

"I know fine well . . . Sadba's here," he said breathlessly, half laughing. "I'm of your band, man! Look harder and maybe . . . you'll know me."

"Silver-arm!" swore the other. "It's the bard! Ha! Pardon! We have not used up all the real enemies yet."

As they looked about them, they saw the demon cat. One of its forelegs was dark with fuming blood. Wet darkness collared its neck and made a patch on the snowy breast. It gathered itself while they looked, and sprang at King Augaire.

Two men with him covered the king with their shields and took the impact. They staggered; one went down. The cat rebounded, to strike the earth in a thrashing frenzy.

The fallen man screamed, for the demon had clawed open his arm from shoulder to wrist. Blood fountained wildly. He tried without success to stop

his life from draining out.

The cat lay still. Sadba's fangs had done what metal weapons could not, and that leap at the king had been a dying effort. Even as the demon's last victim poured his blood into the earth, his killer's flesh turned to writhing vapour. In a few breaths, only the bones were left. They glittered white as salt, clean as though wind and rain had worked upon them for a thousand years.

"We have won!" King Augaire shouted. "The demon is killed!"

Its worshippers, the few who were able, fled into the forest in despair. Three with disabling wounds were taken captive. Eight lay lifeless on the ground. Apart from the king, his granddaughter, and Felimid, five of the victors were standing.

"Dead!"

"The thing's slain! The kingdom is free of it!"

"Gods, the way the flesh seethed and smoked from its bones —"

"Enough!" Augaire said loudly. "You babble like children! Let's have a sensible tally of our wounded. Garrchú, how is it with that man?"

Garrchú knelt by the warrior with the hideously torn arm. "He's dead, lord. Nigh empty of blood, I would say."

Felimid recognised him. He was the surly warrior who had threatened the bard with death.

"As I would be," Augaire said, responding to Garrchú's comment on the dead man's emptiness of blood, "were it not for him and his mate. I'll remember them both. Sadba, where is Sadba?"

They discovered her on the mound. Her entrails hung out of her belly, the side of her neck was in red strips, and the demon's teeth had cut the muscle from her shoulder like intersecting knives. Augaire ran gently searching hands over her, and wept at what he discovered.

"Ah, girl, girl . . . forgive me."

It was not callousness to the deaths of his men. They had known what they were to face. The bitch had attacked out of courage and loyalty, when her master said attack, and she knowing nothing. That lent a special dimension to her fate.

She lifted her head, shuddering. Carina choked, and gripped Felimid's arm. The bard felt tears in his own eyes.

With one hand Augaire caressed the great dog's head. With the other he drew a merciful knife across her throat.

□

THE CHANT DEMONIAC

I am Satan; I am weary,
For my road is long and hard
And it lies through regions dreary
Since the Golden Gates were barred.
(I wait, I wait at the Flaming Gate
I give men death and they give me hate.)

I am Satan, never resting
For the scourge is at my back.
Yonder soul, his crimes attesting,

To the fire, to the rack.
Yet another and another
Will the tally never cease?

Turn from sin, I beg, my brother,
Give a weary demon peace.
I am Satan, I am weary,
By the ever flaming sea;
Ye who tread my regions dreary,
Sinners, sinners, pity me.

— **Robert E. Howard**

Weirdisms

HAND OF GLORY

Some grimoires describe how the sorcerer cuts off the hand of a hanged man. After the ritual of preparation it is treated with wax; it becomes a magical candle. This baleful torch lights the way to hidden treasure . . . and has the power to numb or poison people at a distance.

© Jason Van Hollander - 1989

CLOONATURK

by Mervyn Wall

If you travel the ups and downs of one of the little roads that goes west from Galway, and follow it as it worms its way into the depths of Connemara, you may at last come to the townland of Cloonaturk. You may, but it's unlikely; for there are no signposts and the inhabitants of these parts have an instinctive distrust of strangers, whom they invariably misdirect. Why, I cannot say. Maybe it's that they have no recollection of a stranger having ever conferred a benefit on them, and that they deem it wiser to be on the safe side by hurrying a stranger out of the neighbourhood by the shortest possible route. And even if you do come to Cloonaturk, you're as likely as not to pass through without realizing that you've reached it.

Cloonaturk is just thirty scattered cottages on a wrinkle of stony hill which creeps back from the sea towards the Maamturk Mountains. There's the same crazy-patterned landscape — the walls of loose stones zig-zag all over the place dividing the pale green fields which look no bigger than pocket handkerchiefs. The smallness of everything, the fields, the walls, the roads and the cottages, makes the arc of the sky seem immense, piled high as it usually is, cloud upon cloud. Round the bend of the road the grey Atlantic comes creeping in across the stones. Connemara is not like a part of this world at all, but like a locality which has strayed from a fairy tale. You would easily miss Cloonaturk; as I say, it's only thirty scattered cottages in a waste of rock and bog,

hidden away in a corner of the inlet-worried coast. Even if you were to ask one of the inhabitants if this was Cloonaturk, it'd be doubtful if he'd do more than take his pipe from his mouth, regard you mournfully, and replace the pipe between his teeth.

The population seems to be made up of gaunt, silent, dreamy-eyed men of uncertain age, who meditate every question put to them, but rarely are able to rouse themselves sufficiently to give an answer. There don't seem to be any women, though there's a tradition that there were children once, but that they all emigrated to America.

Since the sixteenth century the inhabitants of Cloonaturk have subsisted entirely on a diet of poteen and potatoes. Poteen is of course an illicit drink; and its distillation should be suppressed by the authorities; but the police have long since given it up as a bad job. The slow-moving inhabitants of Cloonaturk have baffled every excise officer since the reign of George the First, and in the face of this tradition and after seven inglorious raids, the Sergeant in whose sub-district the townland lies, abandoned the matter as hopeless. "Every man and dog in that place," he declared bitterly, "has his inside rotted through and through by reason of the consumption of illicit liquor."

The inhabitants of the townland have always had a deep distrust of officialdom. It had been their experience for centuries that when an official began to take an interest in them, he had

84

85

never anything good in his mind. He usually wanted money, and it took a long time to explain to him that nobody in Cloonaturk had any money. The inhabitants had of course heard of money; some of them had even seen it and could describe it: but none of them had ever handled it. And even if an official wasn't intent on being given money, he was as likely as not to have a dozen uniformed police hiding round the bend of the road; and those lads, you might be sure, were up to no good. They invariably had an assortment of probing rods and spades, and they were quite prepared to spend days wasting their own and everyone else's time digging up half the hillside looking for illicit stills which the inhabitants knew were somewhere else. The official mind was past understanding, and Cloonaturk took a very poor view of it.

It is therefore not surprising that one afternoon when a postman propped his bicycle against one of the loose stone walls which border the road, and came wearily up the track towards Pat's Tommy's cottage, the owner bolted the door and dragging his trestle-bed across the floor, began to barricade himself in. He had just removed his one cup from the dresser to a place of safety, preparatory to moving that article of furniture into position as well, when his eye fell on a long official envelope which had been pushed under the door. He heard the postman's retreating footsteps and realized that he had been outwitted.

For a long time Pat's Tommy stood motionless, gloomily contemplating the envelope; then he slowly shoved the bed back into its accustomed position against the wall, and taking the cup in one hand, he rooted with the other in the heap of peat piled high in the corner. He drew a bottle from its hiding-place and filled himself a cupful of poteen. Late into the night he sat drinking by the fire, filled with the gloomiest forebodings. The following morning he found it necessary to leave the cottage to bring in some potatoes. The unopened letter still lay on the earthen floor. After some hesitation he lifted it gingerly and placed it on the dresser. It remained there unopened until one evening four days later when, smiling slyly, he took it down, tiptoed over to the fire and burnt it.

He went about the little business of his acre of land in melancholy serenity until a week later the arrival of a second letter threw him into the utmost confusion. This time he did not hesitate, but, seizing the envelope, he thrust it into the heart of the glowing peat. But his peace of mind was now gone: a deep depression settled on him, and he waited fatalistically for the arrival of a third letter. It came on a grey afternoon when the soft, thin rain was falling. The words **FINAL NOTICE** were stamped on the outside in broad red letters. Pat's Tommy sat on his stool the whole night through while the fire flamed and glowed and died. He emptied one bottle of poteen and made respectable inroads into a second. About an hour before dawn he sighed, and opening the letter, drew out a printed form. On one side there was a demand for the immediate payment of seven shillings and sixpence for a Dog Licence. On the back in small print were paragraph after paragraph of extracts from Acts of Parliament and a horrifying list of penalties. Pat's Tommy read it all through, finished the bottle of poteen, and went out into the barn and hanged himself.

Cloonaturk received its first intimation that something was wrong when a couple of days later three motor-cars suddenly appeared out of nowhere. Two small gentlemen with bowler hats clambered out of one, and the others disgorged uniformed police and two loose-limbed individuals with hard faces, who immediately pulled out notebooks and started asking everyone questions.

CLOONATURK

It was a fine, sunny morning; and the inhabitants had been mooching about their fields or leaning across the walls smoking their pipes and staring at nothing. Most of the inhabitants did not stay to be questioned: at the first sight of uniforms they hurried back to their respective cottages. But the police manifested exceptional determination and insisted on the arrest of twelve men. When they had twelve, they seemed to be satisfied.

Old Thady, who had a back door to his cottage, managed to make a getaway and fled up the hillside, but he was quickly overtaken and brought back. He was told that he was to be "foreman," whatever that might mean, and he was placed carefully in the first car. The other eleven were packed in somehow, and the three cars started off down the winding road. They travelled for miles until they came at last to the old disused schoolhouse near Cashel. It was the first time that any of the inhabitants had been in a petrol-propelled vehicle, and they didn't like the experience. Indeed, Old Thady at one point tried to fling himself out, and would have succeeded only that one of the policemen happened to be sitting on his coat-tails.

When the old schoolhouse was reached, the twelve Cloonaturk men were ordered out and shepherded inside. They were put to sit on a long bench against the wall, and each one was presented with a notebook and pencil, which, having examined, they stowed away carefully in their tail-pockets. The first indication they had of what it was all about, was when the two hard-featured detectives at the door suddenly took off their hats, and Pat's Tommy was carried in on a shutter. The Cloonaturk men stared. It was true that no one had seen Pat's Tommy for a couple of days, but that was in no way unusual in Cloonaturk, where if a man felt like doing a little really serious drinking, he might retire to his cottage for a week. Their first thought was that the officials had murdered poor Pat's Tommy, but none of them ventured to speak. With such a crowd of officials present, the man who first opened his mouth might well be the next to share Pat's Tommy's fate.

What followed was a nightmare. One of the gentlemen climbed into the school rostrum and from there shouted at the twelve Cloonaturk men until he was crimson in the face. When he was exhausted, the Sergeant took up the shouting. The jury sat staring impassively at whoever happened to be shouting at the time, only manifesting interest when the other bowler-hatted gentleman, who was apparently a doctor, suddenly hung a tube out of his ears and with the other end of it started tapping Pat's Tommy all over. It took two hours' shouting at the Cloonaturk men before it was slowly borne in on them that poor Pat's Tommy had done away with himself. They said nothing, but none of them blamed him. It's usual in many parts of Connemara to "hang a dog against the licence"; that is, if you haven't got the seven-and-six, the only thing to do is to hang the dog. But it was remembered that Pat's Tommy had been fond of the little mongrel, so that his substitution of himself was not considered remarkable.

When the Cloonaturk men realized that none of them was going to be put into gaol on the head of Pat's Tommy's behaviour, they brightened considerably. They nodded their heads when the Sergeant instructed them to do so, and they crowded round to watch Old Thady make his mark on a document which the gentleman in the rostrum passed down to him. The Sergeant witnessed Thady's mark, and the proceedings terminated. The coroner gathered his papers, scowled at the Cloonaturk men, and stumped out of the schoolhouse. They were shepherded once more into the waiting motor-cars and conveyed back to Cloonaturk, where the remains of Pat's Tommy were surrendered to his friends.

The community breathed with relief when the last car disappeared over the shoulder of the hill. Their experience was too recent to admit of conversation, so after standing about for some time in silence, they bore Pat's Tommy awkwardly to Old Thady's house, which, on account of its possession of a back door, was regarded as the most considerable residence. Then they dispersed so as to give Old Thady some hours to prepare for the wake, and one man set out to tramp five miles to the nearest church to inform the Parish Priest that Pat's Tommy was coming along in the morning to be buried.

It was a powerful wake. Old Thady, perhaps on account of his failing eyesight, distilled a poteen that can only be described as vicious. When you took a gulp of it, you could feel the flame striking the pit of your stomach and then forking down each of your legs. While you were wiping the tears from your eyes, you felt your toes opening and shutting. But in spite of the potency of the liquor the men were silent, each slowly turning over in his mind the day's experiences.

On the morrow a little procession of middle-aged men in nineteenth-century tail-coats started along the five-mile road to the churchyard. Pat's Tommy went before on an ass-cart with two men sitting on the coffin.

When the last respects had been paid, the inhabitants of Cloonaturk streamed back, some singly, some in little groups. No one spoke, but with one accord they climbed the track to Old Thady's cottage, in which there was still a large quantity of poteen undrunk. The resumed wake lasted four days. On the second day there was some conversation of a monosyllabic character. On the third day there was some hard cursing as the twelve jurymen began to indicate

to one another what they thought of their outrageous kidnapping by the police. From time to time a man fell asleep in an upright position leaning against the wall, and only awakened when someone fell over his feet. The one who had fallen, usually went to sleep where he lay; while the other who had been awakened helped himself to another drink. Occasionally someone said goodbye to his host and left by the back door, but on making his way round the cottage would find himself at the front door again. Realizing that there was a wake in progress, he would enter and remain for another twenty-four hours.

Long Joe Flaherty, a sad-eyed man with a drooping, black moustache which he had inherited from his father, was the first to get away from the cottage, which he did by slipping in the mud outside the door and rolling twenty yards down the track. He sat up on the ground and looked back at the house with a sense of satisfaction. He distinctly recollected having taken his departure no less than three times, but each time finding himself by some magic back inside the kitchen again with a cup of poteen in his fist. He got carefully to his feet and making his way to the road, screwed up his eyes and searched the sky to see where the sun was. At first he couldn't find it, but at last he discerned it over on his right half-way into the red Atlantic. Therefore it was evening. With a slow lumbering gait he started home. As he crossed the little bridge where the stream comes tumbling down between the stones, a familiar figure turned the bend of the road and came towards him.

"Good evening to you, Long Joe," it said as it passed.

"Good evening, Pat's Tommy," he answered and continued on his way.

He trudged on round the turn of the road and slowly climbed the track to his own cottage. It was only when he was taking off his boots to go to bed, that he remembered the man who had bid him good evening on the road.

"Strange," he said to himself. "I had an idea that Pat's Tommy was dead." But the matter was too complex for further thought. He remembered that he had four nights' arrears of sleep to make up, so taking off his cap, he hung it on the bed-knob and clambered into bed.

When he awoke it was midday. He lay for a long time on his back gazing at the ceiling. At last he struggled out of bed on to the floor and poured out a half-cup of poteen so as to steady himself. Then he went to the door and opened it, stepped out to see what sort of a day it was.

The sky was speckled with vagrant clouds. The mild sunlight lay everywhere; the air was clear. Long Joe's gaze wandered across the tumbled hills and came at last to rest on a small white cottage perched on the rising ground some four hundred yards from where he stood. It was Pat's Tommy's cottage, and as Long Joe gazed idly at it, the door opened, and out came Pat's Tommy with a spade on his shoulder. He was preceded by the little mongrel dog jumping and fawning on its master. Its joyous barking came across the fields through the thin, sunlit air.

Long Joe stood staring, then he turned quickly and re-entering the kitchen, poured himself another drink. Then he went out and had another look. There was no doubt about it. Pat's Tommy was assiduously digging in the potato patch at the back of the house. Long Joe retreated precipitately into his kitchen. Afternoon deepened into evening, and still he sat sipping poteen and staring vacantly in front of him, only stirring from time to time to brush from his moustache with a mechanical hand the little colourless beads of liquor.

Pat's Tommy's cottage was on a height clearly visible from all parts of the townland, so that Long Joe was not the only one who saw Pat's Tommy moving about the fields in his usual way, apparently unaware that he had been sat upon by a coroner and subsequently buried. "Someone should tell him," suggested Old Thady that night as the inhabitants sat in their usual meeting-place in the shelter of a bank at the crossroads. But there was a shaking of heads. Old Thady was known to have a streak of wildness in his character, and anyway such a procedure didn't seem quite proper. Hour after hour they sat in silence smoking their pipes, each man turning over in his mind the events of the preceding week in as far as he could remember them. Everyone had a distinct recollection of having been at a funeral, and several remembered the ass cart going down the road with two men sitting on the coffin. It was felt that Pat's Tommy had been under close observation all the time, and it was not understood how he had managed to get out.

During the following day Pat's Tommy passed several of his acquaintances on the road and bade them the time of day. He even dropped in at one man's cottage and borrowed a pitchfork without the owner's permission. An hour after sunset Old Thady found him in the kitchen helping himself liberally to Thady's poteen. Thady saw no reason for remaining, but retreated through the back door as soon as courtesy permitted. When Pat's Tommy took to joining the men at the crossroads at night, sitting there smoking his pipe without a word, a profound gloom settled on the community. Cloonaturk was never much given to conversation, but it was at the meeting-place at the crossroads that a man was afforded an opportunity of making a remark about the weather or about the government, if he felt it incumbent upon him to do so. Now, nobody ventured to say anything; for naturally enough no one wanted to lay himself open to the possibility of contradiction by a corpse. It was felt that it would be unlucky; so the Cloonaturk men smoked in silence, tapped out their pipes one by one, bade Pat's Tommy good night and trudged home.

It's strange how news travels. A week later a newspaperman from one of the Dublin newspapers arrived at the police station. He wore a shabby waterproof coat and an old battered hat, and his face was bright with whiskey.

"Where's Cloonaturk?" he asked.

The Sergeant scowled at him.

"It's on the coast about twelve miles to the west."

"I hear that a dead man has come back and is walking round Cloonaturk. Did you hear the story?"

"Of course I heard it."

"Is it true?" asked the newspaperman.

"How do I know whether it's true? I wouldn't be surprised at anything that might happen in that place."

"Why are you so violent about it?"

The Sergeant made a mighty effort at self-control.

"Listen here," he said. "I like a romantic story as well as anyone. In fact, I read them to the children. But I like to find my romance between the covers of a book. I have every reason to be indignant when it manifests itself in a part of my sub-district."

"So you believe it's true?"

"Get to Hell out of this," roared the Sergeant.

The newspaperman went out and hired a car. Then he bought himself a half-pint bottle of whisky, as he thought he'd need it before he faced the ghost. When he arrived at Cloonaturk and convinced the inhabitants that he wasn't an official, they became quite friendly. The entire population accompanied him down the road in the failing evening light and pointed out to him Pat's Tommy climbing over a stile, Pat's Tommy milking a goat and Pat's Tommy entering the door of his cottage. The

newspaperman couldn't see anything, but he was conscious of the approach of night and of the cold, damp wind blowing across the grey Atlantic. He shuddered, drank the whisky, and decided to postpone closer investigation until the daylight. He spent the night in Old Thady's cottage drinking Thady's poteen. On the following day he was able to see all that was pointed out to him, and even more.

The newspaperman was a conscientious reporter and, however drunk he was, never forgot his obligations to his paper. He got into the hired car and drove five miles to the church to inspect the Register of Deaths. He avoided an accident more by instinct than by good driving, for his view of the road was much impeded by Pat's Tommy, who accompanied him sitting astride the bonnet of the car. At the church he examined the entry in the register, and back in the town he interviewed the coroner and the doctor. Then he telephoned the story to his newspaper in Dublin.

His editor was sceptical. "I'll hold the story for a few days," he said. "And for God's sake, try to sober up."

"I'm not drunk," squealed the reporter indignantly.

"Were you ever any other way?" growled the editor.

The newspaperman returned to Cloonaturk, but he only lasted three days. He found the pace too hot. He never quite got used to Pat's Tommy buttonholing him on the road and engaging him in abstruse political argument. He was gone from Cloonaturk one morning and was subsequently heard of in various midland towns where he was in process of drinking himself sober in the course of his return to Dublin. When he reported to his office a week later and his editor saw the state he was in, angry words were spoken. But it wasn't until he threw open the door to show Pat's Tommy sitting on the stairs, that his editor gave him the sack, and tearing the Report, flung it in the wastepaper basket.

So the outside world ceased to take an interest in Cloonaturk, and it was left to the inhabitants to employ their own resources in dealing with the phenomenon. They drank more deeply so as to assist thought. To their alarm, Pat's Tommy, who had always been a quiet man, began to manifest every evidence of a nasty and interfering disposition. It became usual for him to enter a house uninvited just as a man was pouring himself a drink, and knock the bottle out of his hand. He took Long Joe by the throat one night and tried to throw him into the river. Worst of all, he began to hide each house's store of liquor, so that it became commonplace for a man to be compelled to spend half the evening in a desperate search, crawling round the floor of his cottage on his hands and knees with his tongue hanging out. This final outrage convinced the inhabitants that action of a revolutionary nature was called for.

"I'll see the priest," announced Old Thady to the haggard inhabitants clustered beneath the bank at the crossroads.

"I'll go with you," volunteered Long Joe, "because if something isn't done soon, there'll be nothing for it but for the whole of us to emigrate to America."

"You're right, Long Joe," said Old Thady, "and I for one don't want to end my days driving a streetcar in New York."

In the parlour of the Presbytery, Father Murphy sat back in his armchair and gazed sternly at the two men who stood in the centre of his carpet firmly clutching their battered top hats, which they had refused to surrender to his housekeeper. There were grim lines about the priest's mouth as he listened to their halting tale. When the story had faded away to its miserable conclusion, he breathed fiercely through his nostrils.

"Kneel down, the two of you," he commanded.

Old Thady and Long Joe looked at one another and then slowly went down on their knees on the hearthrug. They watched anxiously as the priest took out a prayerbook, a pen, and two printed forms.

"I'm going to administer the Pledge against the Consumption of Alcoholic Liquors," he declared, "and I shall require both of you to affix your names to the Solemn Declaration."

A startled look came to the face of each delinquent and remained there.

"Is there no other way you can exorcise Pat's Tommy, Father?" enquired Old Thady brokenly.

"None," replied the priest severely. "I'll visit Cloonaturk on Sunday and administer the Pledge to every man in the townland."

There was a moment's silence; then Old Thady and Long Joe exchanged a mournful glance and rose awkwardly to their feet.

"We're sorry to have troubled you, Father," said Old Thady abjectly, "but we'd rather put up with Pat's Tommy. Maybe in time we'll get used to him."

The priest only remained to watch through the window the two long-coated figures walking slowly across the gravel from his door; then he put on his outdoor clothes himself and went to the back of the house to take out his car.

The Sergeant rose respectfully to his feet as Father Murphy strode into the police station.

"I don't know what the authorities are doing," said the priest angrily. "The whole of Cloonaturk is poisoned body and soul."

"Ah, sure that place —" began the Sergeant.

"I'm not going to waste time talking to you," snapped the priest. "Give me that telephone, and tell me the number of the Superintendent of the Area."

A week later two hundred police, drawn from the neighbouring towns and villages, converged on Cloonaturk from all sides. A cordon was flung around the townland, and four lorry-loads of spades were unloaded. The community was in too wretched a condition to hide anything or to try to deceive anyone. The townland was mapped out in square yards, and digging operations commenced. The inhabitants watched from the doors of their cottages in profound melancholy as still after still was unearthed.

"We made one mistake," said Old Thady. "I've heard that in other parts of the world a bull is always kept in the neighbourhood of a still, and released when them fellows in uniform get too near."

"I've heard that too," replied Long Joe, "and a field where a still is kept, should always have a barbed wire fence around it. I've been told," he added gloomily, "that it's the greatest fun in the world when the bull is let out, to see them police leaving half their pants behind on the top of a barbed wire fence."

"Are you going to prosecute, sir?" the Sergeant asked the Superintendent as the stills were being loaded onto the lorries.

"No," answered the Superintendent gruffly. "It would cause too much of a scandal. The least said about the affair the better."

Pat's Tommy was only seen spasmodically during the succeeding week, as the sense of their grievous loss had a sobering effect on the community. Each time that he manifested himself, he was paler and more shadowy. Ten days later he was seen for the last time. In that unearthly hour between twilight and nightfall Long Joe came on him sitting on the bridge lighting his pipe; but even before the pipe was well drawn, he had faded into nothingness, and Long Joe, gazing where he had been, could see nothing but the stream below the bridge spreading out across the sand as it lost itself in the grey Atlantic breakers.

□

A SCEPTIC WATCHES A WITCH-BURNING

It's a bright day for a bonefire,
The sun slicking mist from a sheen of green fields,
With winter timber ribbed against the sky.
Could you not turn swan and swim the wind-wrinkled river,
Your neck a firm column of impure feathers?
Or be a gull who awkwardly wheels in air and out of water?
The tinder is dry as a judge's eye,
No smoke to smother before flesh withers
In furious scourging by whips of light.
What weeks of pain made you confess to this imaginary wickedness?
To say your soul in a blue exhalation
Flew through the dark of a new moon
Where you danced with the devil's own?
Still, I suppose Hell is the place that all come to,
Whether we follow those pious fellows or find our ways alone.

— Ace G. Pilkington

Horror's most visionary writers contribute
their talents to help children everywhere.

SCARE CARE
EDITED BY GRAHAM MASTERTON
FOR THE SCARE CARE TRUST

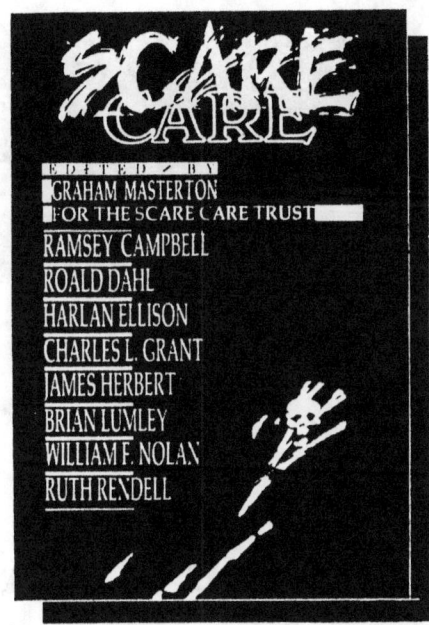

If SCARE CARE had only been an anthology of remarkable horror stories
by the finest writers in the field, it would have been a milestone. It includes
over three dozen harrowing new tales by such writers as Ramsey Camp-
bell, Harlan Ellison, Roald Dahl, James Herbert and Charles L. Grant.

But SCARE CARE is far more than that. It's a special benefit edition to aid
the Scare Care Trust, an organization dedicated to raising money to help
abused and needy children everywhere. All profits derived from the sale
of this book will be donated to the trust.

"An excellent notion! I remember how it was to.be a child, and I'm glad to
see someone standing up for the children."　　　　　—Piers Anthony
$19.95 ★ 0-312-93156-5 ★ 416 pages ★ JUNE

TOR hardcovers are distributed nationally by St. Martin's Press.

WISH UPON A STAR

by Anne Goring

It was a dark place, a deep, dank overgrown hollow in the centre of the wood. He'd named it The Bone Pit after Miss Ellis told them about the dinosaurs. That was when the diggers first started gouging into the hillside for the new bypass and the lumpy, stone-like fossils came up with the sticky yellow clay. A professor or somebody had come from London, and there'd even been a bit on the telly about it. Miss Ellis had been quite excited.

"Think of it, children. Where the houses and the church and the railway station are now was once a steaming swamp full of enormous creatures." She'd reeled off a list of names he couldn't remember and pinned up pictures on the walls. He'd stared at them when he should have been doing sums. The ridge-backed monsters with mouths full of razor-edged, tearing teeth, the ones with long thin necks and tiny, sparrow-brained heads. The terra-somethings that flapped about on leathery wings. "History is all down there

under your feet," Miss Ellis had cried, "Layer upon layer of it!"

Now, in the wood, he looked down at his battered trainers half-sunk in thick, wet leaf-mould. The tops of the trees whipped in the last of the gale. Down here, where the bramble-choked roots scrabbled down towards the water at the base of the pit, his ragged breathing sounded loud in the stillness.

He was thinking of death. Of the dinosaur skeletons sealed for below. Of his father.

He knuckled his eyes angrily. He wasn't a crybaby. He hadn't cried all day. Not through the phone calls, the neighbours mouthing secrets above his head and talking to him and Mam as though they were poorly. He hadn't cried when his mother did, nor during the hours when she wandered about the house ashen-faced, smiling a polite sort of smile to the people who came and went — and all the time her eyes full of black terror.

"It'll be all right," she kept repeating. "I know he'll be all right. We must be brave, Billy. He'd want us to be brave. We'll hear some good news soon." And then, plaintively, turning the sick feeling his stomach into something far worse, something that made him want to claw and bite and kick, "Allen's coming round later. He says the forecast is better. The wind's beginning to drop. Perhaps there'll be some news by the time he gets here."

The water in the pit stirred slowly among drink cans, herniated tyres, and the remains of a mattress that sprouted rusty springs. Dead things. Broken things. Had his father been dumped like this unwanted rubbish? Discarded from the foundering oil rig for the violent sea to swallow into its cold, uncaring depths?

Why did it have to be Dad? Why couldn't it have happened when Dad was safe at home on leave? Why couldn't it have been Allen instead?

Allen was Dad's friend. He worked on the same oil rig. Dad had invited Allen and his girl friend round for a barbecue in the summer. After that, after he'd split with his girl friend, he came to the house more and more. Dad said he was lonely, but then Dad was always inviting people home. He liked company. Mam complained that the house was a bear garden when he was on leave. Sometimes she got flushed and cross and said she just couldn't conjure meals out of thin air for every Tom, Dick, and Harry he felt sorry for. But Dad just laughed and said, "Are you calling me a bear?" And lifted her off her feet and hugged her and rubbed his bristly chin over her face until she screeched and her crossness changed to giggles.

Billy had grinned too, because anyone could see his Dad was nothing like a bear. He was a lion, his Dad. Tanned and golden haired and unafraid. King of the jungle.

But there *was* a bear. A plump, bushy-bearded grizzly with big, hard paws always filled with presents: bottles of wine, chocolates, some new toy that he thought, in his jolly way, that Billy might like. Camouflage.

"Allen's so kind. Too generous for his own good," Mam said.

"A great mate," Dad said. "Pity that girl of his swanned off. He doesn't say much, but I reckon he's cut up about it. Well, we'll do what we can to cheer him up, won't we, love?"

Only Billy knew the truth about the bear. He alone seemed to notice that the smile never quite reached the small black eyes — eyes that were forever restless, darting, calculating, greedy. They watched his Dad with an unpleasant, superior sort of glint. They watched Billy with wary contempt. But most of all they watched Mam. And then they glistened like cold, slithery pebbles; and the fingers on the big, hairy paws wove themselves tightly together until the knuckles stood sharp and white and shining against the skin.

The thick mass of grey cloud above the valley was beginning to thin. Pale shafts of sunlight filtered through the leafless branches. An iridescence coiled along the oily surface of The Bone Pit. Black reflections shifted uneasily in a downdraught of air. Billy shivered. He ought to go. He'd stayed out too long. Mam had enough to worry about. He shouldn't be here at all, anyway. He should be back at the house with the hushed-voice neighbours and the cups of tea.

And Allen.

Allen-Allen-Allen. The creaking branches caught the echo of his thoughts and flung them about. *Allen-Allen-go away-never-come-back-any-other-day.* He put his hands over his ears, but the wood still hummed its song in his head.

The wood knew everything. It had seen everything. Miss Ellis had told them it was very old and had once been a gigantic forest full of wolves and wild boar. Then men began to tear out the trees to make room for their crops and their cows and sheep. They needed timber for houses and barns, for ships that carried them on voyages of discovery. They needed space for villages and towns and cities. Long centuries nibbled and gnawed at it until it was only a scrap of a thing, roughly triangular in shape, at the foot of the hill, criss-crossed with trails made by people and dogs and children. On one side the red-brick houses pressed up against it, his own house closest of all. Above it was the railway cutting; below, the raw yellow gash which would be the new road by next summer.

Billy heard the rattle and clank of machinery. It had gone on for weeks. His mother grumbled about the noise and the mud that the lorries trailed up the lane past their house on the way to the dump. But Billy stood in the garden watching them pass, thinking of dinosaur bones that nobody had spotted, now trapped in their broken loads. He liked the idea of dinosaurs secretly and invisibly passing his house. Sometimes under cover of the engine noise he called goodbye to them as they went on their way to a different burial ground.

The dinosaurs were older than the wood, of course. Much older and far, far deeper than the roots of the trees could reach. Perhaps if the water at the bottom of the pit had been clear he might have spotted a claw or a tooth or a bony knuckle. He could have climbed down there dead easy, fished it out, and taken it to show Miss Ellis. He'd be on telly, then. Mam would boast about him to the neighbours. Dad would be right proud and give him extra pocket money.

The sudden pain doubled him over. He clutched his arms tight around his ribs, wailing aloud, "Dad! Dad! You can't leave us, Dad!"

His foot slid in the leaf-mould against the edge of the pit, sending a cascade of dead leaves and earth into the water. For a few trembling seconds he thought he might follow. He swayed on the brim, flinging his arms wide in an effort to balance. A pebble spurted from under his scrabbling trainer. Then his feet found purchase and his body steadied.

The pebble hit the water with a thunk. Ripples rainbowed outwards, splintering the reflection of his own frightened face. The watery sun fastened on the pebble as it lodged in the muck, a tiny glimmering, bone-white circle — no, not a circle. The disturbed water distorted the image into sharp points and facets.

Billy blinked. It was only a small grey pebble, he knew; but somehow in those filthy, stained waters it sparkled with the intensity of a diamond, a snowflake, a star.

The tree branches sighed and snapped. *Wish-wish-wish-wish.*

His mind churned. People threw money into wishing wells, didn't they? And wishes were granted. That was just a pebble, but sometimes things that looked like pebbles were really fossil bones. And a dinosaur bone was surely more valuable, *stronger* than any rotten tenpee coin.

Dinosaur. The picture swam in front of him. The one on the wall at school.

Pterodactyl. He saw it spelled out in big black letters.

"I wish . . ." he whispered.

He saw the leathery wings, the huge scaly feet as the monster flapped from the cliff edge. He saw it skimming the surface of the sea, the grey spumey breakers reaching up to snare it, but it flapped on to where the rubber life-raft lolloped up and down the waves. He saw his father's bright head dulled by the wet, his face white and drawn, his body sagging, his eyes closed. Billy held his breath.

"No, Dad, No!" he screamed silently. "You mustn't be dead. We need you."

But as the leathery wings flopped and flapped above him, as the great scaly talons reached to snatch him from the dinghy, the man slowly lifted his head and opened his eyes. He looked straight at Billy and he nodded. He was past speech but his message sang out clear and true.

Thanks, son, you did well. I'll be okay. You can go home, now.

It was gone.

Billy looked down at tyres and tin cans poking through oily water. The sun had gone behind the clouds. The star — the pebble — had disappeared in the ooze.

He straightened up. His knees felt funny and his head was swimmy like it had been when he had chickenpox last year. The trees still creaked and sighed; the lorries and diggers still roared in the distance. The wood was the same as it had been.

But something had changed.

He turned from the pit and began to run home along the twisty, beaten tracks through the wood, only stopping when he came to where the trees thinned and he could see his house. A red MG was parked in the lane outside the front gate. Allen had arrived. And Billy understood then what the change meant.

The fear was gone.

His stomach no longer twisted with the smothering dread of those small, darting eyes, of the plump, hairy, gift-bearing paws.

Grizzly bears meant nothing to someone with dinosaurs on his side.

He climbed the back fence and went in through the kitchen door, shutting it softly behind him, walking on light feet through to where faces turned to look at him — to where the clouded atmosphere, heavy with tears, folded in on him.

A couple of neighbours perched on the settee, his mother curled in a chair like a small broken doll. Billy wanted to shout at her that she could stop crying. Dad was okay. He'd seen the pterodactyl rescue him. But he mustn't . . . couldn't. And in any case, Allen leapt up the minute he walked in and bent over Mam, taking her small hands into his big ones. Caressing her palm with his thumb, saying gently, "I'll be away an hour at most, Claire. Then I'll come back and stay all evening. I can kip down on the settee if necessary. You mustn't be alone."

Mam's mouth trembled.

"Kind Allen," she murmured. "Thank you." She gazed unseeingly about her. "You're all so kind. I don't know what I'd have done without you."

Allen came over to Billy on his large quiet bear's feet.

"Billy'll see me out, won't you sonny?"

"I'm not your son," Billy said, coldly.

Allen ruffled Billy's hair with his plump hand. Billy jerked his head away and regarded him with sullen scorn.

Allen's white teeth flashed in a smile. His gaze darted restlessly round the room while his hand moved down to fasten itself on Billy's shoulder. Billy found himself propelled out into the hall in a rush.

Allen's smile faded abruptly.

"You cheeky little sod," he hissed. "Don't think I haven't noticed your attitude. You need a bloody good hiding. Your mother's too soft with you, by half."

Billy wriggled. "Gerrof, you're hurting me."

"I'd hurt you a bloody sight more if you were mine."

"But I'm not, am I?" Billy said. He didn't care any more. He wasn't frightened any more. There was no reason to be. "You're not my Dad. And when my Dad comes back I'll tell him you hurt me and he'll thump you, you'll see."

Fingers bit through the thick wool of his sweater, digging into muscle. Billy squirmed, tears of pain and anger filling his eyes.

"Your Dad?" Allen's voice was laced with contempt, his bear's eyes as slimy as the water in The Bone Pit. "We've heard the last of him. You don't know the North Sea in winter. He wouldn't have lasted ten minutes. None of 'em would. If you're lucky they'll find a body for you to bury." He flung Billy from him so that he fetched up against the banisters. "So don't quote your Dad at me, sonny. You tread very carefully when you're near me from now on. That way, things'll be a whole lot easier for all of us."

Billy didn't think any more. He threw himself at Allen, hammering at him with his fists, choking out the words, "It's not true! He's not dead. He's been rescued. I've seen him. He's on him way home."

Allen trapped his flailing arms in one big paw, dragged him upwards until his feet kicked wildly at the air then let him go so that he staggered and fell backwards onto the bottom step of the staircase.

"Like I said, I'll be back in an hour," he snarled. "And I'll keep on coming back. Now your Dad's gone, your poor mother'll need a man to lean on. That man's going to be me. And if you go telling lies about me to your mother, there'll be worse to come for you. You'd better believe that, sonny boy."

The door slammed behind him. Billy breathed deeply. His arms felt as though they'd been wrenched from his shoulders and painfully stuffed back any old way. But that change, that core of certainty, of strength, he'd felt in the wood was untouched and unharmed. Grizzly bears were powerful, but they didn't stand a chance against dinosaurs.

He knew what he had to do.

He raced up the stairs to his bedroom. The window overlooked the front garden and the lane. He stared down at Allen opening the gate, walking to the car.

Dinosaurs. Which one would fancy a nice juicy grizzly for a snack?

A picture on the wall, the name in big black letters.

Tyrannosaurus Rex.

A glimmer of light in oily water. A snowflake, a diamond, a star.

"I wish," he breathed, "I wish . . ."

He felt it first. The reverberating thump, thump of its feet, then the bellow of rage and lust as it scented its prey.

Billy turned his head to watch the wood where the lane curved against its edge. Saw the trees shake and quiver and break apart at the monster's approach. Not leafless winter trees but richly green like enormous newly-uncurled ferns in which smaller beasts writhed and flittered.

Tyrannosaurus Rex.

It thundered from the wood, towering above the house, its great crested back obliterating the view, telegraph poles snapping like matchsticks against its armour-plated sides. With a howl of triumph it bore down upon its victim.

Allen was getting into the car when he saw it.

Billy saw the expression on his face and laughed aloud.

"You see, old grizzly," he yelled, "you don't stand a chance against a dinosaur."

Tyrannosaurus Rex bent its head.

The massive jaws opened. The inward curving teeth scooped the car upwards. The metal body shrieked its agony, the windscreen exploded, a limb flailed wildly before sagging loose and lifeless amid tatters of upholstery.

Somewhere else, away from the carnage outside, a phone rang, was instantly answered. Calmly Billy heard his mother's distant cry, "He's all right! Oh, thank God! Billy! The helicopter's found your Dad."

He didn't answer. He went on staring into the wild red eye of the dinosaur until the creature lowered its head as though in obeisance and slid back, back among the tangled creeper growth of the sheltering forest.

Other cries. A slamming of doors, a scurrying of people from their houses. A voice, wailing, "That damned bypass! I knew something like this would happen. Those lorries should never have been allowed to use this lane. . . ."

Crushed against the broken telegraph pole lay the mangled red sports car. A lorry had skidded through the garden fence, overturned and spilled its load on the front lawn.

Billy let out his breath on a trembling sigh. His glance slid over the mess of boulders and yellow clay that obscured the lawn. There might be dinosaur bones in that lot. He'd have a good look before they cleared it away. . . .

Deep in the wood the foul black water at the base of the pit stirred. A gas bubble shimmered to the surface and plopped apart. Its passing caused something in the ooze to shift. Tiny points of light glinted briefly, brilliantly, in the pale sunlight, before the dark waters once more sealed it in.

□

COMING IN OUR SPRING 1990 ISSUE!

Our Special *David J. Schow* Issue

— *featuring* —

3 Great New Stories by this Horror Sensation

— *and also* —

Strange New Fiction by

Tad Williams — Darrell Schweitzer — Michael Rutherford

Brian Lumley

THE STARS ARE RIGHT AND GREAT CTHULHU AND
THE OTHER OLD ONES ARE FREE!

ELYSIA: the Coming of Cthulhu
by BRIAN LUMLEY

Is scheduled for publication In December, 1989. Never before published, ELYSIA Is the ultimate climax to all of Brian Lumley's mythos books: the sequel to all the "Titus Crow" novels, the "Theemh'dra" stories, and the "Dreams" novels.

The Old Ones are free at last from their aeon-old prisons and are bent on revenge.... against the men and women of earth, to be sure, but first and foremost against the Elder Gods Themselves. And after the passage of aeons, the Elder Gods have grown.... old!

This book Is profusely Illustrated by STEPHEN E. FABIAN. Deluxe signed edition In a slipcase (lim. to 300), $40; hard cover edition (lim. to 800), $25; trade paper (lim. to 1500), $8.50.

ALREADY IN PRINT by Brian Lumley:
HERO OF DREAMS, SHIP OF DREAMS, MAD MOON OF DREAMS: novels of Hero of Dreams and Eldin the Wanderer. HC editions, $21 each; trade paper, $7.50 each.   THE COMPLEAT CROW: all the shorter fiction about psychic detective Titus Crow.   Profusely Illustrated by FABIAN: HC edition, $21; trade paper, $7.50.   THE BURROWERS BENEATH: the first "Crow" novel, first hard cover edition. Deluxe, $37.50; HC, $22.50.

Plus books by other writers: JOHN COLLIER AND FREDRIC BROWN WENT QUARRELLING THROUGH MY HEAD, by Jessica Amanda Salmonson (HC, $22.50; paper, $7.95); TOM O'BEDLAM'S NIGHT OUT AND OTHER STRANGE EXCURSIONS, by Darrell Schweitzer (HC, $20; paper, $7.50); PULPTIME, by P. H. Cannon (HC $15; paper, $5); SIXTY SELECTED POEMS, by Joseph Payne Brennan (HC $15; paper, $5). For catalog only, send 25¢ stamp.

Add $1.50 for the first book, 50¢ each additional book.
W. PAUL GANLEY: PUBLISHER, P O BOX 149,
BUFFALO, NY 14226-0149

KING YVORIAN'S WAGER

by Darrell Schweitzer

On the morning of his father's funeral and his own accession, King Yvorian had a vision. It came to him as he rode in solemn state on the golden throne of the Eagle Kings, borne aloft at the head of a procession of priests and courtiers by the former king's most trusted bearers. He sat stiffly in his metal-feathered robes, in his helmet that gleamed golden and silver like a second sunrise. All around him the heralds chanted the dirge of the dead monarch, and soldiers marched grimly, clad in black armor, with black banners draped from their spears. The common folk leaned out of windows and gathered on rooftops and walls, waving palm fronds and making their own lamentations. Each strove to outdo his neighbor, to tear his hair more painfully, to shred his garments more wretchedly, to show his face more streaked with tears, for the old king had been a tyrant, and they feared him even when he was dead.

Then, suddenly, the young King Yvorian stood up. His bearers struggled desperately to keep the throne level as the weight shifted, and the people gasped, and the chanters ceased their chanting.

The king spread his arms, and for an instant his robes were like burning wings in the bright morning light.

Someone shouted, "The King is going to fly!" and the whole multitude dropped to its knees, for they knew that the first king of the Eagle Dynasty had flown long ago, soaring into the sun to return with a fiery crown on his head, be-

102

stowed by the gods. Surely, if Yvorian too were about the fly, it was, at the very least, a miracle.

But the King merely stood swaying on the footrest at the throne's front. The beak-shaped visor of his helmet fell down over his face, and for an instant he did indeed look like a divine eagle sent by the gods to rule all the lands of the Crescent Sea.

Then he fell. His knees buckled, his head bowed, and he tumbled forward into the dusty street. His helmet rolled beneath the feet of the stumbling bearers.

The commoners cried out and began to flee in wild confusion. The bearers set the throne down and knelt, covering their faces with their hands. The courtiers and priests milled about, uncertain. Only the soldiers stood, stolidly, guarding their king who shouted words no one could make out and writhed like some drunkard or madman, tearing, hurling his metal-feathered robe aside, clawing at the dirt.

Overhead, shutters slammed closed.

Still the bearers knelt, calmly, knowing they had failed in their duty, while the prefect of the guards struck off their heads one by one. The youngest bearer wept, but he did not try to run away.

A soothsayer pushed his way through the soldiers and also knelt, trying to read the future in the spreading blood, but the prefect struck his head off too, lest he succeed.

Then the priests gathered around the boy-king in their black robes and black, beak-visored helmets, suggesting noth-

ing more than vultures assembled for the feast.

A more prudent soothsayer, watching from a balcony, remarked on this.

The priests dared not lay hands on the King, for they knew that he was touched by the gods, and when the gods touch a ruler so explicitly on the first day of his reign, it is an awesome portent. At such times, the whole history of the nation might be written anew.

And it was a holy thing. They let the vision run its course and waited patiently for more than an hour until the King sat up, dazed, and held out his hands to be helped to his feet. In silence the priests brushed him off as best they could and led him back to his throne. His helmet had been lost somewhere in the confusion. He sat with the wind blowing through his yellow hair. There was dirt down one side of his face.

The priests raised the throne up on their own shoulders.

It was only much later, after King Yvorian's father had been properly laid to rest in the necropolis of the Eagle Kings by the shore of the Crescent Sea, that Kaniphar, the chief priest, took the boy aside and asked him, "Mighty One, what did you see?"

"I saw the gods," said the young King. "I saw them as the poets describe them, huge and insubstantial as clouds, reclining on their couches as they moved men and armies across the face of the world, like pieces on a game board. All the while they were laughing. Then, as they turned and saw that I was among them, a god who had the face of a dog leaned down to me and said, '*Behold, thou shalt wager with Rada Vatu.*'"

"Many are the forms and aspects of the gods," said the priest. "It could have been any one of them that spoke to you."

"It does not matter," said the King. "Tell me of Rada Vatu."

The priest grew pale. "Majesty, I am afraid."

Then the King spoke in a low, grim voice, and for an instant it seemed that the dread former monarch had returned in the person of his fifteen-year-old son. "The foremost of my priests must never be afraid to serve me."

Kaniphar fell to his knees and the King touched him lightly on the head, as if to bless him, but said nothing more, and the high priest was truly frightened.

"Very well then," he said. "You shall learn of Rada Vatu."

So, all night beneath the uncertain light of hanging lamps, the priest and the King pored over ancient books and unlocked many secrets, and spoke of Rada Vatu.

"This One is older and mightier than all the gods," said the priest, "and it is ill luck to even speak his name. For he is the lord of Death and Time and Fate, and those are three of his other names. Sometimes, when the gods are at their games, a playing piece suddenly vanishes from the board. That is because Rada Vatu has taken it. Then the gods are silent and thoughtful, for they know that one day Rada Vatu will sweep them all away with a wave of his hand. In the end the gods are as men, and Rada Vatu erases them like old figures traced in the sand."

"But Rada Vatu shall *wager* with me!" said the king, leaning toward the priest, whispering in a low voice like a hiss.

"Yes, he does that. He is a trickster, and fond of games."

"I shall *beat* him," said the King. He jumped up, knocking his chair over backward. He paced back and forth in his excitement, striking his fist into his palm. "Surely this means I shall be the greatest of the Eagle Kings — !"

"Perhaps so, Majesty."

"No! It means more! It means I'll be greater even than the gods, and Rada Vatu will treat me as an *equal*. He won't snatch any playing pieces away from *me!*"

Now Kaniphar the priest was beside himself with terror and he shook his folded hands and wept, and his voice broke as he begged the King to put aside such thoughts.

"Majesty, know that Rada Vatu is Death and that he comes to each of us at the ending of our days, but not before."

King Yvorian turned to him fiercely. Another vision had come to him, not from the gods, but out of his own mind.

"No, in my case it will be different. Rada Vatu shall come to me on my own terms, like an envoy I have deigned to receive."

Just then the gods looked down from their game and paused. One or two started to laugh, but were swiftly hushed into silence.

The next day King Yvorian (who had appointed a new chief priest that morning) gave the first of a seemingly endless stream of orders. The kingdom was transformed. Royal heralds shouted in every square in every town. Before the palace, trumpeters blew blasts, then the gates swung wide, and the armies of the Eagle King strode forth, to subdue and extract tribute from all the lands bordering the Crescent Sea, from all the islands, from all the cities on the banks of the rivers of the hinterlands.

The wars went on for years. Meanwhile, the people groaned under the exactions of King Yvorian, who taxed away the wealth of the rich and conscripted the poor for their labor.

The King began to build. A palace like none the Earth had ever known rose in the capital of the Eagle Kings. Some said it was the King's very vision, a madman's dream made solid out of stone and wood and glass. Fantastic towers rose, and onion-domed minarets, and among them sat the colossal image of King Yvorian himself on a carven throne, as high as a mountain, carefully placed so that on the first day of the year the sun rose directly behind the King's crown, radiating his glory to all the world. Inside, winding staircases turned so subtly that the eye could not follow them, until they ended up nowhere at all. There were rooms of gold and of silver, and chambers filled with clouds from which strange voices issued, and corridors suffused with red light, with green, and orange and blue. In one vast hall was only darkness, an enclosed abyss, infinite, bottomless. In these endless rooms amid the twisting corridors a whole other kingdom awaited the King's desire, a glittering court populated by bird-headed men and impossible beasts, by beautiful, nearly divine youths and maidens constructed of humming metal and a kind of marble that was somehow soft and warm and seemingly alive. There was, too, a library, with floor, ceiling, and walls, and even the shelves mirrored. The mirrors angled through time. The reflections multiplied the books until the library contained all that ever had been written, or ever would be, to an infinite number.

But nowhere in all the huge palace, which was greater than a city, would the King permit any clock or hourglass or other means of telling time. Nor would he allow anyone who entered there to speak of persons who had died — the new chief priest acted as if he had never had a predecessor — for the palace, he said, was a labyrinth designed to confuse Rada Vatu, and time and death were banished from it.

When he was twenty-five and had fathered a score of sons by his many wives, King Yvorian retired to his labyrinth. He entered alone, without any priests or ministers, for they were not like him, he said, but ordinary men who would inevitably age and be swept

105

away by Rada Vatu. But he, in the prime of his manhood, was to remain ageless forever, so that Rada Vatu would come and wager with him.

For a while, the King spoke to his ministers through a pool in the silver chamber, in which he could see their faces, through which their speech drifted up like something shouted in the depths of a cave. But the greyness of their beards and the weariness of their faces distressed him, until he could bear to look on them no more.

He devoted many years to pleasure in the company of his deathless, lifeless youths and maidens, in rooms filled with strange scents, with vapors and waters that brought impossible ecstasies.

Then he turned to his books, and a faceless automaton read to him the exquisite poetry of the ancients, and the sere, harsh words that are to come in the world's last age, when the sun is already dead and the remnants of mankind retreat into metal pyramids miles high to escape the darkness and the monsters which have inherited the Earth.

And his thoughts were troubled, and he sent the automaton away, then read by himself for a while before withdrawing into the black room, the walled abyss. There he floated, his mind detached from his senses, and he pondered many things. He knew pain then, and shame, and he repented his follies, his excesses, his thousand petty cruelties.

He began to dream, there in the darkness, and his spirit drifted, and it seemed he looked down on the turning Earth for century after century, as the history of mankind slowly passed.

Then he was walking, naked and cold, among the tombs of the gods. He looked down once, and realized that the dust stirring around his feet was not dust at all, but *suns,* countless billions to be kicked aside with each step.

The tombs rose on either side of him

as if to line an endless avenue, black, vaster than worlds, silhouetted against faint stars and glowing nebulae, each of them carven to show some aspect of the god therein: an upraised hand, a bull's head, a cross, a salmon leaping.

Still King Yvorian journeyed along the avenue, among the dust of stars, until the tombs on either side of him were featureless and empty, their doors left open. At last there were no more of them, and he came to those grey, infinite plains which have never known the tread even of Rada Vatu.

His mind emptied, all thoughts, all knowledge, all pride pouring out like water onto the hungry sand — but a single spark remained like a final star in the endless night, the realization, the voice within him: *Yes, I am the greatest of all. I am worthy to treat with Rada Vatu.*

That was enough. It brought him back. He swam up, out of the darkness, out of the dream, out of the black chamber.

He stood in the silver room, by the pool, staring down into the motionless water. He wore only a plain white robe and was barefoot, for he knew that Rada Vatu was never impressed with finery. His own reflection showed himself unkempt but unaged, his yellow hair and beard wild, but his face as unwrinkled as it had been on the day he first entered the labyrinth.

"Surely I am ready," he said aloud. "Surely Rada Vatu will come to me now."

"I have been with you all along," said a voice.

The King whirled around, searching for the one who spoke. But he was alone in the chamber. Carvings of men and beasts stared down at him from the walls, but he knew them incapable of speech. He walked toward a far corner of the room, away from the pool.

"Liar!" he shouted. "I have not allowed you to enter my house until now.

I have shut you out."

"No, I have merely spared you."

"Show yourself!"

Dust and plaster sprinkled from the ceiling, rattling on the marble floor. Then a draught billowed behind a tapestry. A hanging trembled like shaken bones. Darkness and dust whirled together and rose like a miniature whirlwind, then formed the likeness of a man clad in a black robe and barefoot. The face was that of Kaniphar, the chief priest Yvorian had slain on a morning long before.

"You!" He retreated back toward the center of the room.

"It is I." The voice was a cold whisper, like the wind between the tombs of the gods.

Then Rada Vatu tore away his own face like a mask and revealed the glaring visage of the former tyrant, Yvorian's father. And the King retreated farther, until he stood against the edge of the pool.

Rada Vatu removed his own face once more. His head was hollow like a hood, filled with pale blue fire. Two brilliant eyes floated there, like tiny stars.

"Why . . . . why have you come?" said King Yvorian.

Rada Vatu strode to the edge of the pool, leaned down, and touched the water with his hand. The clear pool became blood-dark.

The King scurried away from the pool, across the room. Rada Vatu stood there, gazing into the water, his back to Yvorian.

"Do you not know? I have come to wager with you."

The King regained some of his composure. "Yes. Of course. I knew that."

"And I know all that you do," said Rada Vatu, *"for I can peer into your mind even as I peer into this pool."*

"Yes. A wager."

"Even so. I desire sport on occasion."

"A wager."

Rada Vatu turned around, and the fire of his face was blinding white, and his robes were white too, resplendent as the sunrise. Only his eyes were dark, huge, like shafts into an abyss.

"This is my wager, King Yvorian of the Eagle Land: that you shall cast aside your glories of your own will, that you shall no longer even call yourself a king, that in the end you shall know yourself to be as other men. Until that time, I shall not touch you with death."

"Then I am truly immortal," said King Yvorian. He laughed loud and long. "It is an absurd wager. *I accept!*"

The King rubbed his dazzled eyes, looked again, and saw that Rada Vatu was gone. But the pool was still the color of blood.

Because he no longer feared death or time or the touch of Rada Vatu, King Yvorian emerged from his labyrinth. It was a long journey to the gate. He walked for many days, still clad in his plain robe, barefoot, his hair wild, but wearing the beaked crown of the Eagle Kings. At last he came to a corridor he barely remembered, then into a darkened, pillared hall filled with debris. Rusted chains dangled where lanterns had once hung. Dust and leaves covered a tarnished throne. Some of the great roofbeams had fallen, and even a few of the pillars. He climbed, then wriggled his way toward the outer door. Mice scattered before him, rustling under the leaves.

The door itself was gone, the doorway itself misshapen, like the mouth of a cave.

King Yvorian stepped outside, into the warm sunlight, onto soft grass. To see living grass again and a blue sky and trees rising around him seemed, for the moment, to be more a marvel than all the blackness of the outer spaces, all the infinite suns, all the tombs of the gods.

He walked a little ways, then turned to look back. He saw no palace, no colossal image of himself, no capital city, nor even the doorway from which he had emerged, but only a grassy hillside. Before him, a plain stretched all the way to a line of mountains which rose like an island glimpsed across the sea, a blue smear on the horizon that might be land, or perhaps a cloud.

He found a path and followed it. The sun and wind on his face, the warmth of the earth beneath his feet were all startling, wonderful.

The path turned sharply around the hill. Suddenly a dog blocked his way, barking. King Yvorian jumped back, startled. He had nearly forgotten what such a creature was. He reached to touch it. The dog snapped at his hand, but then retreated, whining, puzzled.

The dog ran to a boy of about eight years and hid behind the child's legs. The boy wore a patchwork of wool and leather. He carried a staff.

"Who are you?" The boy's speech was strangely accented.

King Yvorian stood up straight and said sternly. "Do you not know? I am Yvorian the mighty! I am the king of legends! I rule all these lands!"

"You talk funny," said the boy. He turned and ran down the path, the dog running after him.

Yvorian continued on for several hours, until the sun began to set behind the blue mountains and the air grew cold. At last he sat down, exhausted, marvelling at the motion of the sun and the darkening sky. He slept by the side of the road on a pile of leaves and grass. When he awoke at dawn, he was stiff and sore, and weak with hunger. All these things were stranger to him than any of his dreams or visions within the labyrinth.

That morning he passed through a forest of scrubby trees and reached a village. Huts of stone and wood lined a single street. He walked among them, turning to either side, recalling the tombs of the gods.

Slowly the villagers emerged to stare at him, and they were clad as the boy had been, in leather and wool. They gathered before him, filling the street.

"Bow down before me," said Yvorian. "I am your King, returned to you at last."

At first the villagers just gaped. Some shook their heads. There was a low murmur of whispered questions.

"Behold! I am Yvorian of the Eagles! I am the greatest King of all! I *command* you!"

Then the child from the day before pushed through the crowd, tugged on the sleeve of a village elder, pointed at Yvorian and said, "That's him!"

Some of the villagers began to laugh. Others turned away, embarrassed or afraid. "A madman! A madman!" someone shouted.

The King raged at them. He shrieked for them to be still. He grabbed a man, then another, shoving them to their knees. But each merely leapt up again, laughing and shouting.

Yvorian struck about with his fists, truly like a madman in his fury. The villagers caught hold of him and beat him with clubs, tearing his robe, snatching the crown from his head. He fell to the ground, blind from the blood streaming over his face. Still the villagers kicked him and prodded him with their clubs.

Before he lost consciousness, he heard a woman say, "I wonder who he is, really."

A man said, "Where did he steal that crown?"

King Yvorian wandered for many days, ragged, covered with dirt and blood. He came to other towns, but no one would recognize him as king. Always, people laughed at him, or turned away sadly, or made signs to ward off evil. Sometimes their speech was strange, and he could not make out what they were saying at all.

So the King begged for bread and scraps. Occasionally he got some. More often, he stole. Oftener still, he went hungry.

Then soldiers seized him. This was the final outrage.

"Take your wretched hands *off* me! I am the King. I command all soldiers. I'll have your heads, all of you!"

The soldiers said nothing. Their captain barked a command, and all of them marched off, dragging King Yvorian. They did not wear the uniform of the Eagle Legions, Yvorian noticed. Their armor was not of scales shaped like feathers, but strangely supple plate like nothing he had ever seen before.

They brought him to a wooden lodge inside a stockade, where five judges sat in a semi-circle around a table. The first judge wore a white robe, the second pale blue, the third green, the fourth orange — it seemed to Yvorian that the motif represented the seasons — but the fifth was clad in black and hid his face behind a silver mask fashioned like a skull.

The soldiers cast Yvorian roughly to his knees before the judges. A soldier flipped over an hourglass and the trial began.

"Who are you?" the first judge demanded, leaning forward in his carven chair.

Yvorian staggered to his feet. "I am the king, you fool. I am the mighty and eternal Yvorian, ruler of all the lands of the Crescent Sea, and all the islands."

The judges sat back, pondering.

"What you claim cannot be," said the second after a while. "There is no king here, nor has there been in the memory of any living man. We, the Five, rule the lands. As for the Crescent Sea, it is not known to us."

The third judge laughed. "Perhaps it has dried up."

"*Silence!*" Yvorian shouted. "*You are all ignorant men. Surely you have heard the mighty story —*"

The third judge laughed again. "I know many stories, and I've heard more, but never one about you."

"*I alone of all men have been found worthy to treat with Rada Vatu —*"

The four judges drew back with a simultaneous gasp. Then the fifth stirred, the black-clad one, his silver skull of a mask regarding Yvorian.

"*That* name we do know, but it is never spoken. Your own name is strange to us —"

The King stood still and said calmly, "But it is my name, and I am who I claim to be."

The masked judge banged on the tabletop. The hourglass tumbled to the floor.

"We shall find that out, and much else besides."

The judge waved his hand, and Yvorian was seized by torturers, who tied him to a post and beat him until blood streamed over his back and thighs. They broke his legs with hammers, then turned him on a wheel over a fire. All the while he screamed and gasped, "I am King Yvorian. I am Yvorian, the greatest of all. I built the palace of the Eagles. I conquered all the lands. I am the mighty king. I am Yvorian."

But in the end, after many days, it seemed to him that perhaps he had only heard that name in a story somewhere.

The torturers nailed him to a tree and left him to die. Weeks passed, and he suffered beneath the hot sun and the cold of the night. Crows rested on his shoulders. But Rada Vatu would not touch him, and he could not die. His broken bones mended. His wounds began to heal. People gathered to marvel, to touch him, to bear away some of his hair or a cloth soaked in his blood, that they might be healed.

At last, a fearful torturer came in the night with a ladder and a pair of pinchers. He drew out the nails, and Yvorian fled naked into the darkness.

King Yvorian thought back to the long years within the labyrinth, to the pleasures of his retreat, to the mysteries he had pondered, to his visions within the black room. More than once he tried to convince himself that this was yet another of those visions, more terrifying and painful than most, but a thing which would end.

Yet each morning he woke by the side of a road, or in a field or loft or cave, and he saw his sun-blackened body and his many scars, and he knew otherwise. Even his hands and feet were still marked where the nails had been.

So he retraced his path, avoiding the villages and towns, until he came again to the hillside from which he had emerged. He resolved to go inside once more, dress in his finest robes, and come forth, crown on his head, scepter in his hand and sword at his side, with an army of automatons at his back. He would conquer the lands once again and put the unbelievers to death. Then he would command that his palace be unearthed, that it might stand more resplendent than ever before the eyes of men.

But he could not find the cave mouth. He wandered over the hill for weeks. He could not find it.

Finally, he knelt down and wept. He pounded the earth with his fists.

And a stranger stood before him. The King looked up. The newcomer had the shape of a barefoot man in a black robe, but without any face or head. Only fire filled the robe's hood.

"Who are you?" said the stranger.

"I am King Yvorian, if I am anyone at all."

"Who are you?"

More firmly, the King replied, "I am Yvorian, lord of all the lands."

"Ah," said the other, and departed.

Clad in a kilt and shirt of woven grass, King Yvorian came down from

the hills, into the broad valley where the Crescent Sea had once been in ages past. He followed a yellow-silted stream until he reached a river, and clear water.

Still he was King in his own mind, and each night he dreamt of his palace, and of his old ministers — he could still recall their names, every one, and their voices, and their individual manners, arrogant or servile or cold and expressionless. He remembered building the labyrinth. It seemed that still he heard the noise of hammers. It seemed that just a day or two before he himself had broken the ground with a spade and poured blood on the cornerstone.

And in his dreams his terrible father visited him many times, pacing back and forth, raging, proclaiming that a king is a king until he dies or abdicates, and to abdicate is to die.

"I have not abdicated," said Yvorian, in his dream.

Kaniphar, the chief priest he had killed, stood before him mournfully and said only, "A king lacking a kingdom is no king at all."

"I am still Yvorian," was his only reply. When he awoke from that dream, he was troubled.

Once more he declared his kingship openly in villages and towns along the river. Often he was laughed at or driven away with stones, but in other places men listened silently as he told the tale of his entire life, of his wager with Rada Vatu. This was a tale without an end.

Crowds gathered to hear him. Someone gave him fine clothing, and he threw away his grass kilt and shirt. Still the tale continued. Scribes came to write it down. Then heralds arrived for him, and bore him in a chair across many lands, until he came to a great city of black stone, which stood on a hill overlooking the river where it emptied into the grey, whitecapped sea.

He was placed on a dais in the forum of the city. All around him pillars rose like trees in a forest, bearing up statues of gods and of kings. People swarmed out of black marble houses, out of wooden tenements, out of hovels; rich and poor alike, great lords in their canopied litters, beggars shoving against the levelled spears of the soldiers who held them back.

And Yvorian told his tale, and the people listened, and when Yvorian paused he could hear the wind blowing among the rooftops. When he was done, the old and sick came to him, filing up to where he sat so they might be touched by his healing hands.

This went on for hours. It was nearly dawn when the place was empty but for a single youth, who stood before the dais. The boy was about fifteen, fairhaired, and richly clad. Rings gleamed on his fingers.

Yvorian regarded him.

"It feels so good to be a king once more."

"You are not a king," said the boy. "You are a madman. The mad are touched by the gods, even as kings are, and sometimes their hands can heal, even as those of a king can. Both are holy. But I am prince of this city. When my father dies, I shall be king. You, holy madman, shall remain what you are."

The Prince left him, walking swiftly across the square.

Stunned, trembling, Yvorian rose from his seat and descended the dais. He saw another standing before him in the darkness among the pillars, a barefoot old man in a black robe, whose face rippled when he spoke like a thin, paper mask. His eyes were mere holes filled with fire.

"Are you King Yvorian the mighty?" the stranger asked.

"Yes."

"Are you certain?"

The madman cast off his fine robes and fled from the city, naked. He howled among the hills and in the depths of the forests. He crawled on all fours among the beasts of the fields, grazing. And he wept, and tore his hair, and dug in the earth with bloodied hands, searching for his kingdom.

But still he knew who he was, and when people came upon him he would rise and stand before them in great dignity, and try to tell them the story of King Yvorian. Often he was answered with laughter and stones, but sometimes with reverence. He touched many, and healed them.

At last when he lay shivering in the winter rain, feverish but unable to die, an anchorite found him and carried him to his hut high among the mountains. The holy man clothed him and gave him warm broth, and Yvorian told his story once again.

"It is a fine story," said the anchorite. "It is *true*."

"Does that really matter? The pattern is interesting. It contains a moral."

Yvorian sat still for a while, warming his hands with the cup of broth.

"I am not sure anymore. My mind is filled with so many things, as if I have lived ten thousand years. I think all those things are true. But some of them must be only dreams. How can I tell?"

"Truth may be found both in waking things, and in dreams. So, again, does it really matter?"

"But I have no crown," said Yvorian. "Where is my palace? Where is my kingdom?"

Now it was the anchorite who paused. He sat still for a long time, gazing into the firepit. Smoke rose gently up through the roof. Yvorian looked up at the smoke and the few stars he could see through the hole in the roof. He waited patiently.

"I know where your kingdom is," the other said at last. "If that is what you desire, go to a certain town, as I shall direct you, and obey the first person you meet, whatever you are asked to do.

Then you shall find your true kingdom."

And the King wept once more, for the very first time in his life out of gratitude.

The town the hermit named for him was far away. Yvorian walked throughout the winter and spring. By summer he had reached the edge of a vast desert. His fur clothing was too hot for him and he discarded it, once more weaving garments out of grass.

Slowly, painfully he crossed the wasteland, his grass clothing burned away by the sun, his bare skin darkened like old wood, his hair and beard streaming behind him in the wind like clouds crossing the face of the moon.

He reached his destination in the evening, as the last herdsmen drove their flocks into the town, as little bells rang to call the workmen home from their labors and the priests to their prayers.

A woman was drawing water from a well. She was neither young nor old, and three children clung to her brightly-patterned skirt.

When he saw her, the wanderer did not proclaim himself king. He did not command her to bow down. He only said that he was very thirsty.

The woman looked up, startled. "If you'll carry this bucket for me," she said, "you may have some."

He nodded eagerly. She gave him the bucket and he stared into it. In the failing light he could still make out his own reflection, and he saw a man with a weathered face, whose hair and beard were purest white. He drank.

"And if you will work for me," the woman said, "I'll give you food and clothing. My husband has died, and I need all the help I can get."

Again he nodded, and followed her back to her house.

"You must tell me your name," she said.

112

"I am . . . . Yvorian."

"I've heard that name before. In a story, I think."

"Yes, I know the story. I'll tell it to you sometime."

The children stared at him, wide-eyed.

For Yvorian, every aspect of life in the town by the desert's edge was new to him, a marvel. He was no longer a naked wanderer, but wore comfortable, plain clothes, and ate regularly. That was a forgotten condition he was only beginning to recall. He performed many labors for the widow, whose name was Evadina. He tended her flocks. He cleaned her stable. He drew water from the well many, many times. Never before had he served another. It strengthened him.

After seven years, he married her. This, too, was utterly novel, for he had never loved anyone before in all his long life, or been loved, or even expected to be. It was like an opening of the eyes, an awakening for the first time.

Although he was taken to be a man of at least fifty, he fathered three sons by Evadina. As they grew, he told them, and his stepchildren too, the story of King Yvorian who dwelt beneath a magic mountain far to the west. Sometimes the story concentrated on the king's pride, or his cruelty, or his loneliness; sometimes it was merely a tale of marvels. At the town festivals, he told the story to all who would listen, and people applauded and left coins in his hat.

He tried to write the story down at the request of the priests, who wanted a copy to keep in their temple, but the only script he knew was an archaic one no one could read. Nevertheless, the priests admired his brushwork and sometimes commissioned him to restore the icons of the gods, which hung in roadside shrines and faded from the sun and the weather.

On the night before the youngest of his sons was to go away and live elsewhere with his bride, he told the story of the king for the last time, extending it further than ever before, telling how the king emerged from his mountain and wandered through many lands, shedding his robes and his scepter and his crown, until he found himself better off without them, relieved of their burden, and found a life no king could ever know.

"Father," said the young man. "I have loved that story since I was a child, and now you have made it such a beautiful thing that I think I have only now heard it for the first time. I shall remember you by it always."

The young man turned to go, then paused.

"What is it, son?"

"Still I do not understand. The story, it has no ending."

"Yes it does. Come here." Yvorian rose, and led his son into the bedroom. His son followed, carrying a candle. The old man lay down beside Evadina, the boy's mother, who was already sleeping.

"Father?"

Yvorian put his finger to his lips. "Quiet. Don't wake her." Then he whispered, "This is the end of the story, that the teller came to recognize the end, and he knew that it didn't matter, for in shortly before the end he had gained a great treasure, which was merely a life lived well, and not even Rada Vatu could take that away from him. Slowly, then, Rada Vatu began to touch him, and he started to age, as all men do, but it did not matter."

Then the young man saw that his father was tired and went away. He left the candle burning by the bedside. Yvorian lay still, gazing into the darkness, listening to his wife's breathing as she slept beside him.

After a time, he was aware of another person in the room. A stranger stood by the bed, clad in a black robe. His eyes glowed like fireflies. He held a gleaming axe in his hand.

"Are you not the famous and mighty King Yvorian?"

"No. That is another Yvorian, a character in a story. I tell of him often."

"Ah." The stranger's face shrivelled inward, consumed in fire. The axe rose. *"I win the wager,"* said Rada Vatu.

"Are you certain?"

The axe fell. ☐

THE DEAD TAKE CARE OF THEIR OWN

by Valerie King

May 20

Dear Regina,

I'm writing this while I wait for Lloyd to pick me up. It's hotter than you-know-what in this trailer, and here it is only May! The kids are out playing. Lily is good at keeping an eye on the younger two and keeping them out of my hair which is a relief as I have been on edge lately with all that is going on.

Thanks for the $20 you sent. It came in handy. You are the only one in the family who keeps in touch, and believe me I am grateful for all you do, not to mention that these days yours is the only shoulder I can cry on.

It's just one thing after another around here. Lily's teacher stopped by yesterday afternoon. I didn't take to her at all, let me tell you, though Lily is crazy about her. You know the type, a know-it-all plain Jane. A Miss Evans. She was wearing a long bluejean skirt and no makeup, like some hippy! It makes you wonder who they get to teach our kids. She must make good money. Surely she could afford the price of a lipstick. Anyway she said that Lily is very bright and artistic and she should sign up for this summer art enrichment program in town. I asked her how much it would cost, in my coldest voice. She just looked at me and said, "It's free, Mrs. Darcy. I need you to sign this permission slip."

"And how does Lily get to and from this program?" I asked her cold and sweet. I mean, Regina, you know how my car is on the blink every other day. At which point Miss Evans informed me that there's a free van service the town has organized for the kids. She thought she had me there and waved the sign-up sheet at me almost upsetting my nail polish. But I pretended not to notice and kept on concentrating on my nails. "I'll have to think about it, Miss Evans," I said. "I need Lily here. She's a great help to me, as you can see."

114

THE DEAD TAKE CARE OF THEIR OWN

Miss Evans nodded and said that she could see that. She has an aggravating way about her. She looked around and took everything in: the pile of dishes in the sink, Jimmy's overflowing diaper pail which Lily hadn't gotten to yet, the window that Lloyd broke last week and still hasn't gotten around to fixing. She stared out the broken window at Lily carrying Jimmy with Kyle hanging onto her skirt and then back to me at the dinette polishing my nails. "I'll be in touch with you, Mrs. Darcy," she said. On the way out I saw her talking with the kids, and Lily smiling from ear to ear. I bet she will be in touch, Regina, that type doesn't know when to quit.

I know Lily is smart, a real Darcy like her father. She's looking more like Bennett every day, too. She has that same way of looking at me he did, that still, quiet way he had. Why did he have to get himself killed in that accident leaving me with a 5 year old on my hands and no one to turn to except Earl? After Kyle was born, I found out fast enough what good HE was. At times, I can't help thinking that everyone and everything is against me.

Your twenty came in real handy. What with the social security, and what Jimmy's daddy sends me, we barely scrape by. All Kyle's daddy did was leave me this trailer on a acre of land in the middle of nowhere. I'll never forget how he told me I was bad news before he walked out. I won't say what he was because I'm not one to hold a grudge. Today in town we stopped by the Salvation Army. With the money you sent I got a load of summer clothes for the kids. On the way out, Lily found some old walkie talkies and wanted me to buy them. I told her no way, but the cashier told Lily she could have them for free as she couldn't speak for how well they worked. I was just going to tell the woman not to push her trash off on us, but Lily fiddled with one of the knobs, and all of a sudden, there was a little crackling noise. Lily got them working! She's good that way. The lady still let her have them for free. Afterwards, I treated the kids to sodas and myself to some new Revlon brand nail polish. Always go for the better brand of makeup. It doesn't pay to skimp in that department.

The kids are out playing with the walkie talkies. I can hear Lloyd's truck rumbling up the road. Lily knows enough to feed and put the boys to bed as God only knows when we'll get back once Lloyd starts playing cards. But then, I've trained her to be

115

responsible. Your gift was appreciated.
    -- Your loving sister,
                    Charlene

                                                    May 25
Dear Regina
    Well, I beg your humble pardon! I didn't
understand that the $20 was for Lily's birthday. My
mistake! I offered her the $10 you just sent, but I
won't let her take those art classes. I'm sorry but
kids must learn some responsibility. Now that she's
ten, she's old enough to babysit the boys. Jimmy is
getting to be such a handful, now that he's walking,
almost as bad as Kyle. And Kyle, sucking his thumb and
wetting the bed at age five! My life is no picnic,
Regina. It's always something. It's cooled off a bit
for which I'm thankful. The kids are out playing with
those walkie talkies. They've even made some friends
with a family. I've overheard Lily and Kyle talking to
various children and grownups on those things. I wonder
who they are as we are out here in the middle of
nowhere. Just a lot of fields and that old falling down
cemetery across the road. Funny thing, Lloyd and I were
fooling around with those walkie talkies, and we
couldn't get them to work. They only seem to work for
Lily, I guess. I'm going to surprise her with some
dresses from the Salvation Army with the money you
sent. Wait til I tell you the latest developments with
Jimmy's father. Thanks for the gift.
    -- Your loving sister,
                    Charlene

                                                    June 1
Dear Regina,
    We've been over this territory before! I know I'm
a trained and state-licensed beautician. I know
Carola's Beauty Salon will put me on part time
evenings, but I will not work for that woman period!
She is an impossible tyrant, and what is worse, pushes
the most out-of-date styles. If I could only start my
own salon and siphon off some of her business! She does
good business because she's the only beautician in
town. But on to my news: Jimmy's daddy and his new
wife, the one he dumped me for to marry (me, who was
carrying his child at the time) made contact. It seems
as if she can't have kids! Isn't that poetic something

or other? Wish I had that problem. Ha! Ha! So seeing
how cute Jimmy is they'd like to adopt him from me. In
fact, they offered a good amount of cash up front to
show me they are serious. I'm seriously thinking about
it. They would provide a better home setting for little
Jimmy. After all, they live in a split level ranch.
But, wouldn't you know? Lily suspects something is up.
She has this way of looking at me. I hope she didn't
see their letter. I was careful to hide it from her.
She's only Jimmy's half sister, but she's so attached
to him. And to Kyle, too. When it comes down to it,
she's only related to them through me. I'll draw this
to a close as I feel like a nap before the kids come
in. They are getting so much out of those walkie
talkies. I can't complain about the price now, can I?
    -- Your loving sister,
                    Charlene

                                                June 5
Dear Regina,
    Well, how nice of you to send Lily that shoebox
filled with new art supplies! She is happy as a lark
with her new present and is making you a picture which
I will send on next letter. I allow her to work on her
art after all her chores are done. Once she's put the
boys to bed, bagged the trash, and washed the supper
dishes, she is able to paint and color at the dinette.
She works away into the night, painting pictures and
fiddling with the walkie talkies. Last night it was so
hot, I woke up after midnight and heard whispering and
giggling. There was Lily, sitting at the dinette,
chattering into the walkie talkie. "Lily, come to bed!"
I hollered. "Yes, Mama," she said. But she wasn't quick
enough, so I jumped out of my cot and yanked the walkie
talkie out of her hand. "See you tomorrow!" I could
make out a child's voice above the static. "Who is
that?" I demanded. She told me it was her friend Emma.
"What kind of mother does she have that lets her stay
up all night?" I asked. It irks me how some parents let
their kids get the upper hand. Lily insisted that
Emma's mother, Mrs. Sandler, is a nice lady. "Go to
bed," I told her, which she did. As I was drifting off
to sleep, she asked me the strangest question: "Mama,
do the dead take care of their own? Emma says they do."
"What kind of question is that?" I demanded. It's the
same kind of off the wall remark her father used to
pass. He was so dreamy and impractical. It was just

like him to get himself killed with no insurance. I could be living in a brick, split level and belong to a swim club. Look at me. I'm twenty-eight with three young children living in a dump of a trailer! I'm sorry I'm so low, but Lloyd seems to have vanished off the face of the earth. Thank God I had that operation after Jimmy was born. So that's one less thing to worry about.

-- Your loving sister,
Charlene

June 7

Dear Regina,

So much has happened in the past two days, I feel as if I'm going to burst with happiness! Isn't it something how life can change so quickly? I wish I had a phone, but must make do with a letter -- so here goes. Today in town at a pay phone I called Jimmy's father. He will give me $5000 in cash for Jimmy. The money is mine on the condition that I will sever my ties to the child for good (or words to that effect). He expected an argument on that point. He didn't get one because I was as sweet as pie. I have thought things over, and it is all for the best. I hung up, feeling light as a cloud, turned around, and there was Lily holding Jimmy with Kyle pulling on her as usual. I'd sent them off to buy ice cream, but they got back quicker than I expected. Lily just stared at me in that way she has. I pretended nothing was up. Soon enough, she will see the light. That money will get us out of the trailer into the Riviera Garden Apartments which are now taking children. I'll even let her take that art course. Plus, instead of the old cemetery, they'll have a pool and a recreation room to play in.

Then as we stopped for gas on the way home, the attendant, a short, good looking man, who has been eyeing me for ages, told me he'd be glad to stop by and look under my hood anytime. Wasn't that cute? I like a man with a sense of humor. But he told me he was serious as my car is not in the best of shape, and he doesn't like the idea of me and the kids driving around in a defective vehicle. His name is Curtis, and he's co-owner of the station, not just some attendant. So things are looking up, I must say. I was wearing new eye liner so it pays to look after one's appearance.

Later that day, the kids were out playing, and I was flipping through the Sears catalog daydreaming how

THE DEAD TAKE CARE OF THEIR OWN

I'd decorate the new apartment, when who should barge
in with a stack of summer reading for Lily, but Miss
Evans? What did I tell you about her? She was wearing
what looked like a grey baggy housedress. The woman has
no sense of style whatsoever. She said she just wanted
to drop by and see how Lily was doing, that it was such
a shame that she wasn't in the art program. "Oh, that
might change," I told her. "I'm rethinking my position
on her art lessons." Which brightened up her plain Jane
face considerably. "Where is Lily?" she asked.
"Outside," I informed her. She looked puzzled and said
she didn't see the children anywhere when she was
driving up through the fields. I waved in the direction
of the cemetery. "She and her brothers are probably
over with that Sandler family. She's friendly with
their daughter Emma."

"The Sandler family?" she asked, wrinkling up her
forehead which is something a plain woman like that
should avoid. I told her that they must live on the
other side of the grave yard because my kids were over
there all the time and yakking to them on these old,
broken down walkie talkies they play with.

"There was a Sandler family in these parts over
fifty years ago. They were friends of my grandparents,"
Miss Evans said, looking over to the cemetery.

"That's very interesting, Miss Evans," I told her.
I wished she would leave, but that type can't take a
hint. I needed to refrost my hair, which is a time-
consuming enterprise now that my sink is blocked up.
But she kept talking. She went on and on how her
grandparents' friends, the Sandlers, were all wiped out
in a big flash flood that swept through these parts
half a century ago. It was a big family, I can still
hear her saying, much loved in the community for their
acts of charity and hospitality to the world at large,
quote unquote. There was a ten year old daughter named
Emma who was close to Miss Evans's own grandmother. The
whole thing was so tragic, that to this day her
grandmother still weeps about what happened.

"Sorry to hear about it," I said as politely as I
could, but my mind was on other things such as could
Curtis fix the dumb sink and the window Lloyd broke by
throwing a beer bottle through it?

"There are no more Sandlers in these parts," she
repeated. Her face could have used some blusher, it
looked so pale. Why do some women let themselves go?

She saw that my mind was on other things so she
finally left. I watched her drive off. Good riddance, I

couldn't help thinking. I noticed the walkie talkies
were placed in a neat pile alongside the steps up to
the trailer. I guess Lily and the boys are growing
tired of them as children can do with their toys. I'll
keep you posted on the developments with Jimmy's
father. Do you think there would be enough left over
once we move out of here to start up a beauty shop?
Curtis is coming by this evening, so after I walk this
to the mailbox, I'd better spruce myself up.
     -- Your loving sister,
                    Charlene

P.S. Enclosed find a picture Lily painted of her friend
Emma.

                                        June 8
Dear Regina,
     The very worst possible thing has happened. The
children have disappeared. I haven't seen them since we
got back from town yesterday. It's after two in the
morning as I write this. Needless to say, I can't
sleep. The police have come and gone. They were out
dredging the wells around here. While they have not
ruled out foul play, they seem to think the children
have met with an accident. My head is spinning. Miss
Evans was here with the police, along with Jimmy's
father. I told them about Emma Sandler talking to Lily
on the walkie talkies at all hours, and the detective
and Miss Evans picked up the walkie talkies and tried
to get them working. "They are stone dead, Mrs. Darcy,"
the detective in charge told me. He asked the most
distasteful personal questions about the boys' fathers
and my marital status. He also pried into my financial
and professional background and asked point blank if
the children were insured. He went on to inquire
whether or not I drank. "Nothing stronger than ice
tea," I almost spat in his face.
     "We will be back, Mrs. Darcy," the overbearing
detective assured me. Off they went, leaving me alone
in this dump of a trailer on a hot muggy night with not
a star in the sky. So I sit here writing to you (as I
did just a few hours ago when my life was vastly
different) trying to make sense out of what's happened.
Everything is so still. Even the bugs are quiet. Curtis
said he would come by and sit with me, but I
discouraged that. My heart would not be in it, I'm
afraid.

THE DEAD TAKE CARE OF THEIR OWN

The walkie talkies are lying in front of me on the dinette. From time to time, I turn all the knobs and call out for Lily and the boys. I even call Emma's name, but there's silence, not so much as a burst of static.

The police, well, they can dredge up their wells and their suspects, of which I now know I am counted. Jimmy's father whispered that information in my ear earlier today. He is the malicious type. I am better off without him, I can see that now. Though it's hard to believe I cried my eyes out when he threw me over. But, there's three things I know that I didn't tell that unpleasant detective. One: it was those walkie talkies that caused all of this to happen in the first place. Two: Lily took her art box with her. Her art box and her little brothers. And three: They are all with that Sandler family, whoever they are. Maybe I should add a number four to all of this. It's something I feel in my bones which is this: Lily, Kyle, and little Jimmy are in good hands.

It's the silence that gets to me as I sit here writing this. What I wouldn't give to hear Jimmy's laughter or Kyle's little sing-song voice or Lily giggling into the walkie talkies. Noise that used to drive me into screaming fits. Regina, you are the sensible type. You see things clearly. Where did I go wrong? Am I being punished? And if so, for what? I did what I had to do. I always saw that they were fed and clothed. I never hit them, though I did raise my voice to keep them in line. I wasn't any Joan Crawford. Why would they up and leave?

Lily said something to me before the three of them trooped out of the trailer this afternoon which seems so long ago. How was I to know that it was to be the last time I would see them all? Because, Regina, I know they are not coming back, I just know. I can't for the life of me, sitting here in the silent small hours of the morning, remember what Lily said. Something about the dead. And then she said, "Goodbye, Mama," in that quiet way she has, and hoisted up Jimmy, and walked out of the trailer with Kyle trailing after her. If only I could remember what she said. Why does everything always happen to me?

-- Your loving sister,
Charlene ☐

NO SHARKS IN THE MED

by Brian Lumley

Customs was non-existent; people bring duty frees *out* of Greece, not in. As for passport control: a pair of tanned, hairy, bored-looking characters in stained, too-tight uniforms and peaked caps were in charge. One to take your passport, find the page to be franked, scan photograph and bearer both with a blank gaze that took in absolutely nothing unless you happened to be female and stacked (in which case it took in everything and more), then pass the passport on. Geoff Hammond thought: *I wonder if that's why they call them passports?* The second one took the little black book from the first and hammered down on it with his stamp, impressing several pages but no one else, then handed the important document back to its owner — but grudgingly, as if he didn't believe you could be trusted with it.

This second one, the one with the rubber stamp, had a brother. They could be, probably were, twins. Five-eightish, late twenties, lots of shoulders and no hips; raven hair shiny with grease, so tightly curled it looked permed; brown eyes utterly vacant of expression. The only difference was the uniform: the fact that the brother on the home-and-dry side of the barrier didn't have one. Leaning on the barrier, he twirled cheap, yellow-framed, dark-lensed glasses like glinting propellers, observed almost speculatively the incoming holidaymakers. He wore shorts, frayed where they hugged his thick thighs, barely long enough to be decent. *Hung like a bull!* Geoff thought. It was

almost embarrassing. Dressed for the benefit of the single girls, obviously. He'd be hoping they were taking notes for later. His chances might improve if he were two inches taller and had a face. But he didn't; the face was as vacant as the eyes.

Then Geoff saw what it was that was wrong with those eyes: beyond the barrier, the specimen in the bulging shorts was walleyed. Likewise his twin punching the passports. Their right eyes had white pupils that stared like dead fish. The one in the booth wore lightly-tinted glasses, so that you didn't notice until he looked up and stared directly at you. Which in Geoff's case he hadn't; but he was certainly looking at Gwen. Then he glanced at Geoff, patiently waiting, and said: "Together, you?" His voice was a shade too loud, making it almost an accusation.

Different names on the passports, obviously! But Geoff wasn't going to stand here and explain how they were just married and Gwen hadn't had time to make the required alterations. That really *would* be embarrassing! In fact (and come to think of it), it might not even be legal. Maybe she should have changed it right away, or got something done with it, anyway, in London. The honeymoon holiday they'd chosen was one of those get-it-while-it's-going deals, a last-minute half-price seat-filler, a gift horse; and they'd been pushed for time. But what the Hell — this *was* 1987, wasn't it?

"Yes," Geoff finally answered. "Together."

122

"Ah!" the other nodded, grinned, appraised Gwen again with a raised eyebrow, before stamping her passport and handing it over.

Walleyed bastard! Geoff thought.

When they passed through the gate in the barrier, the other walleyed bastard had disappeared. . . .

Stepping through the automatic glass doors from the shade of the airport building into the sunlight of the coach terminus was like opening the door of a furnace; it was a replay of the moment when the plane's air-conditioned passengers trooped out across the tarmac to board the buses waiting to convey them to passport control. You came out into the sun fairly crisp, but by the time you'd trundled your luggage to the kerbside and lifted it off the trolley your armpits were already sticky. One o'clock, and the temperature must have been hovering around eighty-five for hours. It not only beat down on you but, trapped in the concrete, beat up as well. Hammerblows of heat.

A mini-skirted courier, English as a rose and harassed as Hell — her white blouse soggy while her blue and white hat still sat jaunty on her head — came fluttering, clutching her millboard with its bulldog clip and thin sheaf of notes. "Mr Hammond and Miss —" she glanced at her notes, "— Pinter?"

"Mr and Mrs Hammond," Geoff answered. He lowered his voice and continued confidentially: "We're all proper, legitimate, and true. Only our identities have been altered in order to protect our passports."

"Um?" she said.

Too deep for her, Geoff thought, sighing inwardly.

"Yes," said Gwen, sweetly. "We're the Hammonds."

"Oh!" the girl looked a little confused. "It's just that —"

"I haven't changed my passport yet," said Gwen, smiling.

"Ah!" Understanding finally dawned. The courier smiled nervously at Geoff, turned again to Gwen. "Is it too late for congratulations?"

"Four days," Gwen answered.

"Well, congratulations anyway."

Geoff was eager to be out of the sun. "Which is our coach?" he wanted to know. "Is it — could it possibly be — air-conditioned?" There were several coaches parked in an untidy cluster a little farther up the kerb.

Again the courier's confusion, also something of embarrassment showing in her bright blue eyes. "You're going to — Achladi?"

Geoff sighed again, this time audibly. It was her business to know where they were going. It wasn't a very good start.

"Yes," she cut in quickly, before he or Gwen could comment. "Achladi — but not by coach! You see, your plane was an hour late; the coach for Achladi couldn't be held up for just one couple; but it's OK — you'll have the privacy of your own taxi, and of course Skymed will foot the bill."

She went off to whistle up a taxi and Geoff and Gwen glanced at each other, shrugged, sat down on their cases. But in a moment the courier was back, and behind her a taxi came rolling, nosing into the kerb. Its driver jumped out, whirled about opening doors, the boot, stashing cases while Geoff and Gwen got into the back of the car. Then, throwing his straw hat down beside him as he climbed into the driving seat and slammed his door, the young Greek looked back at his passengers and smiled. A single gold tooth flashed in a bar of white. But the smile was quite dead, like the grin of a shark before he bites, and the voice when it came was phlegmy, like pebbles colliding in mud. "Achladi, yes?"

"Ye—" Geoff began, paused, and finished: "—es! Er, Achladi, right!" Their driver was the walleyed passport-stamper's walleyed brother.

"I Spiros," he declared, turning the taxi out of the airport. "And you?"

Something warned Geoff against any sort of familiarity with this one. In all this heat, the warning was like a breath of cold air on the back of his neck. "I'm Mr Hammond," he answered, stiffly. "This is my wife." Gwen turned her head a little and frowned at him.

"I'm —" she began.

"My *wife!*" Geoff said again. She looked surprised but kept her peace.

Spiros was watching the road where it narrowed and wound. Already out of the airport, he skirted the island's main town and raced for foothills rising to a spine of half-clad mountains. Achladi was maybe half an hour away, on the other side of the central range. The road soon became a track, a thick layer of dust over potholed tarmac and cobbles; in short, a typical Greek road. They slowed down a little through a village where white-walled houses lined the way, with lemon groves set back between and behind the dwellings, and were left with bright flashes of bougainvillea-framed balconies burning like after-images on their retinas. Then Spiros gave it the gun again.

Behind them, all was dust kicked up by the spinning wheels and the suction of the car's passing. Geoff glanced out of the fly-specked rear window. The cloud of brown dust, chasing after them, seemed ominous in the way it obscured the so-recent past. And turning front again, Geoff saw that Spiros kept his strange eye mainly on the road ahead, and the good one on his rearview. But watching what? The dust? No, he was looking at . . .

At Gwen! The interior mirror was angled directly into her cleavage.

They had been married only a very short time. The day when he'd take pride in the jealousy of other men — in their coveting his wife — was still years in the future. Even then, look but don't touch would be the order of the day.

Right now it was watch where you're looking, and possession was ninety-nine point nine percent of the law. As for the other point one percent: well, there was nothing much you could do about what the lecherous bastards were thinking!

Geoff took Gwen's elbow, pulled her close and whispered: "Have you noticed how tight he takes the bends? He does it so we'll bounce about a bit. He's watching how your tits jiggle!"

She'd been delighting in the scenery, hadn't even noticed Spiros, his eyes or anything. For a beautiful girl of twenty-three, she was remarkably naïve, and it wasn't just an act. It was one of the things Geoff loved best about her. Only eighteen months her senior, Geoff hardly considered himself a man of the world; but he did know a rat when he smelled one. In Spiros's case he could smell several sorts.

"He . . . *what* — ?" Gwen said out loud, glancing down at herself. One button too many had come open in her blouse, showing the edges of her cups. Green eyes widening, she looked up and spotted Spiros's rearview. He grinned at her through the mirror and licked his lips, but without deliberation. He was naïve, too, in his way. In his different sort of way.

"Sit over here," said Geoff out loud, as she did up the offending button *and* the one above it. "The view is much better on this side." He half-stood, let her slide along the seat behind him. Both of Spiros's eyes were now back on the road. . . .

Ten minutes later they were up into a pass through gorgeous pine-clad slopes so steep they came close to sheer. Here and there scree slides showed through the greenery, or a thrusting outcrop of rock. "Mountains," Spiros grunted, without looking back.

"You have an eye for detail," Geoff answered.

Gwen gave his arm a gentle nip, and

125

he knew she was thinking *sarcasm is the lowest form of wit — and it doesn't become you!* Nor cruelty, apparently. Geoff had meant nothing special by his "eye" remark, but Spiros was sensitive. He groped in the glove compartment for his yellow-rimmed sunshades, put them on. And drove in a stony silence for what looked like being the rest of the journey.

Through the mountains they sped, and the west coast of the island opened up like a gigantic travel brochure. The mountains seemed to go right down to the sea, rocks merging with that incredible, aching blue. And they could see the village down there, Achladi, like something out of a dazzling dream perched on both sides of a spur that gentled into the ocean.

"Beautiful!" Gwen breathed.

"Yes," Spiros nodded. "Beautiful, thee village." Like many Greeks speaking English, his definite articles all sounded like *thee*. "For fish, for thee swims, thee sun — is beautiful."

After that it was all downhill; winding, at times precipitous, but the view was never less than stunning. For Geoff, it brought back memories of Cyprus. Good ones, most of them, but one bad one that always made him catch his breath, clench his fists. The reason he hadn't been too keen on coming back to the Med in the first place. He closed his eyes in an attempt to force the memory out of mind, but that only made it worse, the picture springing up that much clearer.

He was a kid again, just five years old, late in the summer of '67. His father was a Staff-Sergeant Medic, his mother with the QARANCs; both of them were stationed at Dhekelia, a Sovereign Base Area garrison just up the coast from Larnaca where they had a married quarter. They'd met and married in Berlin, spent three years there, then got posted out to Cyprus together. With two years done in Cy-

prus, Geoff's father had a year to go to complete his twenty-two. After that last year in the sun . . . there was a place waiting for him in the ambulance pool of one of London's big hospitals. Geoff's mother had hoped to get on the nursing staff of the same hospital. But before any of that . . .

Geoff had started school in Dhekelia, but on those rare weekends when both of his parents were free of duty, they'd all go off to the beach together. And that had been his favourite thing in all the world: the beach with its golden sand and crystal-clear, safe, shallow water. But sometimes, seeking privacy, they'd take a picnic basket and drive east along the coast until the road became a track, then find a way down the cliffs and swim from the rocks up around Cape Greco. That's where it had happened.

"Geoff!" Gwen tugged at his arm, breaking the spell. He was grateful to be dragged back to reality. "Were you sleeping?"

"Daydreaming," he answered.

"Me, too!" she said. "I think I must be. I mean, just *look* at it!"

They were winding down a steep ribbon of road cut into the mountain's flank, and Achladi was directly below them. A coach coming up squeezed by, its windows full of brown, browned-off faces. Holidaymakers going off to the airport, going home. Their holidays were over but Geoff's and Gwen's was just beginning, and the village they had come to *was* truly beautiful. Especially beautiful because it was unspoiled. This was only Achladi's second season; before they'd built the airport you could only get here by boat. Very few had bothered.

Geoff's vision of Cyprus and his bad time quickly receded; while he didn't consider himself a romantic like Gwen, still he recognized Achladi's magic. And now he supposed he'd have to admit that they'd made the right choice.

White-walled gardens; red tiles, green-framed windows, some flat roofs and some with a gentle pitch; bougainvillea cascading over white, arched balconies; a tiny white church on the point of the spur where broken rocks finally tumbled into the sea; massive, ancient olive trees in walled plots at every street junction, and grapevines on trellises giving a little shade and dappling every garden and patio. That, at a glance, was Achladi. A high sea wall kept the sea at bay, not that it could ever be a real threat, for the entire front of the village fell within the harbour's crab's-claw moles. Steps went down here and there from the sea wall to the rocks; a half-dozen towels were spread wherever there was a flat or gently-inclined surface to take them, and the sea bobbed with a half-dozen heads, snorkels and face-masks. Deep water here, but a quarter-mile to the south, beyond the harbour wall, a shingle beach stretched like the webbing between the toes of some great beast for maybe a hundred yards to where a second claw-like spur came down from the mountains. As for the rest of this western coastline: as far as the eye could see both north and south, it looked like sky, cliff and sea to Geoff. Cape Greco all over again. But before he could go back to that:

"Is Villa Eleni, yes?" Spiros's gurgling voice intruded. "Him have no road. No can drive. I carry thee bags."

The road went right down the ridge of the spur to the little church. Halfway, it was crossed at right-angles by a second motor road which contained and serviced a handful of shops. The rest of the place was made up of streets too narrow or too perpendicular for cars. A few ancient scooters put-putted and puttered about, donkeys clip-clopped here and there, but that was all. Spiros turned his vehicle about at the main junction (the *only* real road junction) and parked in the shade of a giant olive tree. He went to get the luggage. There were two large cases, two small ones. Geoff would have shared the load equally but found himself brushed aside; Spiros took the elephant's share and left him with the small-fry. He wouldn't mind, but it was obviously the Greek's chance to show off his strength.

Leading the way up a steep cobbled ramp of a street, Spiros's muscular buttocks kept threatening to burst through the thin stuff of his cut-down jeans. And because the holidaymakers followed on a little way behind, Geoff was aware of Gwen's eyes on Spiros's tanned, gleaming thews. There wasn't much of anywhere else to look. "Him Tarzan, you Jane," he commented, but his grin was a shade too dry.

"Who you?" she answered, her nose going up in the air. "Cheetah?"

"Uph, uph!" said Geoff.

"Anyway," she relented. "Your bottom's nicer. More compact."

He saved his breath, made no further comment. Even the light cases seemed heavy. If he was Cheetah, that must make Spiros Kong! The Greek glanced back once, grinned in his fashion, and kept going. Breathing heavily, Geoff and Gwen made an effort to catch up, failed miserably. Then, toward the top of the way, Spiros turned right into an arched alcove, climbed three stone steps, put down his cases and paused at a varnished pine door. He pulled on a string to free the latch, shoved the door open and took up his cases again. As the English couple came round the corner he was stepping inside. "Thee Villa Eleni," he said, as they followed him in.

Beyond the door was a high-walled courtyard of black and white pebbles laid out in octopus and dolphin designs. A split-level patio fronted the "villa," a square box of a house whose one redeeming feature had to be a retractable sun-awning shading the windows and most of the patio. It also made an admirable refuge from the dazzling white of everything.

127

There were whitewashed concrete steps climbing the side of the building to the upper floor, with a landing that opened onto a wooden-railed balcony with its own striped awning. Beach towels and an outsize lady's bathing costume were hanging over the rail, drying, and all the windows were open. Someone was home, maybe. Or maybe sitting in a shady taverna sipping on iced drinks. Downstairs, a key with a label had been left in the keyhole of a louvered, fly-screened door. Geoff read the label, which said simply: "Mr Hammond." The booking had been made in his name.

"This is us," he said to Gwen, turning the key.

They went in, Spiros following with the large cases. Inside, the cool air was a blessing. Now they would like to explore the place on their own, but the Greek was there to do it for them. And he knew his way around. He put the cases down, opened his arms to indicate the central room. "For sit, talk, thee resting." He pointed to a tiled area in one corner, with a refrigerator, sink-unit and two-ring electric cooker. "For thee toast, coffee — thee fish and chips, eh?" He shoved open the door of a tiny room tiled top to bottom, containing a shower, wash-basin and WC. "And this one," he said, without further explanation. Then five strides back across the floor took him to another room, low-ceilinged, pine-beamed, with a Lindean double bed built in under louvered windows. He cocked his head on one side. "And thee bed — just one. . . ."

"That's all we'll need," Geoff answered, his annoyance building.

"Yes," Gwen said. "Well, thank you, er, Spiros — you're very kind. And we'll be fine now."

Spiros scratched his chin, went back into the main room and sprawled in an easy chair. "Outside is hot," he said. "Here she is cool — *krio,* you know?"

Geoff went to him. "It's *very* hot," he agreed, "and we're sticky. Now we want to shower, put our things away, look around. Thanks for your help. You can go now."

Spiros stood up and his face went slack, his expression more blank than before. His walleye looked strange through its tinted lens. "Go now?" he repeated.

Geoff sighed. "Yes, go!"

The corner of Spiros's mouth twitched, drew back a little to show his gold tooth. "I fetch from airport, carry cases."

"Ah!" said Geoff, getting out his wallet. "What do I owe you?" He'd bought drachmas at the bank in London.

Spiros sniffed, looked scornful, half turned away. "One thousand," he finally answered, bluntly.

"That's about four pounds and fifty pence," Gwen said from the bedroom doorway. "Sounds reasonable."

"Except it was supposed to be on Skymed," Geoff scowled. He paid up anyway and saw Spiros to the door. The Greek departed, sauntered indifferently across the patio to pause in the arched doorway and look back across the courtyard. Gwen had come to stand beside Geoff in the double doorway under the awning.

The Greek looked straight at her and licked his fleshy lips. The vacant grin was back on his face. "I see you," he said, nodding with a sort of slow deliberation.

As he closed the door behind him, Gwen muttered, "Not if I see you first! *Ugh!*"

"I am with you," Geoff agreed. *"Not my favourite local character!"*

"Spiros," she said. "Well, and it suits him to a tee. It's about as close as you can get to spider! And that one *is* about as close as you can get!"

They showered, fell exhausted on the bed — but not so exhausted that they could just lie there without making love.

Later — with suitcases emptied and small valuables stashed out of sight, and spare clothes all hung up or tucked away — dressed in light, loose gear, sandals, sunglasses, it was time to explore the village. "And afterwards," Gwen insisted, "we're swimming!" She'd packed their towels and swimwear in a plastic beach bag. She loved to swim, and Geoff might have, too, except . . .

But as they left their rooms and stepped out across the patio, the varnished door in the courtyard wall opened to admit their upstairs neighbours, and for the next hour all thoughts of exploration and a dip in the sea were swept aside. The elderly couple who now introduced themselves gushed, there was no other way to describe it. He was George and she was Petula.

"My *dear*," said George, taking Gwen's hand and kissing it, "such a *stunning* young lady, and how sad that I've only two days left in which to enjoy you!" He was maybe sixty-four or five, ex-handsome but sagging a bit now, tall if a little bent, and brown as a native. With a small grey moustache and faded blue eyes, he looked as if he'd — no, in all probability he *had* — piloted Spitfires in World War II! Alas, he wore the most blindingly colourful shorts and shirt that Gwen had ever seen.

Petula was very large, about as tall as George but two of him in girth. She was just as brown, though, (and so presumably didn't mind exposing it all), seemed equally if not more energetic, and was never at a loss for words. They were a strange, paradoxical pair: very upper-crust, but at the same time very much down to earth. If Petula tended to speak with plums in her mouth, certainly they were of a very tangy variety.

"He'll flatter you to death, my dear," she told Gwen, ushering the newcomers up the steps at the side of the house and onto the high balcony. "But you must *never* take your eyes off his hands!

Stage magicians have nothing on George. Forty years ago he magicked himself into my bedroom, and he's been there ever since!"

"She seduced me!" said George, bustling indoors.

"I did not!" Petula was petulant. "What? Why he's quite simply a wolf in . . . in a Joseph suit!"

"A Joseph suit?" George repeated her. He came back out onto the balcony with brandy-sours in a frosted jug, a clattering tray of ice-cubes, slices of sugared lemon and an eggcup of salt for the sours. He put the lot down on a plastic table, said: "Ah! — glasses!" and ducked back inside again.

"Yes," his wife called after him, pointing at his Bermudas and Hawaiian shirt. "Your clothes of many colours!"

It was all good fun and Geoff and Gwen enjoyed it. They sat round the table on plastic chairs, and George and Petula entertained them. It made for a very nice welcome to Achladi indeed.

"Of course," said George after a while, when they'd settled down a little, "we first came here eight years ago, when there were no flights, just boats. Now that people are flying in —" he shrugged, "— two more seasons and there'll be belly-dancers and hotdog stands! But for now it's . . . just perfect. Will you look at that view?"

The view from the balcony was very fetching. "From up here we can see the entire village," said Gwen. "You must point out the best shops, the bank or exchange or whatever, all the places we'll need to know about."

George and Petula looked at each other, smiled knowingly.

"Oh?" said Gwen.

Geoff checked their expressions, nodded, made a guess: "There are no places we need to know about."

"Well, three, actually," said Petula. "Four if you count Dimi's — the taverna. Oh, there are other places to eat, but Dimi's is *the* place. Except I feel I've spoilt it for you now. I mean, that really is something you should have discovered for yourself. It's half the fun, finding the best place to eat!"

"What about the other three places we should know about" Gwen inquired. "Will knowing those spoil it for us, too? Knowing them in advance, I mean?"

"Good Lord, no!" George shook his head. "Vital knowledge, young lady!"

"The baker's," said Petula. "For fresh rolls — daily." She pointed it out, blue smoke rising from a cluster of chimneypots. "Also the booze shop, for booze —"

"— Also daily," said George, pointing. "Right there on that corner — where the bottles glint. D'you know, they have an *ancient* Metaxa so cheap you wouldn't —"

"*And,*" Petula continued, "the path down to the beach. Which is . . . over there."

"But tell us," said George, changing the subject, "are you married, you two? Or is that too personal?"

"Oh, of *course* they're married!" Petula told him. "But very recently, because they still sit so close together. Touching. You see?"

"Ah!" said George. "Then we shan't have another elopement."

"You know, my dear, you really are an old idiot," said Petula, sighing. "I mean, elopements are for lovers to be together. And these two already *are* together!"

Geoff and Gwen raised their eyebrows. "An elopement?" Gwen said. "Here? When did this happen?"

"Right here, yes," said Petula. "Ten days ago. On our first night we had a young man downstairs, Gordon. On his own. He was supposed to be here with his fiancée but she's jilted him. He went out with us, had a few too many in Dimi's and told us all about it. A Swedish girl — very lovely, blonde creature — was also on her own. She helped steer

him back here and, I suppose, tucked him in. She had her own place, mind you, and didn't stay."

"But the next night she did!" George enthused.

"And then they ran off," said Petula, brightly. "Eloped! As simple as that. We saw them once, on the beach, the next morning. Following which —"

"— Gone!" said George.

"Maybe their holidays were over and they just went home," said Gwen, reasonably.

"No," George shook his head. "Gordon had come out on our plane, his holiday was just starting. She'd been here about a week and a half, was due to fly out the day after they made off together."

"They paid for their holidays and then deserted them?" Geoff frowned. "Doesn't make any sense."

"Does anything, when you're in love?" Petula sighed.

"The way I see it," said George, "they fell in love with each other, and with Greece, and went off to explore all the options."

"Love?" Gwen was doubtful. "On the rebound?"

"If she'd been a mousey little thing, I'd quite agree," said Petula. "But no, she really was a beautiful girl."

"And him a nice lad," said George. "A bit sparse but clean, good-looking."

"Indeed, they were much like you two," his wife added. "I mean, not *like* you, but like you."

"Cheers," said Geoff, wryly. "I mean, I know I'm not Mr Universe, but —"

"Tight in the bottom!" said Petula. "That's what the girls like these days. You'll do all right."

"See," said Gwen, nudging him. "Told you so!"

But Geoff was still frowning. "Didn't anyone look for them? What if they'd been involved in an accident or something?"

'No," said Petula. "They were seen

boarding a ferry in the main town. Indeed, one of the local taxi drivers took them there. Spiros."

Gwen and Geoff's turn to look at each other. "A strange fish, that one," said Geoff.

George shrugged. "Oh, I don't know. You know him, do you? It's that eye of his which makes him seem a bit sinister. . . ."

Maybe he's right, Geoff thought.

Shortly after that, their drinks finished, they went off to start their explorations. . . .

The village was a maze of cobbled, white-washed alleys. Even as tiny as it was you could get lost in it, but never for longer than the length of a street. Going downhill, no matter the direction, you'd come to the sea. Uphill you'd come to the main road, or if you didn't, then turn the next corner and *continue* uphill, and then you would. The most well-trodden alley, with the shiniest cobbles, was the one that led to the hard-packed path, which in turn led to the beach. Pass the "booze shop" on the corner twice, and you'd know where it was always. The window was plastered with labels, some familiar and others entirely conjectural; inside, steel shelving went floor to ceiling, stacked with every conceivable brand; even the more exotic and (back home) wildly expensive stuffs were on view, often in ridiculously cheap, three-litre, duty-free bottles with their own chrome taps and display stands.

"Courvoisier!" said Gwen, appreciatively.

"Grand Marnier, surely!" Geoff protested. "What, five pints of Grand Marnier? At that price? Can you believe it? But that's to take home. What about while we're here?"

"Coconut liqueur," she said. "Or better still, mint chocolate — to compliment our midnight coffees."

They found several small tavernas,

too, with people seated outdoors at tiny tables under the vines. Chicken portions and slabs of lamb sputtering on spits; small fishes sizzling over charcoal; *moussaka* steaming in long trays . . .

Dimi's was down on the harbour, where a wide, low wall kept you safe from falling in the sea. They had a Greek salad which they divided two ways, tiny cubes of lamb roasted on wooden slivers, a half-bottle of local white wine costing pennies. As they ate and sipped the wine, so they began to relax; the hot sunlight was tempered by an almost imperceptible breeze off the sea.

Geoff said: "Do you really feel energetic? Damned if I do."

She didn't feel full of boundless energy, no, but she wasn't going down without a fight. "If it was up to you," she said, "we'd just sit here and watch the fishing nets dry, right?"

"Nothing wrong with taking it easy," he answered. "We're on holiday, remember?"

"Your idea of taking it easy means being bone idle!" she answered. "I say we're going for a dip, then back to the villa for siesta and you know, and —"

"Can we have the you know before the siesta?" He kept a straight face.

"— And then we'll be all settled in, recovered from the journey, ready for tonight. Insatiable!"

"OK," he shrugged. "Anything you say. But we swim from the beach, not from the rocks."

Gwen looked at him suspiciously. "That was almost too easy."

Now he grinned. "It was the thought of, well, you know, that did it," he told her. . . .

Lying on the beach, panting from their exertions in the sea, with the sun lifting the moisture off their still-pale bodies, Gwen said: "I don't understand."

"Hmm?"

"You swim very well. I've always thought so. So what is this fear of the water you complain about?"

"First," Geoff answered, "I don't swim very well. Oh, for a hundred yards I'll swim like a dolphin — any more than that and I do it like a brick! I can't float. If I stop swimming I sink."

"So don't stop."

"When you get tired, you stop."

"What was it that made you frightened of the water?"

He told her:

"I was a kid in Cyprus. A little kid. My father had taught me how to swim. I used to watch him diving off the rocks, oh, maybe twenty or thirty feet high, into the sea. I thought I could do it, too. So one day when my folks weren't watching, I tried. I must have hit my head on something on the way down. Or maybe I simply struck the water all wrong. When they spotted me floating in the sea, I was just about done for. My father dragged me out. He was a Medic — the kiss of life and all that. So now I'm not much for swimming, and I'm absolutely *nothing* for diving! I will swim — for a splash, in shallow water, like today — but that's my limit. And I'll only go in from a beach. I can't stand cliffs, height. It's as simple as that. You married a coward. So there."

"No I didn't," she said. "I married someone with a great bottom. Why didn't you tell me all this before?"

"You didn't ask me. I don't like to talk about it because I don't much care to remember it. I was just a kid, and yet I knew I was going to die. And I knew it wouldn't be nice. I still haven't got it out of my system, not completely. And so the less said about it the better."

A beach ball landed close by, bounced, rolled to a standstill against Gwen's thigh. They looked up. A brown, burly figure came striding. They recognized the frayed, bulging shorts. Spiros.

"Hallo," he said, going down into a crouch close by, forearms resting on his knees. "Thee beach. Thee ball. I swim, play. You swim?" (This to Geoff.) "You come, swim, throwing thee ball?"

Geoff sat up. There were half-a-dozen other couples on the beach; why couldn't this jerk pick on them? Geoff thought to himself: *I'm about to get sand kicked in my face!* "No," he said out loud, shaking his head. "I don't swim much."

"No swim? You frighting thee big fish? Thee sharks?"

"Sharks?" Now Gwen sat up. From behind their dark lenses, she could feel Spiros's eyes crawling over her.

Geoff shook his head. "There are no sharks in the Med," he said.

"Him right," Spiros laughed high-pitched, like a woman, without his customary gurgling. A weird sound. "No sharks. I make thee jokes!" He stopped laughing and looked straight at Gwen. She couldn't decide if he was looking at her face or her breasts. Those damned sunglasses of his! "You come swim, lady, with Spiros? Play in thee water?"

"My . . . *God!*" Gwen sputtered, glowering at him. She pulled her dress on over her still-damp, very skimpy swimming costume, packed her towel away, picked up her sandals. When she was annoyed, she really *was* annoyed.

Geoff stood up as she made off, turned to Spiros. "Now listen — " he began.

"Ah, you go now! Is OK. I see you." He took his ball, raced with it down the beach, hurled it out over the sea. Before it splashed down he was diving, low and flat, striking the water like a knife. Unlike Geoff, he swam very well indeed. . . .

When Geoff caught up with his wife she was stiff with anger. Mainly angry with herself. "That was so rude of me!" she exploded.

"No it wasn't," he said. "I feel exactly the same about it."

"But he's so damned . . . persistent! I mean, he knows we're together, man and wife . . . 'thee bed — just one.' How *dare* he intrude?"

Geoff tried to make light of it. "You're imagining it," he said.

"And you? Doesn't he get on your nerves?"

"Maybe I'm imagining it too. Look, he's Greek — and not an especially attractive specimen. Look at it from his point of view. All of a sudden there's a gaggle of dolly-birds on the beach, dressed in stuff his sister wouldn't wear for undies! So he tries to get closer — for a better view, as it were — so that he can get a walleyeful. He's no different to other blokes. Not quite as smooth, that's all."

"Smooth!" she almost spat the word out. "He's about as smooth as a badger's —"

"— Bottom," said Geoff. "Yes, I know. If I'd known you were such a bum-fancier I mightn't have married you."

And at last she laughed, but shakily.

They stopped at the booze shop and bought brandy and a large bottle of Coca-Cola. And mint chocolate liqueur, of course, for their midnight coffees. . . .

That night Gwen put on a blue and white dress, very Greek if cut a little low in the front, and silver sandals. Tucking a handkerchief into the breast pocket of his white jacket, Geoff thought: *she's beautiful!* With her heart-shaped face and the way her hair framed it, cut in a page-boy style that suited its shiny black sheen — and her green, green eyes — he'd always thought she looked French. But tonight she was definitely Greek. And he was so glad that she was English, and his.

Dimi's was doing a roaring trade. George and Petula had a table in the corner, overlooking the sea. They had spread themselves out in order to occupy all four seats, but when Geoff and Gwen appeared they waved, called them over. "We thought you'd drop in," George

said, as they sat down. And to Gwen: "You look charming, my dear."

"Now I feel I'm really on my holidays," Gwen smiled.

"Honeymoon, surely," said Petula.

"Shh!" Geoff cautioned her. "In England they throw confetti. Over here it's plates!"

"Your secret is safe with us," said George.

"Holiday, honeymoon, whatever," said Gwen. "Compliments from handsome gentlemen; the stars reflected in the sea; a full moon rising and bouzouki music floating in the air. And —"

"— The mouth-watering smells of good Greek grub!" Geoff cut in. "Have you ordered?" He looked at George and Petula.

"A moment ago," Petula told him. "If you go into the kitchen there, Dimi will show you his menu — live, as it were. Tell him you're with us and he'll make an effort to serve us together. Starter, main course, a pudding — the lot."

"Good!" Geoff said, standing up. "I could eat the saddle off a donkey!"

"Eat the whole donkey," George told him. "The one who's going to wake you up with his racket at six-thirty tomorrow morning."

"You don't know Geoff," said Gwen. "He'd sleep through a Rolling Stones concert."

"And *you* don't know Achladi donkeys!" said Petula.

In the kitchen, the huge, bearded proprietor was busy, fussing over his harassed-looking cooks. As Geoff entered he came over. "Good evenings, sir. You are new in Achladi?"

"Just today," Geoff smiled. "We came here for lunch but missed you."

"Ah!" Dimitrios gasped, shrugged apologetically. "I was sleeps! Every day, for two hours, I sleeps. Where you stay, eh?"

"The Villa Eleni."

"Eleni? Is me!" Dimitrios beamed.

"I am Villa Eleni. I mean, I owns it. Eleni is thee name my wifes."

"It's a beautiful name," said Geoff, beginning to feel trapped in the conversation. "Er, we're with George and Petula."

"You are eating? Good, good. I show you." Geoff was given a guided tour of the ovens and the sweets trolley. He ordered, keeping it light for Gwen.

"And here," said Dimitrios. "For your lady!" He produced a filigreed silver-metal brooch in the shape of a butterfly, with "Dimi's" worked into the metal of the body. Gwen wouldn't like it especially, but politic to accept it. Geoff had noticed several female patrons wearing them, Petula included.

"That's very kind of you," he said.

Making his way back to their table, he saw Spiros was there before him.

Now where the Hell had he sprung from? And what the Hell was he playing at?

Spiros wore tight blue jeans, (his image, obviously), and a white T-shirt stained down the front. He was standing over the corner table, one hand on the wall where it overlooked the sea, the other on the table itself. Propped up, still he swayed. He was leaning over Gwen. George and Petula had frozen smiles on their faces, looked frankly astonished. Geoff couldn't quite see all of Gwen, for Spiros's bulk was in the way.

What he could see, of the entire mini-tableau, printed itself on his eyes as he drew closer. Adrenalin surged in him and he began to breathe faster. He barely noticed George standing up and sliding out of view. Then, as the bouzouki tape came to an end and the taverna's low babble of sound seemed to grow that much louder, Gwen's outraged voice suddenly rose over everything else:

"Get . . . your . . . filthy . . . paws . . . *off* me!" she cried.

Geoff was there. Petula had drawn

as far back as possible; no longer smiling, her hand was at her throat, her eyes staring in disbelief. Spiros's left hand had caught up the **V** of Gwen's dress. His fingers were inside the dress and his thumb outside. In his right hand he clutched a pin like the one Dimitrios had given to Geoff. He was protesting:

"But I giving it! I putting it on your dress! Is nice, this one. We friends. Why you shout? You no like Spiros?" His throaty, gurgling voice was slurred; waves of ouzo fumes literally wafted off him like the stench of a dead fish. Geoff moved in, knocked Spiros's elbow away where it leaned on the wall. Spiros must release Gwen to maintain his balance. He did so, but still crashed half-over the wall. For a moment Geoff thought he would go completely over, into the sea. But he just lolled there, shaking his head, and finally turned it to look back at Geoff. There was a look on his face which Geoff couldn't quite describe. Drunken stupidity slowly turning to rage, maybe. Then he pushed himself upright, stood swaying against the wall, his fists knotting and the muscles in his arms bunching.

Hit him now, Geoff's inner man told him. *Do it, and he'll go clean over into the sea. It's not high, seven or eight feet, that's all. It'll sober the bastard up, and after that he won't trouble you again.*

But what if he couldn't swim? *You know he swims like a fish — like a bloody shark!*

"You think you better than Spiros, eh?" The Greek wobbled dangerously, steadied up and took a step in Geoff's direction.

"No!" the voice of the bearded Dimitrios was shattering in Geoff's ear. Massive, he stepped between them, grabbed Spiros by the hair, half-dragged, half-pushed him toward the exit. "No, *everybody* thinks he's better!" he cried. "Because everybody *is* better! Out —" he heaved Spiros yelping into the harbour's shadows. "I tell you before, Spiros: drink all the ouzo in Achladi. Is your business. But not let it ruin *my* business. Then comes thee *real* troubles!"

Gwen was naturally upset. It spoiled something of the evening for her. But by the time they had finished eating, things were about back to normal. No one else in the place, other than George and Petula, had seemed especially interested in the incident anyway.

At around eleven, when the taverna had cleared a little, the girl from Skymed came in. She came over.

"Hello, Julie!" said George, finding her a chair. And, flatterer born, he added: "How lovely you're looking tonight — but of course you look lovely all the time."

Petula tut-tutted. "George, if you hadn't met me you'd be a gigolo by now, I'm sure!"

"Mr Hammond," Julie said. "I'm terribly sorry. I should have explained to Spiros that he'd recover the fare for your ride from me. Actually, I believed he understood that, but apparently he didn't. I've just seen him in one of the bars and asked him how much I owed him. He was a little upset, wouldn't accept the money, told me I should see you."

"Was he sober yet?" Geoff asked, sourly.

"Er, not very, I'm afraid. Has he been a nuisance?"

Geoff coughed. "Only a *bit* of a one."

"It was a thousand drachmas," said Gwen.

The courier looked a little taken aback. "Well it should only have been seven hundred."

"He did carry our bags, though," said Geoff.

"Ah! Maybe that explains it. Anyway, I'm authorized to pay you seven hundred."

"All donations are welcome," Gwen said, opening her purse and accepting the money. "But if I were you, in the future I'd use someone else. This Spiros isn't a particularly pleasant fellow."

"Well, he does seem to have a problem with the ouzo," Julie answered. "On the other hand —"

"He has *several* problems!" Geoff was sharper than he meant to be. After all, it wasn't her fault.

"— He also has the best beach," Julie finished.

"Beach?" Geoff raised an eyebrow. "He has a beach?"

"Didn't we tell you?" Petula spoke up. "Two or three of the locals have small boats in the harbour. For a few hundred drachmas they'll take you to one of a handful of private beaches along the coast. They're private because no one lives there, and there's no way in except by boat. The boatmen have their favourite places, which they guard jealously and call 'their' beaches, so that the others don't poach on them. They take you in the morning or whenever, collect you in the evening. Absolutely private . . . ideal for picnics . . . romance!" She sighed.

"What a lovely idea," said Gwen. "To have a beach of your own for the day!"

"Well, as far as I'm concerned," Geoff told her, "Spiros can keep his beach."

"Oh-oh!" said George. "Speak of the devil. . . ."

Spiros had returned. He averted his face and made straight for the kitchens in the back. He was noticeably steadier on his feet now. Dimitrios came bowling out to meet him and a few low-muttered words passed between them. Their conversation quickly grew more heated, becoming rapid-fire Greek in moments, and Spiros appeared to be pleading his case. Finally Dimitrios shrugged, came lumbering toward the corner table with Spiros in tow.

"Spiros, he sorry," Dimitrios said. "For tonight. Too much ouzo. He just want be friendly."

"Is right," said Spiros, lifting his head. He shrugged helplessly. "Thee ouzo."

Geoff nodded. "OK, forget it," he said, but coldly.

"Is . . . OK?" Spiros lifted his head a little more. He looked at Gwen.

Gwen forced herself to nod. "It's OK."

Now Spiros beamed, or as close as he was likely to get to it. But still Geoff had this feeling that there was something cold and calculating in his manner.

"I make it good!" Spiros declared, nodding. "One day, I take you thee *best* beach! For thee picnic. Very private. Two peoples, no more. I no take thee money, nothing. Is good?"

"Fine," said Geoff. "That'll be fine."

"OK," Spiros smiled his unsmile, nodded, turned away. Going out, he looked back. "I sorry," he said again; and again his shrug. "Thee ouzo . . ."

"Hardly eloquent," said Petula, when he'd disappeared.

"But better than nothing," said George.

"Things are looking up!" Gwen was happier now.

Geoff was still unsure how he felt. He said nothing. . . .

"Breakfast is on us," George announced the next morning. He smiled down on Geoff and Gwen where they drank coffee and tested the early morning sunlight at a garden table on the patio. They were still in their dressing-gowns, eyes bleary, hair tousled.

Geoff looked up, squinting his eyes against the hurtful blue of the sky, and said: "I see what you mean about that donkey! What the Hell time is it, anyway?"

"Eight-fifteen," said George. "You're lucky. Normally he's at it, oh, an hour earlier than this!" From somewhere down in the maze of alleys, as if summoned by their conversation, the hideous braying echoed yet again as the village gradually came awake.

Just before nine they set out, George and Petula guiding them to a little place bearing the paint-daubed legend: "Brekfas Bar." They climbed steps to a pine-railed patio set with pine tables and chairs, under a varnished pine frame supporting a canopy of split bamboo. Service was good; the "English" food hot, tasty, and very cheap; the coffee dreadful!

"Yechh!" Gwen commented, understanding now why George and Petula had ordered tea. "Take a note, Mr Hammond," she said. "Tomorrow, no coffee. Just fruit juice."

"We thought maybe it was us being fussy," said Petula. "Else we'd have warned you."

"Anyway," George sighed. "Here's where we have to leave you. For tomorrow we fly — literally. So today we're shopping, picking up our duty-frees, gifts, the postcards we never sent, some Greek cigarettes."

"But we'll see you tonight, if you'd care to?" said Petula.

"Delighted!" Geoff answered. "What, Zorba's Dance, moussaka, and a couple or three of those giant Metaxas that Dimi serves? Who could refuse?"

"Not to mention the company," said Gwen.

"About eight-thirty, then," said Petula. And off they went.

"I shall miss them," said Gwen.

"But it will be nice to be on our own for once," Geoff leaned over to kiss her.

"Hallo!" came a now familiar, gurgling voice from below. Spiros stood in the street beyond the rail, looking up at them, the sun striking sparks from the lenses of his sunglasses. Their faces fell and he couldn't fail to notice it. "Is OK," he quickly held up a hand. "I no stay. I busy. Today I make thee taxi. Later, thee boat."

Gwen gave a little gasp of excitement, clutched Geoff's arm. "The private beach!" she said. "Now that's what

I'd call being on our own!" And to Spiros: "If we're ready at one o'clock, will you take us to your beach?"

"Of course!" he answered. "At one o'clock, I near Dimi's. My boat, him called *Spiros* like me. You see him."

Gwen nodded. "We'll see you then."

"Good!" Spiros nodded. He looked up at them a moment longer, and Geoff wished he could fathom where the man's eyes were. Probably up Gwen's dress. But then he turned and went on his way.

"Now we shop!" Gwen said.

They shopped for picnic items. Nothing gigantic, mainly small things. Slices of salami, hard cheese, two fat tomatoes, fresh bread, a bottle of light white wine, some fetta, eggs for boiling, and a liter of crystal-clear bottled water. And as an afterthought: half-a-dozen small pats of butter, a small jar of honey, a sharp knife and a packet of doilies. No wicker basket; their little plastic coolbox would have to do. And one of their pieces of shoulder luggage for the blanket, towels, and swimthings. Geoff was no good for details; Gwen's head, to the contrary, was only happy buzzing with them. He let her get on with it, acted as beast of burden. In fact there was no burden to mention. After all, she was shopping for just the two of them, and it was as good a way as any to explore the village stores and see what was on offer. While she examined this and that, Geoff spent the time comparing the prices of various spirits with those already noted in the booze shop. So the morning passed.

At eleven-thirty they went back to the Villa Eleni for you know and a shower, and afterwards Gwen prepared the foodstuffs while Geoff lazed under the awning. No sign of George and Petula; eighty-four degrees of heat as they idled their way down to the harbour; the village had closed itself down through the hottest part of the day, and they saw no one they knew. Spiros's boat lolled like a mirrored blot on the stirless ocean, and Geoff thought: *even the fish will be finding this a bit much!* Also: *I hope there's some shade on this blasted beach!*

Spiros appeared from behind a tangle of nets. He stood up, yawned, adjusted his straw hat like a sunshade on his head. "Thee boat," he said, in his entirely unnecessary fashion, as he helped them climb aboard. *Spiros* "thee boat" was hardly a hundred percent seaworthy, Geoff saw that immediately. In fact, in any other ocean in the world she'd be condemned. But this was the Mediterranean in July.

Barely big enough for three adults, the boat rocked a little as Spiros yanked futilely on the starter. Water seeped through boards rotten and long since sprung, black with constant damp and badly caulked. Spiros saw Geoff's expression where he sat with his sandals in half an inch of water. He shrugged. "Is nothings," he said.

Finally the engine coughed into life, began to purr, and they were off. Spiros had the tiller; Geoff and Gwen faced him from the prow, which now lifted up a little as they left the harbour and cut straight out to sea. It was then, for the first time, that Geoff noticed Spiros's furtiveness: the way he kept glancing back toward Achladi, as if anxious not to be observed. Unlikely that they would be, for the village seemed fast asleep. Or perhaps he was just checking landmarks, avoiding rocks or reefs or what have you. Geoff looked overboard. The water seemed deep enough to him. Indeed, it seemed much *too* deep! But at least there were no sharks. . . .

Well out to sea, Spiros swung the boat south and followed the coastline for maybe two and a half to three miles. The highest of Achladi's houses and apartments had slipped entirely from view by the time he turned in towards land again and sought a bight in the seemingly unbroken march of cliffs. The place was landmarked: a fang of rock had weathered free, shaping a stack that reared up from the water to form a narrow, deep channel between itself and the cliffs proper. In former times a second, greater stack had crashed oceanward and now lay like a reef just under the water across the entire frontage. In effect, this made the place a lagoon: a sandy beach to the rear, safe water, and the reef of shattered, softly matted rocks where the small waves broke.

There was only one way in. Spiros gentled his boat through the deep water between the crooked outcrop and the overhanging cliff. Clear of the channel, he nosed her into the beach and cut the motor; as the keel grated on grit he stepped nimbly between his passengers and jumped ashore, dragging the boat a few inches up onto the sand. Geoff passed him the picnic things, then steadied the boat while Gwen took off her sandals and made to step down where the water met the sand. But Spiros was quick off the mark.

He stepped forward, caught her up, carried her two paces up the beach and set her down. His left arm had been under her thighs, his right under her back, cradling her. But when he set her upon her own feet his right hand had momentarily cupped her breast, which he'd quite deliberately squeezed.

Gwen opened her mouth, stood gasping her outrage, unable to give it words. Geoff had got out of the boat and was picking up their things to bring them higher up the sand. Spiros, slapping him on the back, stepped round him and shoved the boat off, splashed in shallow water a moment before leaping nimbly aboard. Gwen controlled herself, said nothing. She could feel the blood in her cheeks but hoped Geoff wouldn't notice. Not here, miles from anywhere. Not in this lonely place. No, there must be no

trouble here.

For suddenly it had dawned on her just how very lonely it was. Beautiful, unspoiled, a lovers' idyll — but oh so very lonely . . .

"You alright, love?" said Geoff, taking her elbow. She was looking at Spiros standing silent in his boat. Their eyes seemed locked. it was as if she didn't see him but the mind behind the sunglasses, behind those disparate, dispassionate eyes. A message had passed between them. Geoff sensed it but couldn't fathom it. He had almost seemed to hear Spiros say "yes," and Gwen answer "no."

"Gwen?" he said again.

"I see you," Spiros called, grinning. It broke the spell. Gwen looked away, and Geoff called out:

"Six-thirty, right?"

Spiros waggled a hand this way and that palm-down, as if undecided. "Six, six-thirty — something," he said, shrugging. He started his motor, waved once, chugged out of the bay between the jutting sentinel rock and the cliffs. As he passed out of sight the boat's engine roared with life, its throaty growl rapidly fading into the distance. . . .

Gwen said nothing about the incident; she felt sure that if she did, then Geoff would make something of it. Their entire holiday could so easily be spoiled. It was bad enough that for her the day had already been ruined. So she kept quiet, and perhaps a little too quiet. When Geoff asked her again if anything was wrong she told him she had a headache. Then, feeling a little unclean, she stripped herself quite naked and swam while he explored the beach.

Not that there was a great deal to explore. He walked the damp sand at the water's rim to the southern extreme and came up against the cliffs where they curved out into the sea. They were quite unscalable, towering maybe eighty or ninety feet to their jagged rim. Walking the hundred or so yards back the other way, the thought came to Geoff that if Spiros didn't come back for them — that is, if anything untoward should happen to him — they'd just have to sit it out until they were found. Which, since Spiros was the only one who knew they were here, might well be a long time. Having thought it, Geoff tried to shake the idea off but it wouldn't go away. The place was quite literally a trap. Even a decent swimmer would have to have at least a couple of miles in him before considering swimming out of here.

Once lodged in Geoff's brain, the concept rapidly expanded itself. Before . . . he had looked at the faded-yellow and bone-white facade of the cliffs against the incredible blue of the sky with admiration; the beach had been every man's dream of tranquility, privacy, Eden with its own Eve; the softly lapping ocean had seemed like a warm, soothing bath reaching from horizon to horizon. But now . . . the place was so like Cape Greco. Except at Greco there had always been a way down to the sea — and up from it. . . .

The northern end of the beach was much like the southern, the only difference being the great fang of rock protruding from the sea. Geoff stripped, swam out to it, was aware that the water here was a great deal deeper than back along the beach. But the distance was only thirty feet or so, nothing to worry about. And there were hand- and footholds galore around the base of the pillar of upthrusting rock. He hauled himself up onto a tiny ledge, climbed higher (not too high), sat on a projecting fist of rock with his feet dangling and called to Gwen. His voice surprised him, for it seemed strangely small and panting. The cliffs took it up, however, amplified and passed it on. His shout reached Gwen where she splashed; she spotted him, stopped swimming and

stood up. She waved, and he marvelled at her body, her tip-tilted breasts displayed where she stood like some lovely Mediterranean nymph, all unashamed. *Venus rising from the waves.* Except that here the waves were little more than ripples.

He glanced down at the water and was at once dizzy: the way it lapped at the rock and flowed so gently in the worn hollows of the stone, all fluid and glinting motion; and Geoff's stomach following the same routine, seeming to slosh loosely inside him. *Damn* this terror of his! What was he but eight, nine feet above the sea? God, he might as well feel sick standing on a thick carpet!

He stood up, shouted, jumped outward, toward Gwen.

Down he plunged into cool, liquid blue, and fought his way to the surface, and swam furiously to the beach. There he lay, half-in, half-out of the water, his heart and lungs hammering, blood coursing through his body. It had been such a little thing — something any ten-year-old child could have done — but to him it had been such an effort. And an achievement!

Elated, he stood up, sprinted down the beach, threw himself into the warm, shallow water just as Gwen was emerging. Carried back by him she laughed, splashed him, finally submitted to his hug. They rolled in twelve inches of water and her legs went round him; and there where the water met the sand they grew gentle, then fierce, and when it was done the sea laved their heat and rocked them gently, slowly dispersing their passion. . . .

About four o'clock they ate, but very little. They weren't hungry; the sun was too hot; the silence, at first enchanting, had turned to a droning, sunscorched monotony that beat on the ears worse than a city's roar. And there was a smell. When the light breeze off the sea swung in a certain direction, it brought something unpleasant with it.

To provide shade, Geoff had rigged up his shirt, slacks, and a large beach towel on a frame of drifted bamboo between the brittle, sandpapered branches of an old tree washed half-way up the sand. There in this tatty, makeshift tee-pee they'd spread their blanket, retreated from the pounding sun. But as the smell came again Geoff crept out of the cramped shade, stood up and shielded his eyes to look along the wall of the cliffs. "It comes . . . from over there," he said, pointing.

Gwen joined him. "I thought you'd explored?" she said.

"Along the tideline," he answered, nodding slowly. "Not along the base of the cliffs. Actually, they don't look too safe, and they overhang a fair bit in places. But if you'll look where I'm pointing — there, where the cliffs are cut back — is that water glinting?"

"A spring?" she looked at him. "A waterfall?"

"Hardly a waterfall," he said. "More a dribble. But what is it that's dribbling? I mean, springs don't stink, do they?"

Gwen wrinkled her nose. "Sewage, do you think?"

"Yecchh!" he said. "But at least it would explain why there's no one else here. I'm going to have a look."

She followed him to the place where the cliffs were notched in a V. Out of the sunlight, they both shivered a little. They'd put on swimwear for simple decency's sake, in case a boat should pass by, but now they hugged themselves as the chill of damp stone drew off their stored heat and brought goose-pimples to flesh which sun and sea had already roughened. And there, beneath the overhanging cliff, they found in the shingle a pool formed of a steady flow from on high. Without a shadow of a doubt, the pool was the source of the carrion stench; but here in the shade its water

was dark, muddied, rippled, quite opaque. If there was anything in it, then it couldn't be seen.

As for the waterfall: it forked high up in the cliff, fell in twin streams, one of which was a trickle. Leaning out over the pool at its narrowest, shallowest point, Geoff cupped his hand to catch a few droplets. He held them to his nose, shook his head. "Just water," he said. "It's the pool itself that stinks."

"Or something back there?" Gwen looked beyond the pool, into the darkness of the cave formed of the V and the overhang.

Geoff took up a stone, hurled it into the darkness and silence. Clattering echoes sounded, and a moment later —

Flies! A swarm of them, disturbed where they'd been sitting on cool, damp ledges. They came in a cloud out of the cave, sent Geoff and Gwen yelping, fleeing for the sea. Geoff was stung twice, Gwen escaped injury; the ocean was their refuge, shielding them while the flies dispersed or returned to their vile-smelling breeding ground.

After the murky, poisonous pool the sea felt cool and refreshing. Muttering curses, Geoff stood in the shallows while Gwen squeezed the craters of the stings in his right shoulder and bathed them with salt water. When she was done he said, bitterly: "I've *had* it with this place! The sooner the Greek gets back the better."

His words were like an invocation. Towelling themselves dry, they heard the roar of Spiros's motor, heard it throttle back, and a moment later his boat came nosing in through the gap between the rock and the cliffs. But instead of landing he stood off in the shallow water. "Hallo," he called, in his totally unnecessary fashion.

"You're early," Geoff called back. And under his breath: *Thank God!*

"Early, yes," Spiros answered. "But I have thee troubles." He shrugged.

Gwen had pulled her dress on, packed

the last of their things away. She walked down to the water's edge with Geoff. "Troubles?" she said, her voice a shade unsteady.

"Thee boat," he said, and pointed into the open, lolling belly of the craft, where they couldn't see. "I hitting thee rock when I leave Achladi. Is OK, but —" And he made his fifty-fifty sign, waggling his hand with the fingers open and the palm down. His face remained impassive, however.

Geoff looked at Gwen, then back to Spiros. "You mean it's unsafe?"

"For three peoples, unsafe — maybe." Again the Greek's shrug. "I thinks, I take thee lady first. Is OK, I come back. Is bad, I find other boat."

"You can't take both of us?" Geoff's face fell.

Spiros shook his head. "Maybe big problems," he said.

Geoff nodded. "OK," he said to Gwen. "Go just as you are. Leave all this stuff here and keep the boat light." And to Spiros: "Can you come in a bit more?"

The Greek made a clicking sound with his tongue, shrugged apologetically. "Thee boat is broked. I not want thee more breakings. You swim?" He looked at Gwen, leaned over the side and held out his hand. Keeping her dress on, she waded into the water, made her way to the side of the boat. The water only came up to her breasts, but it turned her dress to a transparent, clinging film. She grasped the upper strake with one hand and made to drag herself aboard. Spiros, leaning backwards, took her free hand.

Watching, Geoff saw her come half out of the water — then saw her freeze. She gasped loudly and twisted her wet hand in Spiros's grasp, tugged free of his grip, flopped back down into the water. And while the Greek regained his balance, she quickly swam back ashore. Geoff helped her from the sea. "Gwen?" he said.

Spiros worked his starter, got the motor going. He commenced a slow, deliberate circling of the small bay.

"Gwen?" Geoff said again. "What is it? What's wrong?" She was pale, shivering.

"He . . ." she finally started to speak. "He . . . had an erection! Geoff, I could see it bulging in his shorts, throbbing. My God — and I know it was for me! And the boat . . ."

"What about the boat?" Anger was building in Geoff's heart and head, starting to run cold in his blood.

"There was no damage — none that I could see, anyway. He . . . he just wanted to get me into that boat, on my own!"

Spiros could see them talking together. He came angling close in to the beach, called out: "I bring thee better boat. Half an hour. Is safer. I see you." He headed for the channel between the rock and the cliff and in another moment passed from sight. . . .

"Geoff, we're in trouble," Gwen said, as soon as Spiros had left. "We're in serious trouble."

"I know it," he said. "I think I've known it ever since we got here. That bloke's as sinister as they come."

"And it's not just his eye, it's his mind," said Gwen. "He's sick." Finally, she told her husband about the incident when Spiros had carried her ashore from the boat.

"So that's what that was all about," he growled. "Well, something has to be done about him. We'll have to report him."

She clutched his arm. "We have to get back to Achladi before we can do that," she said quietly. "Geoff, I don't think he intends to let us get back!"

That thought had been in his mind, too, but he hadn't wanted her to know it. He felt suddenly helpless. The trap seemed sprung and they were in it. But what did Spiros intend, and how could he possibly hope to get away with it

141

— whatever "it" was? Gwen broke into his thoughts:

"No one knows we're here, just Spiros."

"I know," said Geoff. "And what about that couple who . . ." He let it tail off. It had just slipped from his tongue. It was the last thing he'd wanted to say.

"Do you think I haven't thought of that?" Gwen hissed, gripping his arm more tightly yet. "He was the last one to see them — getting on a ferry, he said. But did they?" She stripped off her dress.

"What are you doing?" he asked, breathlessly.

"We came in from the north," she answered, wading out again into the water. "There were no beaches between here and Achladi. What about to the south? There are other beaches than this one, we know that. Maybe there's one just half a mile away. Maybe even less. If I can find one where there's a path up the cliffs. . . ."

"Gwen," he said. "Gwen!" Panic was rising in him to match his impotence, his rage and terror.

She turned and looked at him, looked helpless in her skimpy bikini — and yet determined, too. And to think he'd considered her naïve! Well, maybe she had been. But no more. She managed a small smile, said, "I love you."

"What if you exhaust yourself?" He could think of nothing else to say.

"I'll know when to turn back," she said. Even in the hot sunlight he felt cold, and knew she must, too. He started toward her, but she was already into a controlled crawl, heading south, out across the submerged rocks. He watched her out of sight round the southern extreme of the jutting cliffs, stood knotting and unknotting his fists at the edge of the sea. . . .

For long moments Geoff stood there, cold inside and hot out. And at the same

time cold all over. Then the sense of time fleeting by overcame him. He ground his teeth, felt his frustration overflow. He wanted to shout but feared Gwen would hear him and turn back. But there must be something he could do. With his bare hands? Like what? A weapon — he needed a weapon.

There was the knife they'd bought just for their picnic. He went to their things and found it. Only a three-inch blade, but sharp! Hand to hand it must give him something of an advantage. But what if Spiros had a bigger knife? He seemed to have a bigger or better everything else.

One of the drifted tree's branches was long, straight, slender. It pointed like a mocking, sandpapered wooden finger at the unscalable cliffs. Geoff applied his weight close to the main branch. As he lifted his feet from the ground the branch broke, sending him to his knees in the sand. Now he needed some binding material. Taking his unfinished spear with him, he ran to the base of the cliffs. Various odds and ends had been driven back there by past storms. Plastic Coke bottles, fragments of driftwood, pieces of cork . . . a nylon fishing net tangled round a broken barrel!

Geoff cut lengths of tough nylon line from the net, bound the knife in position at the end of his spear. Now he felt he had a *real* advantage. He looked around. The sun was sinking leisurely toward the sea, casting his long shadow on the sand. How long since Spiros left? How much time left till he got back? Geoff glanced at the frowning needle of the sentinel rock. A sentinel, yes. A watcher. Or a watchtower!

He put down his spear, ran to the northern point and sprang into the sea. Moments later he was clawing at the rock, dragging himself from the water, climbing. And scarcely a thought of danger, not from the sea or the climb, not from the deep water or the height. At thirty feet the rock narrowed down;

he could lean to left or right and scan the sea to the north, in the direction of Achladi. Way out on the blue, sails gleamed white in the brilliant sunlight. On the far horizon, a smudge of smoke. Nothing else.

For a moment — the merest moment — Geoff's old nausea returned. He closed his eyes and flattened himself to the rock, gripped tightly where his fingers were bedded in cracks in the weathered stone. A mass of stone shifted slightly under the pressure of his right hand, almost causing him to lose his balance. He teetered for a second, remembered Gwen . . . the nausea passed, and with it all fear. He stepped a little lower, examined the great slab of rock which his hand had tugged loose. And suddenly an idea burned bright in his brain.

Which was when he heard Gwen's cry, thin as a keening wind, shrilling into his bones from along the beach. He jerked his head round, saw her there in the water inside the reef, wearily striking for the shore. She looked all in. His heart leaped into his mouth, and without pause he launched himself from the rock, striking the water feet first and sinking deep. No fear or effort to it this time; no time for any of that; surfacing, he struck for the shore. Then back along the beach, panting his heart out, flinging himself down in the small waves where she knelt, sobbing, her face covered by her hands.

"Gwen, are you all right? What is it, love? What's happened? I *knew* you'd exhaust yourself!"

She tried to stand up, collapsed into his arms and shivered there; he cradled her where earlier they'd made love. And at last she could tell it.

"I . . . I stayed close to the shore," she gasped, gradually getting her breath. "Or rather, close to the cliffs. I was looking . . . looking for a way up. I'd gone about a third of a mile, I think. Then there was a spot where the water was

very deep and the cliffs sheer. Something touched my legs and it was like an electric shock — I mean, it was so unexpected there in that deep water. To feel something slimy touching my legs like that. *Ugh!*" She drew a deep breath.

"I thought: *God, sharks!* But then I remembered: there are no sharks in the Med. Still, I wanted to be sure. So . . . so I turned, made a shallow dive and looked to see what . . . what . . ." She broke down into sobbing again.

Geoff could do nothing but warm her, hug her tighter yet.

"Oh, but there *are* sharks in the Med, Geoff," she finally went on. "One shark, anyway. His name is Spiros! A spider? No, he's a shark! Under the sea there, I saw . . . a girl, naked, tethered to the bottom with a rope round her ankle. And down in the deeps, a stone holding her there."

"My God!" Geoff breathed.

"Her thighs, belly, were covered in those little green swimming crabs. She was all bloated, puffy, floating upright on her own internal gasses. Fish nibbled at her. Her nipples were gone. . . ."

"The fish!" Geoff gasped. But Gwen shook her head.

"Not the fish," she rasped. "Her arms and breasts were black with bruises. Her nipples had been bitten through — *right* through! Oh, Geoff, Geoff!" She hugged him harder than ever, shivering hard enough to shake him. "I *know* what happened to her. It was him, Spiros." She paused, tried to control her shivering, which wasn't only the aftereffect of the water.

And finally she continued: "After that I had no strength. But somehow I made it back."

"Get dressed," he told her then, his voice colder than she'd ever heard it. "Quickly! No, not your dress — my trousers, shirt. The slacks will be too long for you. Roll up the bottoms. But get dressed, get warm."

143

VDF

She did as he said. The sun, sinking, was still hot. Soon she was warm again, and calmer. Then Geoff gave her the spear he'd made and told her what he was going to do. . . .

There were two of them, as like as peas in a pod. Geoff saw them, and the pieces fell into place. Spiros and his brother. The island's codes were tight. These two looked for loose women; loose in their narrow eyes, anyway. And from the passports of the honeymooners it had been plain that they weren't married. Which had made Gwen a whore, in their eyes. Like the Swedish girl, who'd met a man and gone to bed with him. As easy as that. So Spiros had tried it on, the easy way at first. By making it plain that he was on offer. Now that that hadn't worked, now it was time for the hard way.

Geoff saw them coming in the boat and stopped gouging at the rock. His fingernails were cracked and starting to bleed, but the job was as complete as he could wish. He ducked back out of sight, hugged the sentinel rock and thought only of Gwen. He had one chance and mustn't miss it.

He glanced back, over his shoulder. Gwen had heard the boat's engine. She stood half-way between the sea and the waterfall with its foul pool. Her spear was grasped tightly in her hands. *Like a young Amazon*, Geoff thought. But then he heard the boat's motor cut back and concentrated on what he was doing.

The put-put-put of the boat's exhaust came closer. Geoff took a chance, glanced round the rim of the rock. Here they came, gentling into the channel between the rock and the cliffs. Spiros's brother wore slacks; both men were naked from the waist up; Spiros had the tiller. And his brother had a shotgun!

One chance. *Only one chance.*

The boat's nose came inching forward, began to pass directly below. Geoff gave a mad yell, heaved at the loose wedge of rock. For a moment he thought it would stick and put all his weight into it. But then it shifted, toppled.

Below, the two Greeks had looked up, eyes huge in tanned, startled faces. The one with the shotgun was on his feet. He saw the falling rock in the instant before it smashed down on him and drove him through the bottom of the boat. His gun went off, both barrels, and the shimmering air near Geoff's head buzzed like a nest of wasps. Then, while all below was still in a turmoil, he aimed himself at Spiros and jumped.

Thrown about in the stern of his sinking boat, Spiros was making ready to dive overboard when Geoff's feet hit him. he was hurled into the water, Geoff narrowly missing the swamped boat as he, too, crashed down into the sea. And then a mad flurry of water as they both struck out for the shore.

Spiros was there first. Crying out, wild, outraged, frightened, he dragged himself from the sea. He looked round and saw Geoff coming through the water — saw his boat disappear with only ripples to mark its passing, and no sign of his brother — and started at a lop-sided run up the beach. Towards Gwen. Geoff swam for all he was worth, flew from the sea up onto the land.

Gwen was running, heading for the V in the cliff under the waterfall. Spiros was right behind her, arms reaching. Geoff came last, the air rasping in his lungs, Hell's fires blazing in his heart. He'd drawn blood and found it to his liking. But he stumbled, fell, and when he was up again he saw Spiros closing on his quarry. Gwen was backed up against the cliff, her feet in the water at the shallow end of the vile pool. The Greek made a low, apish lunge at her and she struck at him with her spear.

She gashed his face even as he grabbed her. His hand caught in the loose material of Geoff's shirt, tearing it from her so that her breasts lolled free. Then she stabbed at him again, slicing him across the neck. His hands flew to his face and neck; he staggered back from her, tripped, and sat down in chest-deep water; Geoff arrived panting at the pool and Gwen flew into his arms. He took the spear from her, turned it towards Spiros.

But the Greek was finished. He shrieked and splashed in the pool like the madman he was, seemed incapable of getting to his feet. His wounds weren't bad, but the blood was everywhere. That wasn't the worst of it: the thing he'd tripped on had floated to the surface. It was beginning to rot, but it was — or had been — a young man. Rubbery arms and legs tangled with Spiros's limbs; a ghastly, gaping face tossed with his frantic threshing; a great black hole showed where the bloated corpse had taken a shotgun blast to the chest, the shot that had killed him.

For a little while longer Spiros fought to be rid of the thing — screamed aloud as its gaping, accusing mouth screamed horribly, silently at him — then gave up and flopped back half-in, half-out of the water. One of the corpse's arms was draped across his heaving, shuddering chest. He lay there with his hands over his face and cried, and the flies came swarming like a black, hostile cloud from the cave to settle on him.

Geoff held Gwen close, guided her away from the horror down the beach to a sea which was a deeper blue now. "It's OK," he kept saying, as much for himself as for her. "It's OK. They'll come looking for us, sooner or later."

As it happened, it was sooner. . . . □

www.ingramcontent.com/pod-product-compliance
Lightning Source LLC
Chambersburg PA
CBHW070556180626
46817CB00005B/1871